DAMSELFLY INN

A THORNTON VERMONT NOVEL

CAMERON D. GARRIEPY

For Mark,
without whom Joss would not be the man he is.

ACKNOWLEDGMENTS

Where to begin?
Thank you:

To my husband and son, of course, for not tossing me out on the street. Writers are not always easy people to live with.

To my parents, for so many things, including nudging me towards Middlebury College, without which there would be no Thornton.

To Angela and Mandy, for never giving up on me, and never once blowing smoke up my skirt.

To Kim for shining this manuscript up like a boss.

To Paul, whose unwavering faith in my abilities is most likely indicative of madness.

To Heather, Phoebe, and Kate for that long-ago girls' weekend where I truly started to believe in this story.

To the people of Middlebury, past and present, whom I hope will forgive me for borrowing–and taking significant liberties with the fictionalization of–their home.

To Beryl. Cousin Beryl. Beryl Herman. You know who you are.

To the memory of Glenn W. F. Edwards, who always believed I'd write romance novels one day. I wish you were here to read them, my friend.

To my wonderful community of writers out there in the ether, including *but not limited to*
Angela Amman, Eden Baylee, Valerie Boersma, Mandy Dawson, John Dolan, Shelton Dunning, Christine Hanolsy, Marian Kent, Lisa Kramer, Kameko Murakami, Susan Nolen, Kirsten Piccini, Roxanne Piskel, Jessie Powell, Kate Shrewsday, Eric Storch, Andra Watkins, and Liz Zimmers.
You are all cherished here.

DAMSELFLY INN

CHAPTER 1

Joss Fuller was daydreaming about his mother's tomato pie when lightning struck the Damselfly Inn.

He'd watched the storm smudge the horizon on the drive into town, marveled at the tumble of thunderheads sweeping across Lake Champlain towards Thornton, Vermont. By the time he crested the last rise, heading west towards his parents' farm on County Road, the rain was coming down hard.

Driving into the snaps of electricity in the sky and the deep growls of thunder over the valley of pasture and marsh where he'd grown up, Joss was considering a cold beer in front of some pre-season football. That, and the difference between one slice of roasted tomatoes, cheddar, basil, and his mother's ribbon-worthy cornmeal crust, or two.

The bolt that took out the huge maple tree in his parents' neighbor's side yard took Joss by surprise. His first thought was that the Swifts' place had been struck. His second was to haul his pickup back into the road. Between the distraction and the gusting wind, he'd almost ditched the truck. When the limb that shaded the house's third floor snapped like a broken bone, leaving a steaming, ragged wound in the tree, Joss realized the lightning hadn't hit the actual building, but the damage was done. The limb had punched its way through the old Victorian's skin, puncturing the roof of what had once been a thoroughly neglected cluster of attic rooms, complete with clanking plumbing and shadowy gables.

The rain would likely prevent anything from burning, but there could very well have been guests in that attic room. He'd heard from his mom that the new owner–an innkeeper–transformed the cobwebby attic into a bridal suite. Getting an invitation to see it was his mother's new project.

The innkeeper had become a favorite customer at the Fuller Dairy since her arrival in the valley earlier that summer. Joss wasn't sure if his mother was trying to fix him up or whether she just liked the newcomer, but Nan Grady had been a popular topic.

He'd noticed her around. You couldn't not notice someone new in a town like Thornton. With the college kids mostly gone for the summer, new faces stuck out, and hers was a pretty one.

He'd figured on making her acquaintance before too long. His best friend Jack and Jack's sister Kate were the reason she'd relocated to Thornton. It was only a matter of time before they were all in the same place at the same time.

He hadn't figured on the storm intervening.

Joss was already pulling into the Swifts' driveway–not the Swifts' house, the Damselfly Inn, he reminded himself as he passed the understated carved sign–when the lights started snapping on inside the house, marking a trail from the apartment over the garage, down through the kitchen and into the front hall. He was pounding on the front door when the upstairs hall lit up, but the front door was locked, and the rest of the inn stayed dark.

NAN GRADY WAS TRACING glossy lettering across a misdirected postcard when her house split open.

Greetings from Myrtle Beach S.C.! The card was a vintage-styled one, with each drop-shadowed block letter featuring a scene from the beach. She turned it over to read the note, to mull over the intended recipient. The handwriting was young—full and looping.

Danny, it's not this pretty where we live, but the beach is awesome. I miss you. Maybe you can come down here some time. It's warmer than Vermont anyway. Love, Ellie

The postcard was addressed to Danny B. (heart, flower, star), 203 County Road, Thornton, VT. It had arrived that afternoon, nearly lost in the myriad catalogs, flyers, and bills in the mail. Something about the sender's bittersweet tone gave Nan pause. She carried it upstairs to her apartment, meaning to drop it in her purse for her next run into town. She suspected Gary at the Thornton Post Office would know exactly who Danny B. was.

Myrtle Beach sounded like a perfect alternative to the late summer collision of weather fronts currently heaving itself down from the Adirondacks. Outside, the early evening sky had gone gunmetal gray, roiling with clouds. The rain was static, punctuated by sharp cracks of thunder, and Nan could hear the wind buffeting the walls of the old house.

The storm continued its tantrum as it drove eastward, rushing up to and over the Green Mountains like water over a spillway. Rain pelted down, blown nearly horizontal, and the huge maple tree behind the inn groaned in protest.

There would be a mess to clean up in the yard in the morning.

She'd come upstairs to wait out the thunderstorm in the snug comfort of her apartment over the garage.

It was a disorienting feeling still, the newness of owning this grand old house, but living in two rooms that were only attached to it by the stairs off the kitchen, stairs whose walls framed the breezeway between the house and the garage. It was a heady feeling, though, owning the gracious yellow Victorian, opening it to travelers, hosting treasured memories, making a home for herself in this town she was quickly coming to love.

Nan turned the card over one last time, imagining thick South

Carolina heat and the light tease of sea breeze. White heat lit up her living room, throwing everything into Hitchcock-esque relief for a heartbeat; when the thunder shattered the air no more than a half-second later, the lights blinked and the house shook with the impact.

She was on her feet and running for the stairs, pausing only to grab her Maglite from the coffee table drawer, and the card fluttered, forgotten, to rest on the braided rug.

A cold wind tumbled down from the third floor to meet her in the foyer.

With a hard knot of dread already forming in her stomach, she raced up to the third floor landing. She yanked open the door to the Adirondack Suite with her heart pounding.

The scene inside the room struck her like a fist. Rain was pouring in through the remains of the gabled roof, lumber and insulation hanging down like broken bones and torn flesh. The hot smell of ozone was fresh in the air. Shingles and debris littered the floor. The silk drapes whipped and snapped at the sills. A limb from the ancient maple tree that grew next to the house lay across the sleigh bed, its raw end sizzling.

"Oh, god. No," she said aloud to the empty room, her voice swallowed by the noise of the storm. "No."

She forced herself to loosen the death grip in which she held the doorknob. She forced herself to inhale and exhale. If she let herself cry, she would fall apart entirely.

The rain water was pooling in the dips and hollows of the old pine floorboards. She cast around for something to soak up the puddles, for something to catch the deluge. *A paper cup*, she thought with a hysteric giggle, like that song from the Eighties. Shock was making her head fuzzy. She had a bucket and towels in the hall utility closet, but what the hell was she going to do about the hole in her roof?

Out in the hallway, she paused. Someone was banging on the front door; a voice muffled by the storm and three floors of space was calling. She waited, counting the thumping of her heart—one-two, one-two, one-two—but the pounding was persistent.

She jumped when a man's voice called her name from downstairs.

"Miss Grady? Hello! Is anyone up there? Hello?"

She thought of her phone, waiting for her back in her apartment. The man calling knew her name, but she had no idea who she was facing, alone in the dark house in a storm. She gripped the flashlight tightly and started slowly down the stairs.

They all reached the second story landing at the same time. Nan stopped short in relief. Walt Fuller, the dairy farmer from down the road, stood in the second floor hallway in a dripping slicker and muddy boots, with a younger man in a sweatshirt and ball cap at his side.

"Miss Grady? Are you all right?" Walt asked, catching his breath.

Nan almost laughed at the absurdity of the question. Not by a long shot. There was a tree branch in her bridal suite. There were muddy boot tracks on the hallway runner. Panic welled up in her chest again, but she forced it down when she saw Walt's expression. He must have heard the lightning strike, seen her roof, and come running to find out if she'd been underneath it.

She was all right. The third floor was another story.

"I'm fine, Mr. Fuller. The room upstairs–" She started to shake and pressed her hand against her mouth, fearing she might cry after all.

"Come on down to the kitchen, now, Miss Grady. Molly will make tea for you, and Joss here's going to go take a look at your damage." Walt gestured to his companion.

As Walt Fuller put a hand on her shoulder and steered her towards the stairs, she looked back at the younger man. His eyes were the same shade as the thunderheads outside, and he exuded quiet competence in a way that momentarily quelled the panic brewing in her belly.

"I'll be down in a bit." He spoke to his father, but his eyes stayed on her.

In the kitchen, Molly Fuller was boiling water and getting out the tea and teapot.

"I went ahead and poked around your kitchen, hon. I hope that's ok," she said to Nan, before turning to her eyes to her husband. "How bad is it?"

"Joss'll tell us in a minute. I sent him on up." Walt joined his wife at the counter.

Nan was out of sorts watching her neighbor commandeer her kitchen. "Mr. and Mrs. Fuller, thank you–"

"None of that, now," Molly interrupted. "We've barged into your house; we're past formalities. I'm Molly, he's Walt, and we're all neighbors. We take care of our own. Now, I put a fair amount of sugar in this one. It'll help with the shock."

The mug was solid and warm; the tea sweet and strong. She felt the panic begin to dissipate, the knot of dread loosen. She took a deep breath, then remembered her manners.

"I hope you'll call me Nan, then." She watched Walt take his place next to his wife; he fit there like a missing piece. "There are cookies from Sweet Pease on a plate under that pie dome, if you'd like."

Molly smiled. "Your mother raised you well."

"My Gran, actually." Words tumbled out, as much to fill the air as to provide them with her history. "My grandparents raised me. My mother passed away when I was small, and my father was never what you'd call present." She flushed, feeling she'd revealed too much. "Joss... is your son?" she asked, hoping to shift the topic of conversation away from her rootless past.

"He is," answered Molly. "Short for Josiah. Contractor and carpenter, so you're in good hands. He'll get things buttoned up for you tonight, and I'm sure he'll come back in the morning to do a proper estimate, if you'd like." Molly spoke with a certainty that brooked no refusal.

The man himself walked into the kitchen, wiping a hand on his jeans; he carried his wet sweatshirt and hat in the other. Rain clung to his hair, leaving damp streaks on his Thornton Hornets tee as it beaded and rolled off.

"Mom, my ears are burning." There was a smile in his voice.

Something like envy kindled in her heart. The Fullers had that intangible ease that came with closeness and familiarity. They were family.

Molly introduced them, "Josiah, this is Nan Grady. Nan, our son, Josiah Fuller."

"A pleasure, Nan, circumstances notwithstanding." He reached for her hand. "And please," he said with a wry look at his mother, "Call me Joss."

"Joss." She put her hand in his. Their eyes met over the handshake, and a current flared between them. His hands were calloused, warm, pleasantly rough. She wondered how they would feel sliding up her back, running through her hair.

She was sure she must be blushing.

"Well, son, what needs to be done tonight?" Walt asked, interrupting her wayward thoughts. She almost laughed; she was more in shock than she'd realized.

Nan pulled her hand away, but she wasn't sure what to do with it. It took her a moment to realize that Joss was speaking to her.

"Have you got tarps and rope? Tie-downs? I'm going to get up on the roof and cover the hole up until morning. The rain's clearing off, but I don't want to leave that hole exposed. You're lucky," he said. "There's nothing vital in that section of ceiling and the structure's not too badly compromised."

Maybe she'd imagined the heat, the spark between them. Joss didn't seem affected by it at all. Gran had always called her an old soul. She supposed it must be true. At thirty-one, her most devoted relationship was with a century-old house, and the first good looking man she'd taken a moment to notice in six months had set her skin humming.

"I've got some tie-downs in my car, but no tarps." She wished she'd thought to buy them on one of her many trips up to South Burlington for supplies.

"That's no trouble at all." He shrugged and turned to Walt. "Pop, I'll need to borrow some from you, and come back."

"I'll help you get some from the barn," Walt said. "Let's not keep the poor girl up all night."

"I think I'll be up anyway." Nan sighed.

"Nonsense, Nan," Molly said. "I'll stay to help you clean up."

Flustered by her neighbors' generosity, Nan started to tidy the tea tin and sugar bowl. "Please, Molly, Walt." She was embarrassed but resolute. "I can handle it tonight."

Molly's gaze met hers before she got up and cleared the mugs. Nan hoped Molly understood. She needed to fall apart and pull herself back together again in peace.

Molly rinsed out the teapot and dried her hands. She took a key from her pocket and set it on the island. "You're going to want to put that key back under the mat."

Nan stared at the key as Molly bustled out the kitchen door, followed by her men. In all the panic and confusion, she hadn't given a thought to how the Fullers had gotten into the house. She was grateful Molly Fuller had figured out where her spare key was; she supposed beneath the doormat wasn't a very original hiding place.

"Molly, wait!" she called. "Take the key. If I ever need it, I'll know where to look."

Joss, who was the last to go through the kitchen door, turned and took the key from her outstretched hand.

CHAPTER 2

Freshly clad in one of his father's many foul-weather jackets and bearing a stack of tarps and tie-downs, Joss made his way back to the inn. The worst of the storm was past, leaving a steady, steamy rain in its wake.

He couldn't help but wonder how Nan was holding up. His reaction to her had surprised him.

When he'd first seen her on the second story landing, she'd looked wild–frightened and disoriented, her eyes wide and full of panic, her fair skin ghostly with shock. Between the strain of the accident and their unannounced entry, she'd been entitled to at least that much.

He'd been impressed, later, down in the kitchen, when she'd pulled herself together enough to offer cookies to his parents. He'd heard her making small talk with them before he'd come into the kitchen. She reminded him of a Jane Austen heroine, observing the social niceties, no matter the miserable situations in which she found herself.

Most surprising had been the tug of lust he'd felt when she shook his hand. He'd felt that casual touch all the way to his gut, and by the time his father had spoken, his mind had hitched her up onto the kitchen island and buried his hands in her hair, all the better to kiss the color back into her face.

What kind of jackass had fantasies about women in shock?

Joss walked up the granite slab steps to the kitchen door, and was about to knock when he saw her through the glass, sitting on a stool with her back to the door, head down on her arms on the kitchen island, the long line of her neck laid bare, her shoulders shuddering.

Good lord, she's crying.

He took a deep breath and steeled himself. Tears weren't his forté.

WHILE THE RAIN OUTSIDE SLOWED, and the wind continued to push the front eastward, Nan allowed herself to fall apart. She'd meant to at least go back upstairs and look again at the damage with a calmer eye, but as soon as her neighbors were gone she'd succumbed to five minutes of raw weeping. The house settled around her along with a deep longing for her grandmother. When storms had frightened her as a child, Gran had braided her then-long hair and told her it was angels bowling, that Gabriel got a strike.

Three concise knocks on the kitchen door yanked Nan out of her weeping. Her sleeve was soaked from crying and her head ached fiercely. She swiped at her wet eyes, and stood, her back still to the door. Knowing it was Joss at the door didn't make her feel better about the ugly tears, no matter that he was here to help her out of her mess. She crossed the kitchen, drew a steadying breath, and opened the door.

He looked like the type to rescue innkeepers in distress.

The air outside had the crisp clarity a storm left behind. In the glow of the carriage lantern outside the door, he was dazzling. His dark hair, just a little overdue for a trim and shot through with caramel, curled a touch at the tips and framed his face, the way her hands suddenly longed to do.

He needed a shave; the day's stubble threw his mouth into stark contrast. He had a strong jaw and a lush lower lip. He smiled, and she noted one slightly crooked tooth.

God, I must look a wreck, and I'm staring at his mouth like a fool while he stands on my wet kitchen steps.

She forced herself to meet his eyes. "Come in."

That jolt of attraction whipped through her again, settling low in her abdomen and radiating warmth, when he stepped through the door and back into her kitchen.

"I'll be a while on the roof." He took a moment to wipe his feet on the mat. "You going to be okay?"

"Of course." She appreciated the small measure of dignity he afforded her by not mentioning that he'd caught her crying–almost as much as she appreciated the clean boot soles. "I have some calls to make."

He headed up the stairs, his arms full with a tool bag and the tarps. She gave in to the temptation to watch him climb the stairs. The rear view didn't disappoint.

Perhaps it wouldn't be all bad to have someone around fixing the roof.

While Joss was up on the third floor, Nan made the necessary call to her insurance company to report the incident. She hung up the phone with no clear recollection of what she'd said to the company representative. Molly's tea must have worn off. She stared at her phone for a moment, knowing there was one other person who would need to hear the news first from her.

Given Kate Pease's high position in the gossip chain, it would have to be soon.

Joss was back, damp and disheveled, by the time she'd pressed send on the text to her best friend. "It's covered up well enough for now, and I looked everything over. I can work up an estimate for you and bring it by in the morning."

The woman and the innkeeper inside her waged a quick battle over simply hiring him on the spot, just to have him to look at for a few weeks. The innkeeper won out, but only barely. "An estimate would be great."

"If you want me to do the work, I can probably shuffle a few other jobs around, and start by Tuesday." Joss glanced back into the foyer toward the stairs. "You don't want to risk any more water damage."

"Someone will be out from the insurance company tomorrow. Then I'll know my budget." Nan sighed. "I have to get the suite repaired as soon as possible. Lost bookings cost me a lot more than just the construction bills."

"I can take care of you, Nan."

The unintentional double meaning hung in the air for a moment. Nan thought she could easily drown in those gray eyes.

Joss reached down for his bag; his expression was cloudy. "I should let you get some sleep." Straightening, he nudged open the screen door and disappeared into the night.

CHAPTER 3

When Kate's hot pink minivan screeched to a halt in the driveway not an hour later, Nan nearly collapsed with relief.

Kate Pease paused in the driveway, shading her eyes against the flood lamps, assessing the damage. Despite ten years of friendship, Nan was always struck by her best friend's beauty. Where Nan was short and curvy, Kate was all long, lean lines. Kate wore her mane of rich brown waves long and loose, in contrast to Nan's own short, mousy, layers.

Kate was half the county's dream girl, born and bred in Thornton, gone off to Paris to study pastry after culinary school, and back again to take over the local bakery. Beautiful, familiar, but just a bit out of reach; she flirted as easily as she breathed.

Kate came through the kitchen door a moment later. "You okay, sugar plum?"

"I don't even know where to begin. Maybe with the fact there's half a tree in my Adirondack Suite?"

Kate wrapped her in a warm hug. Nan leaned into the woman who'd been the closest thing to family she'd known since her grandparents' passing.

Kate released her with a gentle squeeze and seated herself at the kitchen island. "You know that doesn't actually happen to people, right? Have you called anyone else to help out?"

"I'm fine," Nan replied. "I didn't call anyone…"

Kate frowned slightly, but Nan cut her off.

"I did get a visit from Joss Fuller. He was driving by and saw the whole thing. His parents turned up a couple minutes behind him." Nan pulled a stool out and perched next to Kate. "They were so nice about everything. Joss got up on the roof and shored things up until morning. He said he'd get me an estimate."

"Joss is going to be working here?" Kate clapped her hands. "Nice."

Nan shot down Kate's glee. "I haven't hired him yet. He only left an hour ago."

"You should. He'll draw in every female in a fifty-mile radius. You'll be booked into next year with gawkers. That man is a fox."

"You know him well?" Nan hated that to her own ears she sounded like a schoolgirl with a crush.

"Hell, yes." Kate chuckled. "I grew up with Joss. My brother was friends with him all the way through school. Still is friends with him. They hang out when Jack comes home."

Nan wracked her brain. She would have remembered Joss from amongst Jack Pease's friends. "How have I not met him?"

"I guess we've all been busy this summer. And I don't really hang out with him unless Jack's in town."

"Which has been exactly once since I bought the place."

Kate rolled her eyes dramatically. "I know. Jack's awful, but we love him anyway."

"True story." Nan laughed. Nan knew Kate loved her older brother as fiercely as she teased him, and that Jack inspired a wide and loyal circle of friends.

Kate went on. "Joss has always been a nice guy. Nice and stupidly good-looking. He was an object of desire for pretty much every girl I knew. Now he's got that builds-stuff, works-with-his-hands, rugged thing going. Totally fatal."

"I owe him for bailing me out tonight."

"You should pay him back with dinner *à deux*." Kate toyed with one of the mugs still left out on the island, pinning Nan with a matchmaker's gleaming eye.

Nan snorted, trying to keep her cheeks from flaming. "Hardly."

"You've got to call me when he's up there wearing a tool belt, because I swear to God I'm coming back over."

Nan laughed out loud. She didn't doubt Kate would do exactly that if given the opportunity. "You should come over tomorrow after you close. We'll have a girls' night."

"You're on," said Kate. "See if you can't get Joss started on the roof by then. He can work late; we can turn on the flood lights and have drinks on the lawn with binoculars."

"We'll need snacks, in that case. And blankets. It's getting chilly at night these days."

"Maybe," Kate teased, "I'll test out some new muffin varieties on you."

"You only love me because I'm your guinea pig." Nan sighed.

"And because you'll have a hot contractor working on site."

"I haven't hired him," Nan reminded her.

"You will. He's yummy and the best guy for the job."

"I'm fairly certain the 'yummy' factor shouldn't matter," Nan countered.

Kate giggled. "It very much should." She looked hard at Nan for a moment, eyes crinkling at the corners in concentration. "You know what? We should have a salon day. Wednesday's the day Allison is here?"

"Amanda."

"Amanda, right." Kate plucked at Nan's shaggy hair. "You, my friend, need a cut, and some highlights."

Nan ducked away from Kate's critical grooming. "It's not that bad."

"How long has it been?" Kate pursed her lips in a way that made Nan recall Kate's mother disapproving of the chaos of their dorm room.

"Not that long?" Nan counted back. "We had breakfast at that diner you love in Charlotte."

Kate pushed back from the island. "That was when you first moved in. At the beginning of the summer. And your hair is too short to neglect like that." Kate rummaged in her purse, pulling out her car keys. "Are you empty tonight?"

"What?" Nan stared at Kate, scrambling to keep up. She switched topics so fast Nan's head spun. "For now, I am. Elisha is due in from New York tonight, but there's no one else booked in. Why?"

"That diner stays open until midnight on Saturdays. We are going to get some Commiseration Waffles."

KATE DROVE, making it to the storefront greasy spoon she loved in a shocking twenty minutes. She played the music loud, and they sang along as the night-washed pastures and hillsides passed beyond the windows. The last of the storm was gone and the clouds were parting to reveal the sparkle of the late-summer constellations.

Nan climbed out of the car feeling like her troubles couldn't possibly catch up to her. "You're going to get arrested one of these days."

"Nah." Kate breezed towards the entrance. Inside, there were few seats to be had. The diner was lit up like Christmas, glowing warmly in the violet evening. Kate held the door for Nan. "I went to prom with the Deputy Sheriff."

They were seated by the front windows and handed menus. The booths on either side were packed full of teens and summer students from the college, laughing and finishing the remains of late-night feasts. Nan felt suddenly ancient, and the weight of the night's damage pressed down on her like a yoke.

Kate reached over and squeezed Nan's hand. "It's going to be okay."

Kate never missed a trick. Nan was always amazed by her best friend's ability to read her.

"Is it?" Nan toyed with the trifold menu's laminated edge.

Kate snapped hers closed just as the waitress, a pin-up brunette in a roller derby tee and denim mini skirt, came over with coffee and water. Kate ordered a breakfast sampler to share, then turned to Nan with her Serious Face on.

"Your insurance will cover the damage. Joss won't fleece you."

"No. I know," Nan said. "It's just that right now what I don't need is people getting spooked by some freak accident and canceling, or even the lost bookings for the time that Joss–" She caught herself mid-sentence. She hadn't hired him yet. "That there's work being done."

"You know you can always ask for help." Kate doctored her coffee, heavy on the cream. "My parents, Jack, me. We'll all help."

Grateful tears pricked in Nan's eyes. Her crying jag was only a few hours in the rearview. "Thanks, Kate. Let's hope it doesn't come to that."

The booth was jostled a little as the cohort of high-schoolers made their noisy exit. One of them waved at Kate. "Hey, Miss Pease!"

Kate gave the girl a nod and a smile. "Hey, Kelsey."

The group paused to observe them before loudly wondering why Kelsey bothered with "the bakery lady." Kate went back to her coffee with an eye roll, but Nan felt, not for the first time, as though she would never be known the way Kate was–even if being known meant being "the inn lady." No matter how long she stayed.

Again, Kate caught the shift in her mood.

"Cheer up. There is some serious breakfast food coming our way." She pushed the coffee and water out of the way for the huge plate of mini-waffles, bacon, sausage, and sunny-side-up eggs their waitress set down in the center of the table.

Nan picked a thick slice of bacon from the plate, and did her best to shake off her fears. "I can't argue with that logic."

CHAPTER 4

𝒩an's Saturday was long, weighed down by work and a heavy sky.

She hauled her ShopVac up through the empty inn to the third floor after an early breakfast. Her only guest being more of a lodger and out of town for a few days was a saving grace. It meant not worrying about making a horrendous racket–or cursing like a sailor–while she did what she could to get the third floor cleaned up.

She'd waited until nine to call Anneliese Thompson, the wedding planner who was both her best referral source and newest friend.

It was late notice, but Nan hoped the Anna could help soothe any ruffled feathers resulting from moving the weekend's wedding couple to one of the downstairs rooms. Nan appreciated Anneliese's gift for connecting with people. Her much-coveted services were a fantastic asset to The Damselfly. That Anna had become a friend over the summer was a warm beginning to Nan's new life in Thornton.

Anneliese answered on the first ring.

"Anneliese? It's Nan Grady. I hope I didn't wake Chloe?"

"No." Anneliese laughed. "She's up with the sun, and my parents took her swimming at the State Park this morning. What can I do for you?"

"I have a small hitch with this weekend's wedding party. I don't have a bridal suite."

"What?"

Nan gave Anneliese the worst of the news.

Anna's voice through the receiver was thick with concern. "Are you okay?"

"I'm fine, I promise." Nan pressed her knuckles to her temples, glad Anneliese couldn't see her pale skin and bruised eyes. She didn't look fine, and she knew it.

"I'll call the Grants right now and explain. I'm sure Rebecca won't mind too much. She's been such an easy bride so far."

"Thank you." Nan let a measure of tension go from the knot between her shoulder blades. "I'm up to my neck in cleanup."

"Hey?" This time, Anneliese's concern came through with a touch of snark. "Is Professor Barbie okay?"

Nan giggled in spite of herself. "That's mean. She wasn't even here. She's been in New York for a few days."

"Do you need a referral for a contractor? My cousin–"

"Actually, I think I found one. My next door neighbors' son was over here with them right after it happened. Do you know the Fullers?"

It was Anneliese's turn to giggle. "Molly is my mother's cousin, which makes Joss my second cousin."

"Of course he is."

Anneliese's tone was indulgent. "One of these days, you'll know everyone here, too."

Nan blew out a breath. "So you say."

She hung up feeling like she just might make it through the weekend.

After snatching an hour of restless sleep, she'd readied the five rooms on the second floor for check-in before the representative from her insurance agency had arrived.

Only one thing remained to take care of in the ravaged bridal suite. Nan carried a stack of old sheets upstairs with a heavy heart.

Before Joss–assuming she hired him–could do any work, she'd have to move everything out of the way.

The tarps gave the room an alien, blue cast. Nan drifted for a moment.

She trailed her hand along the natural cherry-wood sleigh bed as she draped it in a white cotton sheet, caught her reflection in the repainted Victorian mirror in the en suite bathroom. Mourning the wilted freesias she'd arranged the day before in a now tipped-over milk-glass vase, she tossed the dead flowers into the trash. The vase she wrapped in the hand-embroidered dresser scarf she'd bought at a church tag sale, and tucked into her laundry basket to take it downstairs. It was whole, as was all of the furniture, by some miracle. As was she.

She was whole, and it was a room. A room that she would have repaired. With the clarity of renewed perspective, she looked critically at the space.

The third story of the house was smaller than the two main levels, and there was already a full bathroom tucked into the gable. Nan had known the first time she'd seen the house that with a lot of cleaning and some elbow grease, she could transform the two small rooms into a bedroom and sitting room.

She'd poured her heart into the third floor, creating a haven for fairytale romance. Splurging on satiny cotton linens for the bed and oversized, lush towels in the bath, searching antique shops and flea markets for the chaise and loveseat in the sitting room, she's spun her dreams of romance and luxury and her inherent practicality into a snug retreat.

The arrival of a pickup truck in the parking lot interrupted her thoughts.

It was chilly under the tarped-off ceiling, but the sight of Joss in his broken-in denim and Thornton College tee shirt had pooled warmth in her belly like a shot of whiskey. She watched him take the porch stairs two at a time, heard the metallic clunk of the mailbox lid. His immediate departure replaced that warmth with something like disappointment.

Anneliese had worked her magic, even with the forecast, which called for clearing skies and milder temperatures by evening. When Nan checked in the bridal party, the mother of the bride cooed over the inn, expressing her sympathy over her storm-damaged room and volunteering her husband to help out. Nan reassured her that she had everything under control.

When the women vanished off to prepare with the hairdresser, she almost believed that she did.

Nan prepared a light tea for the bridal party and a snack on the back terrace for the men before spending a few more hours covering and moving furniture in the Adirondack Suite. Dried out and cleaned up, with the hole covered, the situation didn't seem so dire. The one thing she didn't do was look over the books. For now, she would bury her head in the sand. The potential lost bookings and repair costs would still be there waiting for her come Monday.

In the quiet moments after the sunset had faded into cricket song and stars, Nan took a novel to her office to wait for the wedding party to return from the reception. She opened the windows a little to let in some cool air, and turned up the Mozart violin sonata she'd been playing for the bridal party tea. She tried to concentrate on the story–a lavish and somewhat silly historical romance about a lady pirate and a devastatingly handsome, spoiled gentleman she's robbed and kidnapped–but she kept imagining Rebecca Grant in her wedding gown, dancing with her new husband.

Rebecca left the Damselfly Inn in a long gray limousine, parents and bridesmaids in tow. She was tall and slim, with nearly waist length red curls and green eyes. She'd worn a simple strapless gown with silver embroidery and amethyst jewelry. Her bridesmaids had worn lavender and silver.

Nan pushed a few limp strands of hair off her forehead. Thoughts of the striking bride, glowing with happiness, reminded her of every-thing she wasn't. She wasn't tall; she certainly wasn't willowy. Her style—though Kate might argue the use of that term–was practical and easy, hardly romantic.

She smiled, remembering the father of the bride, eyes shining, in his black formal wear as he ushered his wife, daughter, and her entourage into the limousine. His weathered hand on his wife's violet silk wrap touched an achy spot on Nan's heart.

Her own mother, lost long ago to vices she'd been unable to overcome, would never wear silk to her wedding. Her father, lost even longer ago to the lure of quick cash and short cons, was an unlikely escort down any aisle. Despite living with both of them until she was two, she only remembered seeing her father once in her twenty-eight years.

One afternoon when she was small, he had come to find her at her grandparents. Her grandfather had stood on the front porch with a thirty-ought-six leaning against the wall behind him, and quietly told her father he wasn't welcome. She'd never told Granddad she'd seen her father get out of his car and start up the sandy driveway.

Nan envied the bride her beauty and her loving father, but summoned her pride in The Damselfly and whispered her dreams to herself like a mantra. That night, her inn would shelter newlyweds. Tomorrow, when the bride and groom ate their first breakfast together as man and wife, it would be from her kitchen. And that would be enough for now.

She'd been up to Thornton College several times since arriving in town, so she could picture the ceremony in the chapel. They were to be married by the professor who'd introduced them years ago; a man who was also a Justice of the Peace. They would dance and eat Kate's cake under a tent on the Chapel Lawn.

She shouldn't spend so much time poring over wedding details with Anneliese. The visions Anna painted became a too-vivid backdrop for daydreams. She could clearly see herself wearing a gown and dancing under a fairy-lit tent, Kate in a fabulous cocktail dress, romancing some handsome, hapless wedding guest. When the groom, tall and strong in white tie, his gray eyes twinkling in the fairy lights, took her in his arms for their first dance, he bore a striking resemblance to Joss Fuller.

The rough hand on her cheek, the mouth on hers, each became Joss's as her fantasy spun out.

The daydream was dissolved by the laughter of the bridal party returning. She put aside the barely-read book and stood up. There was a delighted giggle, then applause from the foyer. From the doorway to her office, Nan caught a glimpse of the red-haired bride being swept up the stairs in the arms of her tuxedoed groom.

None of the bridal party saw her standing there as they made their way upstairs to their rooms, so Nan quietly locked the front door and went to her apartment, resolved not to indulge in adolescent wedding fantasies about men she barely knew, even if she was half-asleep at the time.

Joss would have preferred to spend Saturday night up at his cabin in the woods of Catmint Gap, but his mother had asked him to fix her screen door. When she offered him the leftover tomato pie he hadn't gotten the night before, he'd surrendered. His stomach growled hopefully; his mother was the best cook in three counties and had the fair ribbons to prove it.

On his way to his parents' place, Joss slowed as he passed the Damselfly Inn. Before the storm, he'd passed the Swifts' former home almost daily, noting the new owner's progress with mild curiosity. He'd noted the Victorian's cheerful new coat of yellow paint, Mrs. Swift's perennial beds looking tidy and well kept, and the new carved sign out front. He'd recognized the artistry that proclaimed the Damselfly Inn's presence; the local carver was a friend and occasional employee.

He'd watched the Swifts' grandkids grow up, just a few years behind him, and he knew the property like the back of his hand. He'd done some handyman work on the house in recent years, when the maintenance was too much for Mr. Swift. It pleased him to see that the new owner was keeping Mrs. Swift's flowers.

Joss wondered if Nan knew the house's story. His grandfather's grandfather had owned the land on which it sat, had been the one to sell off the parcel to the railway heiress who'd commissioned the three-story Victorian, complete with a carriage house, servants' rooms in the attic, and five bedrooms, each with a private bath. A shocking amount of excess, previously unheard of in the valley. He made a note to ask her if she knew about Faye Bartram.

Joss pulled into his parents' driveway, about a tenth of a mile down the road, and looked back at the house, more curious now about its proprietor.

His parents were in the parlor when he came in, feet in the moccasins his mother insisted on in the house.

"Mom, Pop," he said, dropping down on the couch with his mother.

"Don't get comfortable, Joss. That screen door is driving me crazy, and yesterday's storm didn't help." Molly said. "I've had flies in the kitchen all week."

He picked himself up, kissed his mother on the cheek, and went to assess the situation on the back screen door.

With the door off the hinges and laid across a pair of ancient sawhorses from the barn, he set to work with his hand-planer. In the still air, he heard the faint strains of violins floating from the direction of the Swifts'–he corrected himself–the Damselfly Inn.

He hadn't met Nan Grady before last night, but he knew from his parents that she bought her milk and eggs from their farm. He knew she was friendly with Katie Pease. Town gossip reported that she had been frequenting tag sales and craft shows all summer, making friends with local artisans.

His cousin's teenaged son, Ian, and some of his friends, had done some mowing and painting when she'd moved in. From Ian, he knew she paid fairly and fed the boys well.

She hadn't called him or any of the tradesmen he knew, so he assumed she hadn't needed carpentry. He knew the house was in good shape. Getting it ready for paying guests should have required little more than landscaping and paint, but she must have taken care of that little on her own.

Before too long, he imagined she would need a referral for something. The windows weren't new, and neither was the water heater. It would only be neighborly to drop in and offer some advice, assuming she was still willing to speak to him after seeing his bid on the third floor repairs.

With the screen door snugly back in place, Joss joined his parents in the kitchen. His mom was bringing the tomato pie and a radish salad to the dining room table.

"Go wash up, Joss. And bring the pitcher of lemonade with you when you come back."

"Yes, ma'am," he said with a wry smile, earning a withering look from his mother.

Once Joss had brought his parents up to speed on his current projects–and helped himself to a third slice of tomato pie, talk came around to the rest of the family.

"Your cousin came by this week," Molly said.

"Which one?" He was related on both sides to big families, most of whom were still in the county. His cousins numbered in the dozens.

"Anneliese."

"How is she?" he asked.

"She looks better, less haunted," Molly said. "And that Chloe is just a sweetheart."

"She's a great kid," Joss agreed.

"Anna referred a wedding party to our new neighbor. Seems she's impressed with the inn's potential," Molly added.

"Seems everyone met your new neighbor but me," he said.

"Nan's a nice girl," his father remarked.

"Your father's got a bit of a crush," Molly teased. Walt's ears went pink. Joss laughed.

"She puts me in mind of a pretty brunette I married." Walt reached for the pie dish.

"Oh, you." Molly flushed like a school girl.

"Mom, can I take your plate?" Joss asked, half-standing with his own empty plate in hand. "I'll start the dishes."

"You'll stay and let me beat you at gin, Joss?" his mother teased as he started the warm water.

"Sure, Mom."

He took his time with the dishes, contemplating the view to his parents' nearest neighbor. Though the inky silhouettes of the evergreens between the two houses obscured his view, Joss could see lights burning on the front porch and in the west-facing corner room on the first floor of The Damselfly. He wondered what kept her in that one room, assuming it was Nan with the lights on, when every other light in the house was dark.

His mother pulled him out of his reverie. "Josiah, did you fall into the sink? These cards aren't very good at dealing themselves, and your father's about to fall asleep."

Staying for a game of gin-rummy with his folks was hardly a hardship, and he would stop at the market on his way back up the mountain. A steak, a good beer, some loud music, and his drafting table sounded like the perfect way to spend a Sunday.

THE VOICE RINGING out across the market was the kind a smart man avoided. For Joss, it was a more dangerous sound than any he knew. In a small town market, when you were the only man—hell, the only other person—shopping, and that kind of voice was calling your name, even a smart man had to answer. Answer, and know who he was speaking to.

"Joss?" the voice trilled. "Joss Fuller?"

The voice was attached to a blonde, steaming his way like an aerobically sculpted cruise ship.

"Yes," he replied, eyeing the blond warily. In his basket was a six-pack of copper ale and a New York strip; dead giveaway, he realized, for a single guy with no pressing social engagements for the rest of the weekend.

The cashier was a few steps away. He cast a glance at the nearby shelves, hoping for a distraction. There was something familiar about her, but his memory couldn't place her.

"Don't tell me you don't remember me, Joss." Her smile gleamed;

her lips were perfect. "Elisha McNair? We had a class together, first semester at Thornton?"

Elisha. The woman coalesced with the girl in his memory. He'd dropped into the seat next to hers before an English Literature Survey lecture. Her ponytail had swung fetchingly over her shoulder, and she'd looked amazing in running clothes. They'd hooked up later as a result of too much beer at an open party at one of the frat houses. Nothing more had ever come of those hungry, hot kisses in the loud, crowded basement, but the memories were there.

"Elisha. It's been a long time."

"Not that long …" The look she gave him was frank; he knew he'd been appraised and found acceptable.

Small talk was going to happen, whether he liked it or not. "How are you? What brings you back to Thornton?"

"I'm well." Elisha looked more than well, he thought. She looked incredible. "I'm guest lecturing in sociology at the college this semester. I'm actually just on my way back into town. I had to run down to Manhattan for a meeting with my editor." She paused, and Joss could almost see her flipping back through the years. "Your family owned a dairy farm, right? Are you still involved in that?"

"Not these days, Elisha. I'm a general contractor now. In fact," He suppressed a trace of impatience in his voice and shifted his basket to his other arm. "I've got to start early tomorrow, and it's a ways back to my place. It was really great running into you."

Elisha's eyes rested on the telltale contents of his basket before flicking back up to his face. Her laugh was playful.

"You're retreating off to some man-cave for a steak and a beer. Tell me you'll stay in town and have a late dinner with me instead? I barely know anyone anymore." She flashed that smile again. "We could catch up."

Something in her tone hinted at more than dinner.

"Another time, maybe," he said. "I had a late night, a client emergency, last night. I'm not good company right now."

"I seriously doubt that." She tucked her platinum waterfall of hair behind her ears, then reached into her purse for a silver card case. "I'm staying in the valley, at the Damselfly Inn." She took out a card and handed it to him. "Give me a call about dinner some time."

The Damselfly Inn. His parents' next door neighbor. Perhaps his newest client. Of course. And she'd been in New York, so she hadn't been there. "I'm sure we'll run into one another then. My folks own the farm next door, and I gave Ms. Grady an estimate on the damage."

"Damage?" Even her frown was attractive. "What happened?"

There was concern in her voice. He wasn't proud that it surprised him. "The house took a beating in the storm that blew through last night."

"Oh, no! I only just got back. I had no idea."

"The third floor suite took a tree limb through the roof and ceiling."

"Is Nan okay?" Elisha reached out to touch his arm, but there was nothing flirtatious in the gesture. "It's such a beautiful room. What a shame."

"Yeah." Joss found himself reevaluating Elisha by the moment. "The house is pretty sturdy, and Nan was in her apartment when the limb came down."

Elisha's million-watt smile returned. "Well, I'm sure she's glad to have the repairs in such capable hands. Now, I'll let you get home."

As he drove through downtown Thornton, Joss plugged his mp3 player into the truck's sound system. He surfed through the albums list until he pulled up some old U2 to keep him awake as he drove east and up into the mountains.

Dorm room lights at Thornton College twinkled in his rearview mirror. The music brought back evenings spent listening to a glorified boom box is in a shared dorm room, sketching and researching for his art major, indulging in an unexpected appreciation for Dickens and Austen, struggling with chemistry, and thinking about girls like Elisha McNair. He wondered if he would have appreciated Nan Grady's subtler charms back then. Bono crooned away, and Joss felt a pang of nostalgia for that carefree life.

He couldn't believe what he'd said to Nan the night before–that line about taking care of her. He'd only meant the roof, but something about the soft light in the kitchen and the late hour, something about her eyes, wide and golden, had made his voice go rough with desire. The words had come out sounding like an entirely different kind of promise; the kind of promise he didn't make lightly.

Joss slowed the truck for a cluster of students crossing the street outside Temple, the closest bar within walking distance of campus. They were singing the fight song in drunken harmony.

His thoughts drifted as he drove south, away from the college, towards his current life. It hadn't been seamless, the transition from local boy, to college kid, to local guy. He'd had to get away to come home again. This time a few years ago he would have been out on the Lower East Side with his two best friends, chasing down a lead on hot girls, cutting edge art, or cheap, plentiful alcohol. Possibly all three if it were a promising Friday night.

That was before Jack's offer from Kearney-Mulligan in Boston. Before he and Seth had fallen out over art and ambition. Before Joss had come home, disillusioned, to lick his wounds and start over.

The nostalgia faded as the truck sped out of town towards his cabin up on Catmint Gap. He had the contracting business to pay the bills. He had a workshop in one of his father's unused barns and as much side work as he wanted making furniture. He opened the window and let the whip of September air carry off his nostalgia. His life in Thornton might not be so carefree, but it was still relatively simple.

He made the turn onto the mountain road, smiling at the sign for the Damselfly Inn, 8 Miles. Just when he thought his life was exactly where he wanted it to be, he had one woman slipping into his thoughts, and another trying, evidently, to slip into his pants.

It was enough to drive a man deep into the woods with some beer and a steak.

CHAPTER 5

Come Sunday, Nan was up early, baking off Kate's raspberry danish and preparing her favorite thyme and caramelized onion frittata. Coffee was holding in her thermal carafe, and a stoneware bowl holding the first of the valley's local apples waited for her guests on the long farm table that occupied one side of the roomy kitchen.

The table looked exactly as she felt it should, as she'd dreamed it would. If she ignored the third floor, she could congratulate herself on her very first weekend in the wedding accommodations business.

Maybe someday, she'd host the wedding too.

The best man was the first up. She took in his sleep-wrinkled cheek and heavy eyes and kept her voice low. "Good morning."

He pushed back his floppy hair, looking like Hugh Grant in *Four Weddings and A Funeral*, and smiled sleepily. "Good morning."

"Can I pour you some coffee?" she offered. "The breakfast menu is on the table."

"Just coffee for the moment," he said, taking a mug from her hands. "I'm sorry, I didn't catch your name last night."

"Nan Grady. You're Rebecca's brother? James?"

"I am," he said. "My fiancée, Liv, is on her way down. We're going to head up to Montreal after breakfast. Spend a few days."

"Does she shop? I can give you some great tips," Nan said. "Restaurants, too."

"That would be great," James replied.

"What would be great?" the aforementioned Liv asked, coming into the kitchen. "That coffee smells amazing."

Nan set out the coffee accompaniments and poured Liv a mug.

"I saw your mom upstairs, hon. She was checking on Pepere," Liv said to James. Nan heard voices on the stairs and mentally prepared for breakfast service.

She was happily busy, fixing plates, making small talk and freshening coffee cups for the next hour. As the other guests were finishing up, the groom wandered into the kitchen.

"Good morning, Miss Grady."

She smiled at his bleary charm. "It's Nan, and congratulations. From the sounds of it, it was a great party."

He grinned. "Yeah."

Rebecca was a lucky woman. "Would you care for coffee?"

"In fact," he said, "I was hoping to take a tray up for Rebecca and me. I thought it might hit the right note." He looked around, as if daring anyone to tease him on this of all mornings.

The father of the bride chuckled, and put an arm around his wife's shoulder.

"Son," he said, "It sounds like you'll take to married life just fine."

Everyone laughed. Nan turned away and began preparing a tray for him, unexpected moisture welling in her eyes.

Up to her elbows in post-breakfast dishes, with her guests happily fed and sent on their adventures, Nan looked up to see Elisha McNair's sparkling, luxury rental pull into the driveway.

Thornton College's most recent guest lecturer had foregone an apartment closer to campus and was spending the semester at The

Damselfly. Nan was grateful for a steady booking, and Elisha was a fairly easy guest. Low-maintenance and stunning. Nan had half a mind to ask her to pose for website photographs. Elisha's platinum hair fell thick and straight over her shoulders, and her intense turquoise eyes and Vogue cover body would sell as many overnights as the dramatic autumn foliage.

As if she'd been conjured, Elisha came in from the foyer, her heels clicking fashionably on the hardwood.

Nan tamped down the urge to smooth the wrinkles in her fatigue-green painter's jeans and lamented her pinned-back hair and dish-water splashed clothes. Elisha was effortlessly chic, a tribute to athletics and good genes; Nan couldn't help comparing herself. Especially when she'd started her day, hours before her guests joined her for breakfast, inspecting the second floor hallway ceiling to make sure there were no lingering signs of the storm damage. Some small water stains has sprung up on the landing ceiling, but the spots dried quickly and stayed dry. She was confident they could be re-primed and painted with no lasting ill-effects.

The guest rooms would have to wait until turndown.

Elisha dropped jingling keys into a Coach purse, bringing Nan back to the here-and-now. "You're a million miles away."

"Morning, Elisha. Was your drive okay? You were out late."

"I holed up in a back booth the Riverview Tavern. Had some dinner and worked on my edits for an hour or two when I got back to town." Elisha leaned against the counter next to the sink. "I heard what happened. Are you okay?"

Nan kept her eyes on the dishes. The kind inquiry forced her emotions to the surface, and she had no interest in crying in front of Elisha. "I am. The Adirondack Suite, not so much." She pushed the topic away. "How was New York?"

"Fantastic. I had dinner with my parents, met with my agent." She smoothed a hand over one snug, denim-clad hip with a triumphant grin. "Did some shopping. Speaking of which, I need to bring it all in."

"Can I help you with your things?" Nan asked.

"Sure, thanks."

Nan followed Elisha out into the sunny driveway. She indulged in a moment of raw material lust at the full set of Louis Vuitton luggage in the trunk.

"Isn't it hard to leave Manhattan? This is about as far from The Upper West Side as you can get." Nan hoped her comment didn't sound as envious as she felt.

"It's not hard at all," Elisha answered. "I love it here. It was my home for four years, after all." Her eyes lit up. "Oh! I ran into an old flame at the little market across from the stone church. I stopped in on my way to the Riverside. Turns out, he's contractor in town, and he is even better looking than he was in college. He mentioned the inn was damaged in the storm and hinted he might be working here. You can give me the dish on him. Is he seeing anyone?"

Joss. Nan sucked in a breath."I don't... really... know him. We only met recently."

"We had a class together as freshmen. He was all wholesome and dreamy with those big hazel eyes. He was a fantastic kisser." Elisha gave Nan a conspiratorial glance. "Maybe I should relive a little of my youth while I'm here?"

"Why not?" A lump of disappointment lodged in Nan's throat.

"I don't have that in New York, you know? Going to the market to get a few things and running into someone I know."

Nan's mood plummeted. The one man for whom she'd felt even a tug of interest in years had history with one of her guests. Not just any guest, but a glamorous, leggy guest who wanted to relive her youth. She summoned a last ration of patience. "I'm considering hiring him to repair the storm damage."

Elisha went ahead, pausing to peer up the main stairs. She took Nan's breath away, silhouetted in the light pouring down the stairs from the windows on the landing.

Nan followed with her bags, as Elisha turned back, lips curved with all the sly delight of a cat in a canary cage. "I knew when I took this position that it was the right thing to do. I was certain I was meant to come back to Thornton."

∼

Nan had all the guest rooms turned over when Penny from Coulson's Nursery texted her a photo of their potted chrysanthemum display.

Heads up! Sale on today!

After a quick mental shuffle of her to-do list, she pushed her feet into her clogs and shrugged into a fleece pullover. Rows of steely clouds were gliding in from the Southwest. It might not mean rain, but the milder temperatures were giving way to a distinctly autumnal chill.

Coulson's was just north of the center of town on the same industrial avenue as the local brewery and adjacent to one of the county's two lumber yards. Nan was loading four good-sized pots of orange and dusty red mums into the back of her station wagon when Joss's truck pulled in nose to nose with her car. She nearly hit her head on the raised rear hatch when Joss said hello.

"I'm sorry." There was gentle humor in his eyes. "Scaring Penny's clientele isn't something I try to do."

Nan shoved the last pot into place and shut the back of the car. "I'll be okay."

Joss pocketed his hands and glanced back at the mum display. "I was going to pick up a pot for my mom after I grab a couple things at Robidoux's."

Nan's heart squeezed a little. "That's sweet of you."

Joss leaned a denim-clad hip against her car. "How are things at the inn?"

"Better." She took a deep breath. Did he know how good he looked? "I had a chance to look at the estimate, and my insurance rep emailed me some preliminary numbers. Given the urgency of getting things moving, if you're still able to start on Tuesday, you're hired."

"I'll be there bright and early." He straightened, his attention shifting to the lumber yard. "That means a few more things for my list at Robidoux's."

Nan pulled her keys out of her pocket. "I shouldn't keep you."

"It's no trouble. I wasn't up to much at all, but another client needs something switched up while I'm over there tomorrow, so here I am." Joss tapped the rear hatch. "I can stop by The Damselfly on my way over to drop off my mom's flowers and help you unload those."

The offer flustered her. "Oh, no. That's okay. I've got it."

Joss offered his hand. "Then I'll see you on Tuesday."

Nan clasped her fingers around his, and that same streak of heat flew along her skin. "Tuesday."

He jumped the low chain that separated the parking lots and headed into the hardware store portion at Robidoux's. Nan caught herself staring far longer than she should have.

Tuesday was going to be interesting.

CHAPTER 6

*K*ate excelled at being consulted in matters of Nan's personal appearance. She'd been bossing Nan around since the day they'd met, moving into student housing at NECI.

Today was no different. The salon plot Kate had hatched on Friday night was scheduled for midweek, and Nan was tasked with finding some possible styles for her stylist–and Kate–to review.

Amanda Lloyd, Nan's part time help, was a Thornton College junior who'd stayed in town for the summer prior to her last year at the college. Nan was hopeful that Amanda might continue her position after classes started. She was responsible and good with the guests, and seemed genuinely interested in the often menial and repetitive work required to keep the inn going.

She left Amanda manning the office while she played hooky, picked Kate up outside the bakery, and drove them up to Burlington under a bright sky scattered with tall, silvered clouds.

Under the smock in the stylist's chair, hair combed flat against her head, Nan was caught between vanity and frustration. The stylist was shaping an imaginary cut around her head, talking excitedly with Kate about what would suit Nan best.

"She won't blow dry it, so we have to work with the natural wave," Kate was saying.

"Okay." The stylist plucked at the ends of Nan's hair. "It looks like there was some texture cut in a while ago, we can work with that. I'm thinking a casual bang and layers around her face?"

"I am sitting right here, you know," Nan said, trying not to sound as helpless as she felt.

"Yes, you are, sugar plum." Kate made a reassuring face. "And we are going to make you gorgeous. Sit tight."

"So we're doing highlights today?" The stylist was already reaching for her color cart.

"Yes! Now for color." Kate clapped her hands like a toddler.

Kate and the stylist conferred over the color swatches before presenting Nan with two choices. She fingered the artificial locks of hair gingerly. She was a grown woman. Couldn't she choose her own highlight color?

"I like the honey color. A lot," she admitted ruefully. Kate always knew what suited her.

While the stylist mixed and foiled, Kate got serious about the other area in which she excelled, getting information out of her relatively private best friend.

"How are the repairs going?" Kate's tone was casual, but Nan knew Kate's tactics. This push and pull of information was old hat between the two of them.

"So far, so good?" Nan sipped from the mug of herbal tea she'd been given when she sat down. "He was up there all of yesterday setting up and making lists."

"I was only half kidding about coming over to watch him work." Kate gave the stylist a knowing glance. "This guy is one dishy contractor, even if he's basically my other brother."

"You can't distract him, Kate." Nan sounded prim, even to her own ears.

"Are you planning on distracting him, then?" Kate's eyes sparkled wickedly over her water and lemon.

"No!" Nan flushed a little. "I've got too much riding on the work getting done."

"That the only reason?"

Nan nearly choked on her tea.

Kate was never one to miss Nan's tells, or to hold back. "You like him, don't you?"

Nan backpedaled. "He's a nice guy."

"Nice is for the pharmacist at the Rexall," Kate said. "Joss Fuller is hot."

"Hot or not, Kate, he's not looking at me," Nan said, trying for nonchalant. "He's got some history with my guest."

"Professor Barbie?" Kate asked.

"The one and only," Nan replied, chuckling at the nickname her girlfriends had devised. "Elisha called him an 'old flame.'"

"Damn!" Kate nearly dropped her water glass. "You've been sitting on gossip like this for what…days?"

Nan had the grace to look impishly ashamed. "She was talking about how she knew the timing was right for her to be back in Thornton. I can't see how the deal isn't sealed. Whether Joss knows it or not."

"So, Joss and the platinum sociologist," Kate mused. "It's a shame," she added as the stylist packed up the color cart and turned the timer on for Nan's highlights to set. "I've known Joss a long time, and I'd have said you were just his type."

ABOUT THE TIME Nan and Kate could see the tip of the Thornton Congregational Church spire rising up from the town common, they had listened through Kate's new KG Project album. Nan was trying not to play with her newly styled hair.

"I want Moira Kennedy's voice in my next life." Kate unplugged her phone from the jack in Nan's car and dropped it into her voluminous purse. "Do you mind stopping by my mom and dad's? My mom hemmed a couple of pairs of jeans for me."

"How does someone whose legs go up to her armpits need pants hemmed?"

"I buy them extra long so I can have them exactly right for different shoes." Kate looked at her as if she were a complete idiot. "So, can we drop in real quick?"

"No problem. As long as you don't mind hanging out at the inn for a bit before you go home. I want to grab a couple of those tracks." Nan signaled her VW, and turned onto Chapel Street where the Peases had, according to family legend, lived since the first John Pease had parked his tired horse on the plot of land next door to the Cartwright homestead.

Nan parked her car behind John Pease's.

"We should stay for dinner. My dad is grilling. There'll be plenty. They still cook like Jack and I are living at home and bringing home strays."

The foursquare Mansard-style house that Kate grew up in sat about twenty feet off the street, flanked by a pair of heirloom apple trees. The grass was kept meticulously trimmed and watered, and the front porch always welcomed guests with potted annuals and a cozy swing. Nan longed to leave the car behind Mr. Pease's Jeep Cherokee and join the family, but she shook her head with a smile.

"I told Amanda I'd be back by five." She hoped Kate didn't see the wistful sheen in her eyes. The Peases had always been warm and welcoming; it should have been so easy to slip into their close family circle, but Nan didn't quite understand how to do it.

Kate would say feeling like an outsider was all in her head.

"Okay. Your loss, though. Dad's burgers are ridiculous." Kate opened the car door just as her father came out the front door. Nan didn't resist giggling at John Pease's *Step Back: Dad's Grilling* apron.

Kate launched herself into her father's hug and smooched him extravagantly on the cheek before running inside, screen door banging the frame behind her.

John came down the stairs to say hello, so Nan lowered the window while the car idled. "Katie wasn't too hard on you, was she?" He chuckled affectionately. "She's a force, that girl of mine."

Nan laughed at the understatement. "She keeps me on my toes."

"How's innkeeping treating you? I took Cora for a drive past your place a couple of weeks ago. Looks great."

"Thanks, Mr. Pease." Nan warmed under the praise.

"Nan," he said sternly, "I've known you for coming on eleven years. It's John. Or Dad."

The warmth turned to embarrassed heat. "I'm sorry … John."

"Don't you dare apologize. You're family."

Kate bounded down the porch stairs, hair flying, with a short stack of folded denim under one arm. "Daddy, leave Nan alone. Your burgers'll burn." She shooed her father back toward the house and climbed back into the car. "To The Damselfly!"

She waved over her shoulder until they turned the corner onto College Street and the house disappeared from view.

THEY PASSED Joss's truck headed away from the inn on their return. Kate leaned across Nan's lap to honk the horn and wave through the driver's side window.

"Kate!" A blush bloomed on Nan's chest.

To make matters worse, Elisha and Amanda were talking outside when they pulled in.

"Hi, Nan." Amanda was glowing. "Professor McNair thinks she can get me into her three-hundred level class for the fall."

The young woman took in Nan's shame-stained face. "Are you okay?"

Kate burst out laughing, giggled her way past everyone and went inside.

"I'm fine," Nan said, pasting on a smile for Elisha's benefit. "And that's great about the class. What's the subject?"

It was Elisha who answered. "The sociology of publishing. We're going to explore gender identities and the balance of power in the world of publishing using some current bestsellers and a few twentieth century masters. I'm looking forward to it."

"Sounds great," Nan said. "Amanda, did anyone call?"

Amanda tore her gaze away from Elisha. "The messages are on your desk."

Nan left student and teacher to bond over the sociology of publishing.

Her hand was on the door when the sound of shattering glass exploded from the back of the house and Kate screamed. She found Kate bracing herself against the pedestal sink in the powder room at the end of the first floor hall. The small bathroom was peppered with bits of glass. A rough stone the size of a softball lay against the far wall. The window glass was broken in a couple of places. The eyelet lace curtains fluttered in the air moving through the ruined window.

"Are you all right?" Nan's shoes crunched on the broken glass.

Kate looked up, eyes wide, her creamy complexion gone grayish, and offered Nan a watery smile. "Scared the shit out of me."

Both women dissolved into hysterical giggles.

Elisha and Amanda weren't far behind.

By the time the Thornton PD arrived, Nan had herded everyone into the kitchen for tea.

"For now, I'll take a report and start canvassing." Sergeant Pete Lowry spoke with a slow deliberateness. His inspection of the property was thorough, and the young officer riding with him took photos and notes throughout their visit. "Ms. Pease didn't see anything on account of the curtain, and the three of you were on the front porch. I'll check with the Fullers, see if they noticed anything, but you don't exactly have neighbors out here, and without witnesses? It's not exactly C.S.I. up here. We're not set up to take prints off a garden stone."

"If I think of anything, Sergeant, I'll be sure to let you know," Nan promised. "In the meantime, can I have the window repaired?"

Sergeant Lowry looked around the kitchen. "Do you have someone who can handle the repair?"

Nan winced. That phrase was starting to get repetitive. "I do. Joss Fuller is already going to do some work here, I'm sure he can help me."

"He's a good kid. You'll be okay." Lowry seemed the kind of man Nan had always wished for as a father. Sturdy without going to paunch, with kindness and humor in his eyes. His salt-and-pepper mustache matched his regularly trimmed hair.

"Are you sure you won't have a cup of tea? Or coffee?" Nan offered.

"No thanks, Ms. Grady. I'm going to file your report." He pressed his lips together, furrowing his brow. "I have to ask you, though I can't imagine. Do you have any idea who might have done this?"

CHAPTER 7

Joss was outraged by the entire mess. "Who the hell chucks a rock through antique glass like that?"

"I wish I knew," Nan said. "Sergeant Lowry asked me the same question last night."

Joss sat across the kitchen island from Nan, hands wrapped around a mug of her truly excellent coffee. He'd come straight down from Catmint Gap when she'd called him about the broken glass. It was only a hair after seven. There was rain in the extended forecast; he wanted to get the roof buttoned up for her as soon as possible, but the window was going to have to take precedence.

He'd have to be careful not to make a habit of spending the first half hour of every day at the inn lingering over her coffee. And her company.

"Next time something like that happens, let me know sooner. I could have come down last night."

"You've already done enough emergency work around here."

Low, early morning sunlight streamed into her kitchen. The rich shine on the long farmer's table warmed up the still-chilly kitchen. Autumn was definitely in the air, and Joss had noted leaves beginning to give up green for gold on his way down the mountain.

Nan's eyes looked tired, he thought. He recalled the way she'd pulled herself together the night of the storm; he figured she wouldn't want him to fuss over her too much. He decided not to think about why he wanted to fuss over her in the first place. He went for easy humor. "Kate must be pissed."

He was rewarded with a wicked grin from Nan. A spark of laughter lit up her caramel eyes. Her movements were swift and graceful, her body wonderfully compact and feminine. He couldn't help admiring the way her layered cotton tees stretched over her curves when she reached into the fridge for cream for his coffee.

"She was pretty pissed," Nan agreed. "I think she wanted to head out into the marsh and hunt down the vandal." She smiled again at Joss. "I should have realized before this past weekend that you two knew each other."

"Her brother Jack and I've been buddies since we were kids. I've known her whole family forever." Joss wanted to see Nan's smile again. "She's a tough cookie."

"Yeah." Nan was all business again when she refilled his mug. "How long do you think it'll take to repair the glass?"

"I can get it done tomorrow. I'll measure and order the glass from the hardware store this morning, pick it up tonight on my way home. I can do the replacement first thing tomorrow."

Some of the weariness in her expression brightened into relief. "Oh, good."

He didn't fight the impulse to reach out for her hand. "You're sure you're okay?"

He felt her pulse jump under her skin. She didn't meet his eyes. "I'll be fine."

Fine wasn't okay. He'd been around enough women to know the difference. "If you need anything at all, you can call me, or my parents. You know that?"

Her eyes were shiny when she looked up, but she didn't pull her hand away. "Thanks, Joss."

"I mean it." He wanted to reach for the lock of hair that fell from behind her ear, but a door closed, followed by footsteps on the main stairs, and the moment dissolved. Her hand was gone; she was gathering up the coffee tray, presumably for whoever was on the stairs.

JIM AND CAROL CALLAHAN came into the kitchen as Joss was leaving.

"Good morning," Nan said, setting down coffee mugs at the farmer's table. Jim Callahan stood by the fireplace. His wife sat and paged through a back issue of Vermont Magazine from their room.

"Did you sleep well?" she asked. When they answered in polite monosyllables, alarm bells rang in her head. "Can I get you coffee or tea?"

"Yes, coffee for both of us," Carol Callahan said. "Jim, sit down."

Neither of them asked about the breakfast menu. The silence sat down like a third guest at the table.

"Ms. Grady," Jim Callahan began. Nan's stomach turned sourly. "I think we're going to be checking out. We're just not comfortable..." His words trailed off and he glanced significantly at the door to the foyer beyond. Nan was acutely aware of the sounds of Joss's measuring tape from the powder room.

"I hope you'll reconsider," she said, desperate to keep the pleading from her voice. "I'd be happy to take a night off your bill. I'm so very sorry your stay was affected by yesterday's incident."

She watched the couple exchange a series of nods and glances. It struck her that even in such a moment, she envied them the unspoken language of a well-established marriage.

"We appreciate the gesture, Ms. Grady," Jim Callahan replied, "but we've already booked rooms in Charlotte for the rest of the week."

They sipped at their coffee for another moment or two, before Carol Callahan closed the magazine and stood up. "I think we should just check out. I'd like to see that winery on the way up to Burlington." She looked pointedly at her husband. "Why don't you bring down the bags?"

"Mrs. Callahan, if you'll just follow me out to the office?" With her back to her lost guests, she blinked away tears and took a deep breath.

CHAPTER 8

Joss made the call to the hardware store from the front seat of his truck. He rested his feet in the driveway gravel. By the time he'd measured for the powder room glass and a few things up on the third floor, the sun was fully up and the muggy warmth of a September morning had drawn him outside. He couldn't see the Adirondacks from his vantage point, but the Green Mountains were at his back. His parents' pastures bordered the inn on two sides, new-growth woods on the third, and a marshy thicket grew alongside County Road on the fourth.

The valley was home. He knew the land, the silhouettes of the mountains, the shadows the clouds painted over the hillside pastures. In another life, he would have been out with Pop, tending to the dairy herd. He could see the lazy girls now, dotting the expanse of the East pasture, sunning their Jersey hides.

The Damselfly stood back some from the road. The property line on the Fuller side was marked by a sparse stand of pines and birches. Otherwise, tall marsh grasses and, farther out, his family's dairy pastures left the house relatively exposed.

How was it no one had seen whoever threw the stone yesterday?

The slap of the screen door snapped him from his reverie.

Elisha McNair came out the Inn's front door in wind shorts and a racerback tank. She wore a pair of earbuds and a tiny, nearly antique iPod clipped to her top. Seeing him sitting in the cab of his truck, she started down the stairs, waved, and pulled the earbuds out of her ears.

Manners dictated that he get out of his truck and talk with her, even while instinct told him to duck and cover.

She jogged over to the truck. He hopped out and shoved his hands in his pockets.

"Good morning, handsome," Elisha said, smoothing her already flawless ponytail and stepping in close.

"Elisha," he acknowledged. "Going for a run?"

"Between Nan's breakfasts and that fabulous looking pastry shop in town, I'm going to blow up like a balloon if I'm not careful." She ran her hands over her belly and hips.

Joss was a cautious man, but he wasn't dead. He knew when a beautiful woman was making an effort for him, and he couldn't help but appreciate hers. "I don't think you've got anything to worry about there."

Elisha tilted her head back to smile at him, shading her eyes from the sun.

"You flatterer," she smiled, touching his arm and shifting her body towards him. "So you're going to put the inn back together again?"

"Appears that way." He inched back along the seat. "Were you here yesterday when the rock came through the window?"

"I was." Her playful smile faded. "Poor Nan. And her friend!"

"And none of you saw anyone?"

A puzzled wrinkle formed on Elisha's flawless brow. "No. Why?"

"I was just thinking you can see to my folks place on one side, even with the trees, and the pastures are wide open." He looked over his shoulder into the marsh grass. "Whoever it was must have taken off into the marsh."

By the look on her face, Elisha had put two and two together quickly. "Someone who knows the property well, then."

Joss nodded.

Elisha shuddered. "I don't think that makes me feel any better."

"I'm sure it was just a one-time thing." Joss cast a glance at the house, thinking of the sweet woman inside. Who could have a reason to target her?

Elisha's gaze caught on the kitchen windows and a secretive half smile flirted with the corner of her lip. "Of course," she said, reaching up to put in her earbuds. "But just in case, it's nice to know there's a capable man around the place."

She stretched up on her toes and kissed his cheek, before turning and jogging down the driveway, turning right and heading down the state road towards the dairy.

He had to admit, the view was pretty good. Joss grabbed his Sawzall and his tool belt and headed towards the house.

"Come on in. It's open," Nan called, in response to his knock.

He found her at the sink, literally up to her elbows in dishwater.

"Do you need anything?" There was a chill in her tone.

"Nope. Are you okay?"

She turned to him with a pursed lips and a raised eyebrow. "Fine, thanks," she said, stacking a baking tray on the drying rack.

He looked for his coffee cup, and found it next to the sink, among the dirty dishes. So much for a refill. "I'll be up on the roof if you need me."

"Sure," she said. "I'll put fresh coffee on as soon as these dishes are done. Feel free to help yourself."

As Joss continued through the kitchen towards the main entryway, he had the distinct impression he'd been dismissed.

NAN WAITED until Joss left the room before exhaling. She'd felt like a voyeur watching the exchange from the kitchen window. They made a striking pair: Joss in his Carhartts and tee shirt, leaning against the doorframe of his pick-up, his eyes coasting over Elisha's toned physique, and Elisha looking like a model for a fitness gear catalogue in her LuluLemon and Asics. They glowed in the September sunshine, standing together in her driveway. She wanted to look away, but she felt foolish being so conscious of her reaction to seeing them together.

Since their impromptu meeting at Coulson's she'd been telling herself he couldn't really be that attractive, but every time, seeing him was like hitting an invisible wall: it surprised and humiliated her, knocked the wind right out of her. She was glad that she had a day full of mundane tasks to keep her occupied; she was going to need the distractions to keep her mind off Joss being in the house, off of the sight of Joss and Elisha, pressed into the side of Joss's truck.

She started off in the basement laundry room. She was switching bed linens to the dryer when she heard Joss in the kitchen above her. With the washer and dryer humming, she made her way upstairs.

He was outside rummaging in the cab of his truck.

Midmorning, Nan walked upstairs with the leftover pastries from Elisha's breakfast. From here on out, she wouldn't overdo it on the baked goods while Elisha was her only guest. The writer clearly didn't get her statuesque good looks from too many danish.

On the other hand, a friendly offering to Joss wouldn't go astray. She was a grown-up, and he might appreciate a snack. She approached the third floor with a little trepidation. She hadn't meant to be cool to him earlier, but awkwardness and the disappointed ache from the Callahans' departure had gotten the best of her.

Joss was cutting out damaged sections of wallboard when she came into the suite. His back was turned, and the noise from his saw drowned out her sudden sneeze. Standing amidst the swirling dust, she was glad she'd thought to wrap up the plate of pastries. She set the plate down on the plywood work surface Joss had set up, and tiptoed out again.

Elisha returned from her run, stopping to stretch on the driveway. Nan couldn't help but assume Joss would see her from his vantage point on the third floor. Shaking off the jealousy, she pulled out her recipe books. Time to come up with some sample menus for Anneliese, who was thinking big thoughts for The Damselfly's future.

She offered Joss a cup of coffee when he came downstairs a little later. "I was all set to have you come upstairs and tell me where to put all that furniture." His smile was sheepish.

"I took most of it apart and moved it myself over the weekend. I needed to feel like I was doing something. I hate feeling helpless, but most of this is way beyond my meager carpentry skills."

"I appreciate the prep work. It means I get off to a faster start."

"Which is good news for me." Good news lightened her mood even further.

"I'm going to start by replacing the broken joist. It's the only structural damage. The branch missed the ridge beam, which is really good news for you. Should keep time and costs down. The materials for the roof should be delivered tomorrow, and I'll make that a priority."

"I guess I was lucky?"

He answered her with a brief nod as he sipped the coffee. "If you need anything, come on up and ask."

"I'm going to do my best to stay out of your way," she said.

Elisha clacked in on impossible heels. "Joss."

Nan wondered unkindly if Elisha practiced that polished purr. She felt unreasonably short and grubby in the other woman's presence.

Elisha eyed the fresh-brewed coffee before eyeing Joss. "Are you staying for coffee?"

Joss stood and set his coffee cup down. "I'm afraid I have to get back to work. Nan, I'll check in with you before I go." He nodded as he turned for the door. "Ladies."

Elisha shrugged prettily. "I'm off then. Have a wonderful day, Nan."

Nan couldn't shake the feeling that there was something simmering under the surface of their exchange.

"You're sure it's okay if I'm here?" Nan sat at Kate's desk with a paper cup of tea, watching Kate press gum paste petals for an order of birthday cupcakes.

Kate's attention never left the delicate molds. "It's fine. Promise."

Nan watched Kate work: her dark hair was twisted back in a white baker's cap, her face scrubbed clean. The sleeves of her fuchsia chef's coat were rolled back to give her room to work. Her fingers were quick, her movement focused, but the look on her face was closer to the expression of a new mother watching her child.

Nan sipped a spicy herbal tea blend while Kate twisted floral wire around the petals and stood them in a styrofoam block to dry. The process was fascinating.

"Not that I'm not always glad to see you, sugar plum," Kate said, wrapping the leftover gum paste in plastic wrap and sealing it inside a plastic container. "But what brings you in this morning. I'm guessing from the fidgeting, it's not a purely social call."

Nan promptly stopped wagging her foot. "I'm worried, Kate."

Kate pulled off her cap and joined Nan by way of perching on the corner of the desk.

"I had guests cancel their stay and leave." She flicked a nail against her cup's plastic lid. "Three nights. They booked in somewhere in Charlotte because of that rock."

Kate pulled her into a one-armed hug. She smelled of sugar and laundry soap. "Hey, don't sweat them. One milquetoast couple does not mean failure."

"Milquetoast?" Nan giggled in spite of herself.

"Yes." Kate rested her cheek against Nan's head and gave her a little squeeze. "I'm not just a pretty face. I have words, you know."

"Really old-fashioned ones, anyway." Nan looked up at her best friend. "You really think I'm okay?"

"I really do." Kate's expression hardened. "And we'll get to the bottom of this. All of us together."

Nan felt a pang of nerves along with the heady warmth of Kate's inclusion, but she put on her brave face.

"Now." Kate shucked off her chef's coat and dropped it over the back of the chair Nan was sitting in. "Speaking of 'us,' how's having Joss around the place?"

Temping? Frustrating? Fascinating? "Interesting."

"Do tell. I love 'interesting.'" Kate spoke while making her way between two racks of pastries toward the door to the dining and retail space. "But give me a minute to grab us some more tea."

Nan drained her cup and braced herself to admit she was more than a little jealous of her bombshell guest.

CHAPTER 9

Once a week, regardless of bookings–or vandalism–Nan washed the linens. Kate teased her for being overly structured, but it wasn't easy for one woman, even with a part-time helper, to stay on top of the housework required by the inn. So, even if a room hadn't been occupied all week, on Fridays she changed the bed sheets and switched the towels.

All that laundry was easier to tackle with the prospect of paying guests ahead, so on this particular Friday she was happily distracted by her own daydreams.

The finished rooms laid themselves out in her imagination like a map. She populated them with perfect guests: an older couple planning a vow renewal and second honeymoon, leaf-peepers, Thornton College alumni.

She'd turned over the second floor, and washed a load of kitchen linens, leaving only the Adirondack Suite's sheets and towels. Even with all the linens in storage in the closed-off bathroom, she felt compelled to include them in her weekly routine.

Hope sprang eternal.

She planned to slip in through the dust barrier, deliver the clean towels to the bathroom, and head back downstairs without getting in Joss's way. She didn't want him to think she was hovering.

Her wishful thinking crashed to the floor, along with the whole stack of fresh towels, when Joss opened the bathroom door, nearly knocking her over.

Her *dammit* was distinctly un-innkeeper-like.

Joss dried his hands on the legs of his jeans and bent to retrieve the fallen towels. "I'm sorry. I didn't realize you were there."

"It's okay." She took a towel from him and snapped it out, grimacing at the fine sheen of plaster dust on the French terry.

"I have a meeting with an architect, and I didn't want to show up covered in dust." He halfheartedly dusted one towel off. "Can I at least help you re-fold?"

She shook her head. "It's really okay. I wasn't paying attention when I opened the door."

Joss held his hand out. "My mother taught me. I promise not to botch it."

She handed him one of the few that remained in her arms, mussed but still clean.

A curious sense of intimacy filled the air; it was like slow-dancing, folding towels with him in close confines of the bathroom. It was altogether too easy to imagine–as she laid an oversized bath sheet against her chest and flicked the corners inward to overlap in the middle–wearing the towel against her damp skin, feeling callused fingertips slide over her shoulder to release the plush fabric.

"I am sorry," Joss said, bringing her back to the moment.

"It's really okay." Nan stacked the towels on the toilet seat and hoped her fantasy hadn't played out on her face. "Do you have a minute to show me what you've been doing?"

"Sure. Anything for the client." Joss held the dust barrier aside for her.

He brought her over to the spot where the limb had broken the roof and ceiling. The hole in the roofing was gone, and she could see fresh lumber and plywood in the dim light above the ceiling.

"From the outside, you shouldn't be able to tell there was damage, except that the new shingles look new." There was certainty and quiet pride in his voice. "I've sistered in a new joist and done the strapping for the ceiling. It'll be closed in by next week."

It was easy to appreciate the work through his eyes. She understood his satisfaction, and it struck a chord with her. Even if she didn't understand the finer points of framing, she had a working knowledge of carpentry. Granddad made sure she knew how to swing a hammer; she could tell she was listening to someone who not only knew what he was doing, but loved it.

"So, I'll bring in the electrician and the plumber next, make sure everything's all set before we hang blue board. Then plaster, and paint." Joss paused. "Do you have a painter?" he asked, reaching into his pocket for his wallet. "I can recommend one or two good ones."

Nan shook her head. "No, I'm a pretty decent painter and I've got a good reserve of all my colors. I'll do it myself."

"I could help you out with it," he offered. "Off the clock. A neighbor helping out. You've got a lot going on with this place already."

A happy thrill coasted down her spine. She smiled up at him. "I'd like that, Joss. If you're not too busy."

He pocketed his wallet. "Just let me know when."

"I will."

She didn't want to lose the moment, but Joss's phone was pinging. He had a meeting. She had an inn to keep, and the moment slipped away as he excused himself.

"I've got to head out" He paused at the doorway. "Take care."

Nan stood under the newly reframed ceiling until his truck left the driveway. It took her longer than she liked to remember what it was she'd been planning to do next.

A RAINY WEEKEND came and went, leaving mild days and clear skies. While the work continued upstairs, and the weather was fine, Nan took advantage of the early autumn sunshine. She was working in the annual beds in the front yard when Molly Fuller walked up the road.

"Morning!" Molly waved as she crossed the lawn.

Nan looked up from under the brim of her straw hat to watch Joss's mother approach. She carried a basket over one arm and what appeared to be a small stool in her other hand.

Nan knew her nearest neighbor to be a practical and determined business woman. Anytime she mentioned being the Fuller Dairy's neighbor, someone added a piece of the Fuller family's history. By all accounts, Molly ran the business end of the dairy with the same ruthless Yankee frugality that she had used to keep her family fed during the leanest years. They were some of the lucky ones. Many Vermont dairy farmers had struggled and ultimately failed to keep their herds and land. Molly had jumped on the organic bandwagon early and pushed their small farm to stay competitive. Fuller's Dairy offered CSA shares, supplied local restaurants, and was a presence all around the county at Farmer's Markets.

Nan had seen for herself that Molly was also a kind and generous neighbor. It was clear to Nan where Joss's integrity came from.

"Hi, Mrs. Fuller," replied Nan. "How are you?"

"Oh, well enough, and I told you. It's Molly." Molly set the stool down on the front walk, next to the garden beds. "How are you, and that roof of yours?" She settled down on the stool and placed the basket at her feet.

"Joss is doing a great job. The insurance check is due any day, and it should cover all of the work, so I'm only down the lost business." The relief of speaking it aloud pushed her words out in a rush.

"I imagine that takes some of the weight off your shoulders. Can you recover, with all this coming so close to the opening?" asked Molly.

"I'll have to, won't I?" Nan sensed approval in Molly's gaze. "What can I do for you?"

"I brought over a few things for you." Molly unwrapped a folded gingham tablecloth.

"Oh, wow," Nan said, her smile blooming.

"Strawberry jam from this summer's crop," Molly continued. "Pear butter from last year's canning, and some cheeses. This label sources milk from local places, including ours. I figured if you like them, your guests just might, too."

"That's a great idea, Molly," said Nan, visions of homemade strawberry preserves on warm croissants and afternoon cheese plates in the parlor filling her head. The local angle would go over well with tourists.

"I also want you to have this stool." Molly stood again, stepping aside so Nan could get a better look.

Nan inspected the piece with fresh eyes. It looked like an old fashioned milking stool, but one that had grown right up out of the forest floor. It was practical, certainly, but there was magic and warmth in the twining form and glossy finish.

"Joss makes them from reclaimed timber. Some of it he cleared up at his place on Catmint Gap," Molly said.

Nan saw the pride aglow in Molly's face. "Joss makes furniture?"

"He does. I only wish he'd do more. He's got an artist's eye when it comes to woodworking, and his talents get lost on these contracting jobs."

"I wouldn't say that," Nan said, thinking of the care and precision she'd seen in his work.

"He works out of one of the old barns on our farm." Molly knew how to tell a tale. "He actually majored in visual arts at Thornton."

Nan's eyes went wide. Molly grinned.

"He did a lot of found object sculpture at first, and then it started looking like furniture. By the time he graduated, he was rivaling the fancy pieces at the craft guild." Taking her cue from Nan's delighted expression, Molly launched into a proud-Mama brag. "Frankly, at the time, it drove his father and me nuts. There we were, killing ourselves to give the boy that education, mortgaging the farm he didn't even want to the hilt, and he was making sculptures that looked like milking stools out of tree limbs and lacquer."

Nan laughed. It was hard to imagine Molly and Walt as anything but proud of their son.

Molly went on with the story. "A few years out of college he sold a few pieces to an art dealer for enough money to convince him he should take a shot at New York City. Folk art, they called it. He made milking stools and demilune tables in a studio in Brooklyn and shared a place with a couple of friends."

Nan could picture him in a woodworking studio, but not in a SoHo gallery.

"There was some falling out after Seth and Jack–do you know Jack Pease?" When Nan nodded, Molly continued. "Anyway, Joss came home…" Here the older woman paused, as if she'd said too much.

"He got his license and made some solid contacts here in the valley. Next thing he knew, he was running a contracting business, and the handmade stuff slowed down." Molly picked up the stool and handed it to Nan. "Now he sells a few pieces a year. Occasionally donates one to the Booster Club for a fundraiser." She bent and caressed the wood gently. "It's hard for me to admit his father and I thought it was a bad idea at the time."

Nan curved her hand along the contours of the seat. The man was a good neighbor, a reliable and trustworthy contractor, not to mention easy on the eyes. Now, a folk artist?

"Anyway," Molly said, "I was hoping maybe you could set this one somewhere in the house. Maybe drum up a little interest?"

"I'd be happy to, Molly. It's a beautiful piece." Nan remembered her manners. "Can I invite you in for tea? Or something to eat? I've got coffee or soda if you'd rather?"

"No, hon, I've got to get back to the farm," said Molly, "but I appreciate you putting in a good word for us with your guests."

"Of course." When Molly hugged her, she smiled to herself. "And I'll be by on Monday to pick up my order."

"Looking forward to the visit," Molly called back with a wave. Nan watched Molly walk along County Road as far as the dairy before bringing her new treasures inside.

~

LATER THAT EVENING, with the work done, Nan took a mug of tea into the parlor. She'd laid the first fire of the season in the fireplace–just a small one to ward off the chill. Her novel lay on the arm of the sofa, still unfinished; she was looking at the milking stool. She'd set it by the fireplace, near an old dairy pail that held kindling. She found herself tracing the lines of the piece with her eyes, watching the flicker of firelight on the satiny finish. The knobs and bends of the lacquered branches were sensual in their way, and the slice of tree trunk that formed the seat had a forest's biography ringed into it.

To be able to envision such a thing, and then to conjure it out of reclaimed timber and fallen limbs. To think, he had that talent in him. What other wonders was he hiding?

Despite the flutter of nerves he inspired, she was at ease in his presence. He drew her out; he piqued her curiosity.

Nan thought of his family, his roots in Thornton. Everything she'd craved, growing up in her grandparents' house with the shadow of her parents' mistakes over her like a caul–despite her grandparents' unflinching love. Her own family's roots ran deep in their Mass-achusetts mill town, but they were tarnished by scandal. Her grand-parents' generation had a long memory. Easier to deny those roots and move on, transplant herself somewhere the soil was more forgiving.

She knew from Molly that the Fullers went back generations in the Champlain Valley; Walt's ancestors fought the British on the Lake when the country was in its infancy.

Even dreams hadn't been able to tear Joss from his hometown.

She heard Elisha's feet in the room upstairs and did her best to banish thoughts of Joss. There was another tie. The stunning professor had roots here, too, roots she seemed interested in cultivating.

Nan feared she was no match for the other woman's stunning looks–or their shared history.

CHAPTER 10

Joss enjoyed the feeling of being in the midst of a challenging job. He liked to pull up to a site in the morning, knowing his tools and the work were waiting for him. He liked progress, loved the process of problem solving repairs and remodels.

He had always loved seeing a client pleased with the progress, but in the case of Nan Grady, he was like a school kid with a science project. He wanted to show off. More than a little.

He kept telling himself it had nothing to do with her being a pretty woman.

In the meantime, he tried to keep his head in the game. He had other projects in the works, and the Hills' barn had been put on hold for Nan's repairs.

He had called up a few guys he knew and trusted with framing work and sent them to continue the restoration of Ellen Hill's beloved barn, but he needed to check in on them every few days for his own peace of mind.

Hill Farm perched on a rise, southwest of Thornton. Ellen's grandfather sold the working part of the farm to a developer in the Fifties, but the parcel she lived on retained its privacy. The cluster of mid-century homes were hidden by birch woods and fir stands. On a clear day, you could catch the sparkle of Lake Champlain from her third floor. The barn remained, adjacent to the house, and Ellen relentlessly fought age and decay in the barn the way some women fought it off in their appearance.

"I admit, Joss," Ellen was saying, "I was a little concerned when you told me you were going to sub out the framing."

"But you're happy with the progress?"

"I am."

Joss silently thanked his makeshift crew. He owed those guys a little something extra. "Have you made a decision about the roof? Will I be patching the existing roof, or are we going to redo the whole thing?"

"I want it uniform, Joss. And a little better quality than the current roof," she said, thumbing through a binder she carried with her to all their meetings. She showed him a photograph of the shingles she preferred.

"These are great, but they're going to up your end cost," he warned.

"Money isn't the issue here, Joss. Preserving this barn is."

"Of course."

Ellen closed the binder. "Do you mind my asking when you'll be back on the job, Joss?"

"No more than another week or two, and I'll be checking in as I go. I'll have to introduce you to Nan Grady, Ellen. You two would get along famously."

"I like her already for saving Meg Swift's gardens."

He arrived at the inn later that morning to a fresh pot of coffee and a danish on a plate with a note from Nan saying, "Help yourself."

Not every client was so considerate, he'd mused, but then again, not every client was in the hospitality business. When he came downstairs around midday, planning to head over to the farm to scrounge in his mother's fridge for lunch, he found Nan in her kitchen, humming to herself over her work.

"Hey," he said, by way of announcing himself.

"Hi, Joss," she said, looking up from a bowl, whisk suspended in her hand. "How's everything going up there?"

"Fine," he said. "Just taking a trip out to grab some lunch."

"I'm in the mood for an omelet." She dipped the whisk back into the bowl, whirling the eggs into foam. "If you want, I can make one for you, too?"

"I wouldn't want to trouble you." He hoped she'd call his bluff.

"It's no trouble," she reassured him. "Have a seat."

She lowered the whisk and finished frothing the eggs in the bowl. "I was thinking chèvre and chive. Does that work for you?" she asked, turning back to the four burner professional range opposite the island.

"And I've got some smoked salmon, if you'd like," she added, pouring half the eggs into the pan.

"Sure." Sometimes there were miracles on a weekday morning.

She had two additional eggs whisked into the bowl before he'd even sat down.

"Margaret certainly didn't put that range in," he commented. "It's a beauty."

"I picked it up cheap from a restaurant closing sale down in Rutland. It was worth losing a few cabinets to make space." She ran a satisfied hand along the edge. "I love it."

"You did all that yourself?" He had to admit, the idea surprised him.

Nan laughed. "No, Kate's dad helped me take out the two cabinets, and the guy who sold it to me drove it up here."

Of course he had. Joss understood the impulse.

He watched, fascinated, as she swirled the eggs in the pan, sliding herbs and cheese into the eggs as they set. Her movements were swift, graceful, efficient. She left the pan for a moment, and pulled the salmon out of the fridge. She flaked a bit of the fish off the butcher paper and into the pan, folded the omelet, and slipped it onto a plate.

With one hand she slid the plate across the island, while she scraped out the pan with the other, and started the process over again.

Her own omelet only took a moment, so he waited for her to sit.

"You learned to cook at NECI, right?" he asked, picking up a fork full of eggs.

"Yeah," she answered. "It's where I met Kate. And Kate drew me here."

Joss hummed appreciatively as his brain and stomach simultaneously registered the bliss of a perfect omelet. His eyes drifted closed, he breathed deep. For a few moments, their forks scraped contentedly through the eggs.

"This is amazing," he said, fork poised over his plate. "Why do your guests ever leave?"

"I keep hoping they won't want to," she laughed. "That's what makes them want to come back."

"You said Kate drew you here. You weren't always set on this area?"

"I knew I wanted to stay in New England. I grew up on the Mohawk Trail, and other than my internships in Arizona and Florida, I've lived in New England all my life. But here? Thornton?" She paused. "I fell in love with the town through Kate's eyes, and then I saw this house for sale."

"You make it seem easy, but it's got to be grueling." He scooped up the last of his omelet.

"I love it, but it's demanding, and it never won't be. It's a huge commitment. Sometimes I wonder what possessed me to try this while I'm still–"

Single hovered unspoken.

Joss set his fork down gently on his plate. He snuck a glance at her. She was blushing, fidgeting with her fork. He wanted to sit all day with her, to hear her vision for the inn. He wanted to watch her move, study her grace, but the third floor was waiting, and he knew she was counting on him to get the suite back into working order again.

Time to exit, then, and spare her dignity.

"I've got to get back to it. You need those rooms." He plucked a mug from the mug tree, keeping his tone light. "Can I grab some coffee? You've got a talent there."

She took the mug from him, but her gaze only skated over his. "I'll get it."

Nan offered the mug back to him with an awkward smile. He took it and went back to work, refueled not only by the eggs, but by Nan herself.

~

WITH THE WALLBOARD HUNG, Joss thought, the room looked pretty good. He stepped back into the center of the room to take in the last couple weeks' work. He wondered if Nan would actually call him about the paint.

He would be sorry to be done with this job. He knew Nan needed the room finished, he was satisfied with the work he'd done, but he'd enjoyed her as a client, enjoyed getting to know the woman behind the innkeeper.

He thought back to the room the night of the storm, the acrid scent of burning wood, the limb laying incongruously on the bed. He'd admired the classic lines of the old sleigh bed, recognized it as a second hand piece–knowing Nan, probably from the big flea market up in Charlotte. Standing there in the room, refurnishing it in his mind, he realized he wanted something a little more quietly fanciful–a little more like Nan herself–for the space.

The lines drew themselves in his imagination. A four poster, perhaps with a canopy frame. A glowing natural finish. Graceful, curving lines, unexpected in a traditionally boxy form. As the bed took shape, the strong, bending grain of birch came to mind.

But would Nan accept a gift like that? She struck him as proud, independent, and unused to lavishness.

He wondered if she'd take it at cost instead.

The project was already flourishing in his mind. If she wouldn't take it, if it came out the way he was envisioning it, he could probably sell it through the craftsmen's guild in town or Linda's gallery in Warren. Lin was always after him to do larger pieces.

He sincerely hoped that wouldn't be the case.

∽

Twilight fell before Joss finished on Friday night.

The Damselfly was empty save the two of them; Elisha was in meetings at the college, and the rest of the rooms awaited check-ins the next afternoon.

Nan ate a salad in her office while she updated the inn's website. Joss's quick knock on the open door yanked her out of an HTML fog. "You're done?"

"For tonight." He dusted his hands off on his cargo pants. "Sorry to be rattling around so late, but I've got the electrician coming by tomorrow."

"Please, don't worry about it." The truth was, she liked knowing he was upstairs, even if her attraction to him left her on edge, overly aware of his presence.

"Can I take this to the kitchen for you?" Joss asked, picking up her empty salad plate.

Nan stood, reaching for the dish, but he smiled, and turned out of the room. She caught up with him at the sink. "You don't have to do that."

"Don't tell my mother that." Under the pendant light that hung over the sink, his eyes were shadowed. "Besides, I wanted to."

Nan sensed a shift in the atmosphere.

Their hands brushed as she took the dishes from him. Awareness shimmered over her skin and she almost dropped them. She set the plates down in the sink with extra care and looked up at Joss.

He was looking down at her with those gray eyes the way her traitorous imagination had pictured him looking at Elisha. She felt she should say something, but the words wouldn't come and the silence stretched out between them.

She simply hadn't considered this possibility.

His thumb was brushing against her knuckles, the pressure so light it had taken a moment to register. He reached out with the other hand and caressed her cheek, cupping her jaw in his calloused hand. Slowly, so slowly, he brought her face up, lowering his mouth to hers.

Their lips touched, just a feather-light pressure, and the tension of the evening drained out of Nan all at once. Joss caught her sigh with his mouth, this time with a little more purpose. She opened her mouth against his, tasting his lips with her tongue, and felt his hand leave hers to comb through her hair.

Joss's hands skimmed down her neck, over her shoulders, down her back to pull their bodies closer, and Nan gave in to the pleasure. The kiss deepened, and Nan ached to feel more of him.

She couldn't remember ever abandoning herself to a kiss like this. Her hands seemed to move of their own volition; her fingers wound in the hair that brushed his collar. She spread her palms against the warm skin of his neck, drew them towards his chest, enjoying the strength under his soft cotton shirt.

Strength that had as much to do with the man as with his profession.

The crunch of tires on the gravel outside, followed by a loud, metallic clatter on the stones, had her pulling away from him, her breath hitching a little as her heartbeat began to slow. Joss looked slightly shaken, as well.

"Elisha must be back." She sounded like a breathless girl. A car door slammed outside.

"That was unexpected," Joss said, grinning crookedly.

"Which part?" Her laugh was shaky, but Joss pressed a gentle kiss to her forehead.

Elisha burst through the kitchen door. She pulled up short when she saw Nan and Joss at the sink. "I think I just saw your vandal."

"What?" Nan and Joss both barked the word at her, but Joss reacted faster.

Outside, the headlights of Elisha's rental car illuminated three hastily painted words sprayed across the garage doors in dripping black:

GO AWAY BITCH

*J*oss stalked the floor in front of the parlor fireplace. His scowl reflected Nan's anxiety back to her. In the fifteen minutes since Elisha had discovered the graffiti, Joss had barely spoken. Nan hadn't seen her only guest since she'd vanished upstairs to put her things in her room.

In the meantime, Nan had called the Thornton police before turning on every exterior light she had.

Joss stopped, picked up a pottery Holstein and turned it his hand. "I don't think you should be alone here tonight."

Nan left her perch on the arm of a nearby wing chair. She liked that little cow; she'd bought it her first semester at NECI at a Vermont Hand Crafters' festival. "I don't think I'm in any danger of being spray-painted to death." She took it gently from his hand and set it back on the mantle.

He circled his hands around her forearms, drawing his palms down over her sleeves and lacing his fingers with hers. "Someone has attacked your home twice. I don't think it's crazy of me to suggest you call Kate and ask her stay with you." His next words were softer. "I don't want anything to happen to you."

"She's hardly going to be alone." Elisha stood in the parlor doorway, arms crossed, hip resting on the jamb. Her tone was kind, but it hinted at irritation nonetheless.

Nan tugged her hands out of Joss's.

Joss's soft expression hardened, a flush crept up his neck. "I'm sorry, Elisha. I don't mean to imply–"

Elisha smiled at him in the way mothers smiled at their sticky-faced toddlers, but her voice was politely biting. "Of course you didn't mean to imply that I'm not sufficiently capable of taking care of myself, or even that I'm not in fact in the building."

"Christ." Joss muttered under his breath; Nan bit back a smile. Further sniping was interrupted by the front doorbell.

"I'll get the door." Nan shot Joss a silent plea. "Elisha, thank you."

Elisha sat in the wing chair whose arm Nan had only recently vacated. Joss walked Nan to door.

She put a hand on his arm. "I'll call Kate. She'll come."

He squeezed her hand lightly. "Thank you."

KATE WAS unboxing muffins and pouring coffee for Joss and Elisha when Nan came into the kitchen. She had nothing to offer Pete Lowry in the way of information, but at least now that Kate was here, she could offer him a snack for his trouble.

Kate pushed a mug her way. "I never knew innkeeping was so exciting, sugar plum."

Nan let her frustration come to the surface. "I could do with less excitement."

Elisha was waiting elegantly across the long farmer's table with Joss. She looked up at Nan with a questioning tilt to her perfectly plucked brows. "My turn?"

Nan nodded, feeling suddenly frumpy. Elisha rose from her seat and went to give her statement to Sergeant Lowry.

Joss stood as well. "I should get going. I'm glad you're here, Katie."

Nan could feel Kate's eyes on her when she met him at the door. "I'll walk you out."

"'Night, Joss." Kate chimed from her spot near the coffee.

Nan prayed he didn't catch her best friend's cheeky wink.

Outside, the air was cool and mild, the stars close overhead. They walked side by side to Joss's truck, their bodies close but not quite touching.

Joss was the one to break the quiet. "I can come by tomorrow and help you clean up."

"Are you sure? I don't want to spoil your Saturday." Nan blushed, feeling like a schoolgirl.

He turned to her. "I want to."

"Okay." She threaded her fingers together awkwardly.

Joss leaned in close. His breath shivered over her skin. "You should know that I'm going to think about you between now and then."

He kissed the corner of her mouth, lips lingering near hers for a whispered goodnight, before climbing into the truck's cab. Nan stood in the driveway, feeling that touch for a long moment after he'd gone.

Kate's knock on the window reminded her to stop dreaming in the moonlit driveway. Kate's expression when she was safely inside the house let her know there would be no secrets.

"I get the impression I'm interrupting something."

Nan felt the grin split her face. "No. Elisha and my graffiti artist took care of that a while ago."

"What happened?" Kate grabbed two steaming mugs and dragged Nan to the farmer's table. "Did you kiss him?"

"Not exactly …" A flutter rose up from Nan's belly in the telling. "He kissed me."

"And?" Kate's curiosity wasn't so easily avoided.

"And he's a very good kisser."

Kate tucked her feet up under her knees, assuming the girl-talk posture she'd adopted back when they shared a room at the New England Culinary School's Essex Junction campus. Her expression was stern, but Nan knew the sparkle of mirth in her eyes. "Just how long has this been going on?"

"About two hours," Nan replied. When Kate pursed her lips in disbelief, Nan was quick to check the reproduction clock on the wall. "Seriously. I mean, yes, I was attracted, but I thought …"

"I love when you're wrong." Kate was gleeful. "So, what happened?"

At first Nan didn't know quite what to say. Their kiss, while full of promise, wasn't a movie moment with fireworks and violins. She was out of practice at dishing, but as she spoke she got lost in the reliving. Joss's gray eyes in the low light, the comfortable intimacy of being alone together in the house, the magic she sensed brewing between them, the sweet reality of his warm lips over hers.

Kate's answering smile was soft. "He's made a romantic out of my practical Nan."

Nan snorted. "Not yet. It was a kiss. I'm hardly looking at *Modern Bride*."

"You might not be," Kate said slyly, "but a solid majority of the women in this town would in your shoes."

Nan sighed. "And a solid majority of them would probably be better suited for him."

Kate plunked her mug down. "What?"

"I keep thinking that he's so much a part of this place. Family, friends, history, education. And I'm still so much a stranger."

"Screw that." Kate swigged the dregs from her coffee cup. "You're fast on your way to being at the heart of this town. Everyone who knows you loves you. She unfolded her endless legs. "And you're practically a Pease by association, which is like being best friends with the prom queen."

"Like being best friends with the prom queen?" Nan giggled. "You were the prom queen."

Kate bowed slightly. "Yes. Indeed I was. A dubious honor which your handsome contractor never shared."

"I hope not," Nan managed between increasing laughter. "I can't picture him in a tiara."

"You know what I mean." Kate tried for reproachful, but only managed to give in to the giggles herself.

～

JOSS WAS BACK bright and early, with a gallon of primer and a fresh roller in the back of his truck.

He smelled eggs frying. Nan was at the stove when Kate let him in. "Morning, Joss."

"Morning, Katie. Nan."

Kate's mischievous grin spoke eloquently of slumber-party secrets and female laughter. Nan's cheeks were pink when she turned to say hello. He hoped it wasn't all due to proximity to the hot stove.

"Smells amazing. What's the occasion?"

"No occasion. There are humans in the kitchen." Kate slipped a companionable arm around his shoulders. "She's incapable of letting us fend for ourselves."

The toaster popped, adding the scent of English muffins to the room. Joss inhaled deeply. "I'll take it."

The hair framing Nan's face curled slightly in the steam from the frying pan. She was dressed for work, in a paint-stained, button-down shirt and jeans. Her sneakers had seen better days.

She was perfect.

When she sat him down in front of a fried egg sandwich and a mug of strong coffee, he would have installed a brand new garage door for her on the spot.

"So Joss," Kate asked around a bite of sandwich, "have you heard anything about this new woman Jack's been squiring about town?"

"Nothing I'm repeating in mixed company," Joss said, feeling a hot flush rise up the back of his neck.

Kate guffawed; Nan tilted her head, but her eyes widened slightly. He'd forgotten she knew Kate's older brother. "Sorry, Nan."

"I'm aware of Jack's…" Nan wrinkled her nose with a wry smile. "Reputation."

"Right." Joss looked into the depths of his perfectly fried egg, wondering just exactly how much Nan knew about Jack Pease.

"I'll just have to badger it out of him myself," Kate said, rising to clear her plate. "He can entertain me on the phone while I drive down to Rutland to meet with the Calvados guy."

"Calvados guy?" Joss watched Nan gravitate toward Kate's news, the question colored with curiosity and what he could only describe as food-nerd joy.

"Oh! Did I not tell you?" Kate spent a full five minutes extolling the virtues of some apple grower in Cavendish who was producing his own apple cognacs in the Norman style. "Shit," she said, looking at her phone. "I gotta jet. Have fun, you two."

With a wicked grin, she was gone.

"Why is Katie meeting with a Calvados guy?" Joss took Nan's plate from her. The gesture was familiar; Joss loved the two bright spots of color that rose on her cheeks.

"Have you ever had her Tarte Tatin?" Her lashes settled on her skin as her eyes drifted shut. "It's divine—she soaks the apples in Calvados, and that lovely spiked apple flavor in the Crème Anglaise is –"

He couldn't resist the hushed reverence in her tone. The way she talked about Kate's pastry was seductive as hell. Before she opened her eyes, he circled her waist with one arm and drew her close, whispering close to her lips. "I'm sure it's delicious."

He'd meant to keep it playful, but she melted into him. Her body went pliant in his arms and she smiled against his mouth. While the hand at her waist gathered up her worn cotton shirt, he brushed her cheek with his free hand. She smelled like clean sheets and sunshine and something lemony, and he wanted nothing more than to kiss her until they were both breathless with it.

She shivered when his fingers grazed the warm skin at the small of her back. He felt her sharp inhale, then she shifted her mouth against his, drawing him deeper into her flavor.

When his libido kicked into overdrive he forced himself to pull back. His pulse was racing, his breath coming hard. He hadn't anticipated the fire, and his reason felt a bit charred around the edges. "Hey."

She laid her head against his chest; he squeezed her in a quick hug.

"We should think about tackling that garage door before your guests get here. After all," he smiled and kissed her one last time, "I have my professional reputation to think of."

She answered his smile with her own. "As do I."

CHAPTER 12

"I've left the phones with you, but I don't expect a lot of phone traffic this evening. Ms. McNair knows her way around, and the online booking software will handle itself." Nan cast her eyes around the room, as if to secure everything simply by seeing it. She imagined this was how mothers felt, leaving their children with a sitter, though in fairness someone wasn't usually vandalizing your baby.

"I think I can handle a phone booking, if someone calls." Amanda pulled up the form on Nan's computer screen, her nearly turquoise eyes twinkling with wry humor.

Amanda's recently adopted blonde pixie cut was clearly an homage to a young actress's similar cut; Nan realized it made her inn-sitter seem far older than her just-shy-of-twenty-one years.

"Do me a favor, because I'm paranoid and mildly crazy." Nan gave a self-deprecating chuckle. "If someone does actually call to book a stay, write it all down separately as well as putting it in the system?"

"Consider it done." Amanda picked up a pen and tapped it on a legal pad. "Hopefully along with my chemistry homework."

A baritone honk from the driveway distracted them from Nan's note-giving.

Kate was crossing the driveway in the slanting late afternoon light, looking back over her shoulder and waving at Walt Fuller's rusty Chevy pickup driving away.

"Looks like Kate just got here. In my neighbor's truck." Nan gave the office one last look. "So, you'll be okay?"

"I'll be fine," Amanda confirmed. "Have a great time, Nan."

"Thanks." Nan left Amanda in the office. The front door flew open ahead of Kate, who sailed in and hugged her.

"Walt stopped into the bakery to get Molly some chocolate cherry cookies just as I was heading out. I figured I'd hitch a ride. He's such a sweetie."

Nan looked her over. Kate was wearing a fitted jacket over a lacy camisole and inky denim slung snug and low on her slim hips.

"How do you fit underwear under those?" Nan asked wryly.

"Who say's I'm wearing any?" Kate winked outrageously.

Nan had no choice but to laugh at Kate's antics. "So, where are we going, without your underwear?"

Kate looked out the open window at the sky, washing from pale blue to gold as the sun sank; Nan could swear Kate was scenting the possibilities on the breeze coming in.

"Back into town, to Temple. Dee's got a great band playing tonight–some guys I knew from high school. They'll draw a crowd from the whole valley. We are going to dance and persuade some man to buy us a shot… or five." Kate's tone was perfectly sincere.

"I should get dressed, then." Nan matched Kate's gravitas.

Kate followed her into the bedroom, keeping a watchful eye as Nan grabbed a pair of peep-toed wedges with a low heel. Nan pawed through her closet, settling on dark green tee shirt. She pulled on her favorite jeans, shook out her hair, and swiped lip gloss over her dry lips.

She did a little turn for Kate, who gave her a cursory once over.

"You'll do," Kate sighed. "Come on, we'll take your VW into town, and you can crash at my place tonight."

Nan shot her a look.

"Hush," Kate touched a finger to Nan's lips before she could protest. "You'll call Amanda later, and tell her to lock up and head home. You'll get up with me; I'm training a new morning baker on the five o'clock shift. You'll be back here long before Professor Barbie surfaces from her beauty sleep."

VINTAGE SIGNS HUNG over the booths, colored lights draped the back of the bar, mismatched linens and cutlery lent the tables in the dining area a homey charm. The band had drawn a crowd, and the good time was already in progress when Nan and Kate arrived.

The last of the dinner crowd was just finishing up. At the tables up front, Nan recognized the manager of the co-op market eating with his two teenaged kids. There were a few locals occupying the dozen bar stools, working guys whose businesses kept the town running, and a whole lot more college boys bellied up to the empty spaces at the bar.

Temple's dance floor would be raucous by the time the kitchen closed. Nan paused to say hello to the co-op manager; when she looked up, Kate was already halfway to the bar.

"Dee!" Kate hollered, waving. Deirdre Temple sauntered over, pushing a heavy tangle of blonde curls off her face.

"Katie Pease!" she laughed. "You've been busy. I haven't seen you in here in weeks."

"*Mea culpa*, friend. I'm here now," Kate reassured. "And I brought Thornton's hostess-with-the-mostest in with me."

Nan caught up to Kate and scooted in next to her at the bar.

"What'll it be, girls?" Deirdre asked. The touch of brogue in Deirdre's delivery never failed to charm Nan.

"I'll have a Manhattan with two cherries." Kate shot her friend an I-dare-you look. "Nan?"

Nan shook her head a fraction. "Dark and Stormy, Dee."

"I'll be right back," Deirdre said, before turning to the scruffy man next to them. "Robbie, you need another, babe?"

"Nah, Dee. I'm okay."

"Bullshit you're okay. But I'll bring you the check."

The scruffy man watched Deirdre saunter away with visible longing.

"Robbie?" Kate asked, touching the man's shoulder.

"Yeah, Kate?" Robbie replied, his eyes still on Deirdre's swaying hips.

"When the papers are signed, you ask Dee out to dinner, over at Nan's place. The Damselfly Inn. On County Road."

Robbie looked blearily at her over his empty bottle. Nan raised a brow at Kate but said nothing.

"I'm dead serious, Robbie Shaw."

"Okay, Kate. Okay." Robbie acquiesced with a defeated shrug and the ghost of a smile.

Deirdre returned with their drinks. Nan started to dig into her pocket. Robbie put out a hand to stop her.

"I got it." He pushed a ten across the bar with a hopeful smile for Dee. "Kate and her friend are on me."

Kate kissed Robbie's cheek, winked at the bartender, and grabbed the drinks. She maneuvered her way toward the patio out back, where a few empty tables waited. She nudged Nan into a chair and folded herself into one.

"What was that back there?" Nan fished the lime from her drink and squeezed the juice over the ice before dropping the peel back in.

"What? With Robbie?" Kate was all big eyes over the rim of her martini glass.

Nan nodded.

"I used to make out with Robbie when we were in high school." She plucked one of her two cherries out of the drink. "He's a sweetie. Married the wrong girl right out of Thornton Union. She left him last year, for their mechanic."

Nan sighed.

Kate pushed the other cherry to the bottom of the glass, muddling it a little with the toothpick. "He has a crush on Dee. Comes in here every night, drinks one sad beer, and goes home alone to the freshly emptied split-level Jessie made him buy."

"So you're bossing him into asking her out?"

"More or less." Kate said with her know-it-all smile. "And bossing you into expanding into dinner on the terrace or in that sweet little bay window nook in your parlor. Now, spill."

"Spill what?" Nan replied, trying to sound casual.

The grilling she was about to get regarding Joss was interrupted by the arrival of two young men who didn't look old enough to buy the beers they were carrying.

The spokesman of the pair, blonde and self assured, spoke first. "Hey."

Kate silently dared them to take her on. Nan knew it was a game, and one Kate would crush them in, and momentarily pitied the two boys.

Nan replied with an easy smile; they were sweet to try flirting with Kate. "Hi."

Spokesman flashed her a smile that probably cost his parents more than her monthly income. "My buddy Liam here wants to know what you're drinking, and if he can buy the next one."

Nan was taken aback. "Me?"

Liam flushed deeply and shot Spokesman a withering look. "Sorry."

Flustered, Nan opened her mouth to speak, but Kate replied for her. "She's spoken for, gentlemen."

Liam silently dragged his friend back into the crowd, and Nan rounded on Kate.

"Spoken for?"

Kate was unapologetic.

"I left you alone with Joss on Sunday. Did you put the moves on him?" Kate waggled her eyebrows. "Don't you dare hold out on me."

Nan attempted a neutral expression. "I'm not holding out. Nor am I spoken for."

Kate pressed on. "I know for a fact there was kissing the night before, and I'm not blind or stupid. I could tell he was into you at breakfast."

Nan concentrated hard on the condensation beading and dripping from her glass.

Kate went in for the kill. "You really like him."

Nan felt the red stain of embarrassment on her cheeks. Kate had always seen right through to the heart of her.

"Oh, my god. What happened?" Kate pressed. "Please tell me you seduced him in the kitchen or something wonderful like that!"

Nan's blush deepened. She had a healthy swallow of her drink, letting the alcohol burn down her throat. She was torn between wanting to confess everything to Kate and wanting to keep her feelings close. As soon as she shared them, they became something to be examined, analyzed. Then again, Kate already knew they'd kissed, already had a sense of the giddy pleasure she took from Joss's interest.

Out with it then. "He kissed me again."

Kate didn't miss a beat. "And you just stood there thinking, 'Is he done yet?'"

Nan rolled her eyes. "I kissed him back."

"So, you've made out twice with the most eligible bachelor in town?" Kate clarified. Neither woman noticed the bartender saunter over with a second round of drinks for them.

"You don't say? Who's that now?" Deirdre asked, a conspiratorial smile on her face.

"Mum's the word, Dee." Kate whispered, finger laid theatrically over her lips.

Dee gave them a wide grin, followed by miming locking her lips, before turning back for the bar.

"Oh, god. Kate..." Nan groaned.

A few hours later, collapsed in a heap of borrowed pajamas and blankets on Kate's bed, Nan finished a glass of water and set it on the nightstand. "My feet hurt."

Kate rolled over and bolstered a pillow under her cheek. "You need better dancing shoes, then."

"When I recover, you can take me shopping."

"So ..." Kate lay back against her pillow and closed her eyes. "Was reeling in the dream man of half this town's population part of your master plan?"

"It's not like that, you know," Nan began. "I'm not reeling him in."

Kate cracked one eye open.

"It's not," Nan tried again. "I'm not. I mean–"

"You like him," Kate finished for her. "He's a good guy, sugar plum. You could do a lot worse."

"It was just kissing, Kate. It's not like we're dating."

"He hasn't 'just kissed' anyone in the last couple years, hon. In this town, I'd hear about it if he did."

"I'm painfully aware of that," Nan replied. She snuggled in next to Kate and gave in to sleep.

CHAPTER 13

*J*oss was whistling along to vintage Creedence when he pulled into Nan's driveway. True to his word, he had been thinking about her. He'd been thinking about taking her out–dinner, a date.

He'd been thinking about kissing her again.

Nan's VW was gone, so he set about unpacking his tools from the truck. He could check in with her later in the day, see how she felt about bad pizza, cheap beer, and a second-run movie at the Marquis.

The front door was unlocked, which surprised him. It was early for anyone to be coming and going that way. Nan, he'd noticed, mostly used the kitchen door, and Elisha the same. He hadn't noticed any other guests in residence, so the open door bothered him. He shouldered his bag and picked up the case that held his finish tools.

Joss was about to turn the last corner before the second story stairs when he heard a door swing open behind him. Elisha came out of her room, turning to lock the door. She was again dressed for running.

He had to admire her dedication.

"Morning."

Elisha was frosty. "You might want to keep it down until Nan's guests have had a chance to get a cup of coffee."

Her cool accusation rose the hair on his forearms. He hadn't made any noise to speak of. "Aren't you her only guest?"

With a cranky huff, she dropped her room key into the slim pocket of her wind jacket and strode away down the hall.

He blew out a breath. Complicated. Whatever this thing was with Nan, it would be complicated as long as Elisha was around, he thought as he climbed the stairs to the third floor.

He opened the suite and swore roundly.

The plywood work surface he'd set up on sawhorses was tossed over, the tools he'd left there scattered across the floor.

The new plaster was slashed and cracked. The trim stock was gouged and haphazardly broken up.

What the hell?

He pulled out his phone, brought up Nan's number, and hoped she was somewhere close by. She answered on the fourth ring.

"Nan, it's Joss. I just got to the inn, and I think there's been a break-in. Where are you?"

"I'm in the car, on my way back from... Did you say a break-in? Where's Elisha? What happened?"

"Elisha just went out for a run. She saw me on the stairs on my way up to get started, accused me of being too loud, too early." Joss surveyed the room again. "I think she probably heard your visitor."

"What happened?"

"Tools scattered, some damage to the trim stock and the walls. Doesn't look like anything but the suite was hit."

Nan exhaled audibly. "Oh, no."

"I'm going to call Thornton PD, see if I can get Pete Lowry back over here. I'll meet you outside."

He paced by the window waiting for Nan, tallying the time and expense to mend the damage.

Lowry's cruiser followed Nan's Jetta into the driveway; Joss jogged downstairs to meet them. When Pete Lowry hefted himself out of the driver's seat, Joss relaxed a little. Pete had been his Little League coach, and in more recent years Joss had redone the Lowrys' upstairs bathroom. It was a relief that he was the officer involved. Pete acknowledged the younger man with a nod, and Joss walked over to open Nan's car door for her.

"More trouble, Ms. Grady?" Sergeant Lowry glanced at the cleaned and primed garage door.

Nan was unable to tear her eyes off the window of the suite, three floors above. She glanced at Joss. "Yeah, but I don't know what exactly happened."

Standing next to her, Joss could feel her need to get inside tugging at her.

Lowry reached into his pocket for a small notepad. "Let's go on in and have a look."

Joss's heart broke for Nan when she saw the damage. Her eyes filled and her chin trembled, but she held herself steady. He caught her miserable expression as she took it all in. He thought he understood. It was more personal, this vandalism. An accident, a force of nature, that he could comprehend. But he knew he too would take–did take–this gesture far more personally. It was baffling.

Pete took photos of everything with his phone before ushering them out, this time careful not to touch anything that might have prints on it.

Joss gave Lowry his statement in Nan's office while Nan waited in the kitchen. When he joined her, he could see the stress in her eyes.

"I should have been here," she said. Her guilt was palpable.

"I'm glad you weren't." He closed the space between them and hugged her. "What if something had happened to you?"

Lowry cleared his throat from the foyer door. "Ms. Grady, did you have the locks changed when you bought the property?"

"No." Her eyes widened and he reached for her hand.

"There's no sign of forced entry." He frowned. "I think our vandal had a key."

IN THE HOURS after Pete Lowry's assessment of the situation, Nan felt that work needed to go on. She pressed Joss to let her go on with her day, promising she would find him if she needed anything.

Joss's mind was only half on his work. Despite their relatively new acquaintance, and his admitted bias, he couldn't wrap his head around why someone would target Nan, or the Damselfly Inn. The house had moved from one quiet owner to another, and Nan was proving to be a welcomed addition to Thornton.

Who could possibly want the inn or its keeper to feel threatened? And why?

He'd invented more excuses to check up on Nan than was in any way necessary, and when Elisha's car hadn't made an appearance by quitting time he was determined not to leave Nan alone at the inn.

He found her in her office. "Is Elisha back yet?"

Nan looked at him curiously.

"It's just... I don't want you to be alone." He felt awkward for invoking Elisha.

"She has dinner in town fairly often, or goes out with other faculty members. I don't expect her anytime soon; though she could always surprise me."

"Come over to the farm for supper then. I'll bring you back before it gets too late." He pushed his hands into his back pockets to still them. Asking Amy Kovaleski to the prom had been a less fidgety prospect. "It feels wrong, leaving you here."

She shuffled a stack of papers and dropped them into an open drawer in her desk. "Joss, I don't think I'm in any danger tonight."

He couldn't describe it to her, but the whole scenario had bells going off in his head.

"Come with me. My mom loves to feed people, and she likes you." He strove to sound casual, hoping his mom's legendary cooking was too much to resist.

She took a deep breath. "Okay. I will. Give me ten minutes?"

He sensed an unspoken misgiving, but she shut down the computer and left her desk.

When she passed him to leave the office he laid a hand on his arm.

Her smile only touched the corners of her mouth, but her eyes seemed less sad. "Thanks."

With Nan beside him in the cab of his truck, he drove the quarter mile to his parents' farm. He felt better, but she still seemed preoccupied, watching the pastures that separated her property from theirs with a grim expression. He resisted the urge to take her hand, clenched lightly on her thigh.

The drive lasted only moments, but her silence made it seem longer. He cut the engine and hopped out of the truck, making his way around the front of the cab. She let herself out, thwarting his effort to get the door for her, so he closed it behind her and followed her up to the back door.

CHAPTER 14

*N*an assumed the frantic whirring of her thoughts was audible, if Joss' careful treatment of her in the car was any indicator, but when he gently steered her through the back door of his parents' house, she forgot to be upset.

To say Molly Fuller's mud room was charming was an understatement. A well-worn braided rug under her feet, a cheerful green hall bench, and baskets of hats and mittens ready for the coming fall enveloped her as she walked in. The warm glow from the schoolhouse light eased the tension in her shoulders as Joss helped her out of her coat and hung it on a peg above the bench.

"Mom's always been a stickler for no shoes in the house." He deftly plucked a pair of sheepskin slippers out of a basket and handed them to her. "She keeps spares for guests."

Nan slipped her feet out of her clogs and into the soft slippers. They were a little big, and she remembered shuffling around her grandparents' house in Granddad's slippers as a child.

Walt Fuller was sitting in a leather armchair, smoking a pipe and tying what looked like fishing flies by the light of an apothecary's lamp. He looked up and smiled around the pipe at Nan and Joss. He finished a fiddly bit of work and set it down, before taking out his pipe to stand up and welcome Nan.

"Molly!" he called, "Joss is here with Nan Grady."

Her reply floated in from the kitchen along with the tang of tomatoes and garlic. "Send Nan in here once you've said hello."

Nan kissed Walt on the cheek and followed Molly's voice towards the kitchen. She turned at the kitchen doorway to give Joss a questioning look. Joss shrugged and grinned, leaving her to his mother.

She found Molly washing the last of a considerable pile of pots and pans in the old farm sink. Much like the mud room, the kitchen was a welcoming room, full of warm light–and rich aromas.

"Molly," Nan said. "I'm sorry to crash dinner."

"It's a nice surprise." Molly set a clean dish on the rack and dried her hands before reaching for a tin labeled Tea.

"Would you like some?" Molly pulled mugs from a glass-front cabinet as the kettle rattled a little over the gas flame.

"Very much." Nan looked around for a sugar bowl, and found it on the counter.

Molly pulled two chairs out from the kitchen table and gestured Nan into one. "To what do we owe this pleasure, hon?" She gave the younger woman a searching look. "Is everything all right?"

Nan took a breath, not sure where to begin or how much to tell Joss's mother.

The kettle whistled, and Molly got up, dropped bags of tea into the mugs and poured the water. She brought the mugs over and sat again, placing her work-chapped hand over Nan's, and looked hard at her. "What is it, Nan?"

"It's complicated."

Molly's answer was simple and perfect. "I can listen to complicated, or I can let you have some peace."

"No." Nan rubbed her temples. "It's just… Someone is vandalizing my property, and it's getting worse. It feels really personal, and I'm scared." She took a sip of the tea, concentrating hard on the column of steam swirling up from the surface of the liquid. "I only have the one guest right now. I lost a booking after the first incident. If word gets out..."

Molly sighed. "By anyone's standards, that's a lot."

Out in the parlor Joss laughed. Walt's gravelly chuckle followed.

Molly's attention was momentarily drawn to her men. "Those two."

Nan's attention was drawn to the lights she'd left burning at the inn. "I should be there."

"Maybe where you should be is here. Leaning on your neighbors."

"I let Joss talk me into coming over here because he's right; I don't want to be alone right now."

"Drink your tea, hon." Molly squeezed her fingers gently. "We'll get the rest sorted out."

The two women sipped in silence. Nan felt more of her anxiety loosen its grip. It was impossible to be stressed in a room smelling of Molly Fuller's lasagna.

Joss' entry into the kitchen broke the companionable silence. "What's for supper, Mom?" He kissed the top of Molly's head as he passed her on his way to the fridge. He didn't wait for an answer as he took two bottles of beer out of the fridge.

Molly pinned him with the half-stern glare reserved for doting mothers. "Use your nose."

Joss rolled his eyes and returned to the den.

Molly chuckled; Nan followed him with her eyes.

Once Joss was again out of earshot, Molly sighed affectionately. "I love that boy to death."

"It shows, Molly. He loves you both just as much. It's nice to see." Nan blinked, embarrassed by the prickle of tears in her eyes. She knew full well Molly Fuller was no fool. She was certain Molly had seen her watching Joss. Certain Molly knew just what she was thinking.

Molly smiled, patted Nan's hand, and got up to check the oven. The mouthwatering smell of warm cheese and spicy tomatoes wafted out, and Nan's stomach rumbled in anticipation.

"I'm glad he brought you over." Molly slipped her hands into a pair of oven mitts and pulled the casserole out. "Walt and I've been meaning to invite you, but we thought maybe you had your hands full."

Nan flushed and fiddled with her bracelet as Molly slid a foil-wrapped loaf of bread into the oven. The scent of toasting garlic mingled with the decadent fragrance of the homey kitchen, reminding Nan of her manners. She hopped up from her seat, and let Molly put her to work.

The next hour passed too quickly. Nan couldn't remember a better meal, even when she was eating her culinary school homework. The conversation was laced with the secret language of family, but the Fullers knew how to make a guest feel welcome. The obvious respect and humor between Molly and Walt seasoned the evening perfectly.

While spearing a runaway lettuce leaf, Nan looked up to find Joss watching her with a heady blend of tenderness and wanting. She held his gaze for a beat. He flushed a little, and looked back to his father, who was recounting a conversation with the mailman about the college kids who rented an old farmhouse down the road. Nan let the intensity of that glance wash over her.

She was dismayed when the meal ended, but delighted when Walt, and consequently Joss, offered to do the dishes.

"You're just showing off for company!" Molly teased.

"Not every day we have a pretty girl over to dinner," Walt said dryly, with a mischievous twinkle in his eye. He switched a dishtowel at her in a move choreographed by more than thirty years of dinners in the same kitchen.

When the dishes were done and the surfaces wiped down, Nan felt Joss's eyes settle on her while he dried his hands. The tenderness was still there, but there was hunger now, too, despite their full bellies.

JOSS HAD BEEN WATCHING her carefully all night and he'd seen her transform from a woman rattled by uncertainty to the graceful, hospitable neighbor he knew her to be. His mother's magic was a formidable power.

He'd also seen the mirrored longing in Nan's eyes when they'd locked with his across his parents' table.

He'd assumed he had a handle on the attraction that smoldered between them, but that glance had fanned it into something hot and insatiable. He wanted her.

"Mom, Pop?" He waited for his parents' attention. "Thanks for dinner. I'd love to keep Nan here half the night playing a killer game of Monopoly with you two, but under the circumstances, she doesn't want to have her only guest come back to an empty inn. I think I'll drop her off and head up the mountain."

"Of course, Joss." Molly shot him a look, silently calling him out on his intentions for the rest of the evening. Joss led Nan out to the mud room before she saw the grin his parents exchanged before following them.

He helped her into her jacket, acutely aware of the clean, citrusy scent that clung to her. His mother hugged them goodnight, Walt shook his hand and chuckled when Nan kissed his cheek.

Joss walked her out to his truck in silence, scenarios flashing through his head as he handed her up into the cab and closed the door. He imagined bracing her up against his truck and plundering her mouth there under the full moon. He longed for her to reach across the cab to unlatch his door and meet him with a hot kiss.

In reality, she did reach over to open his door for him, but slid back over, keeping her hands to herself.

"Dinner was perfect," she said. "Thank you."

"I know I kind of hauled you over here, but I couldn't just leave you over there alone." He turned the key, bringing the engine to life and turning out the cab light.

He reached across the console and took her hand. He stroked her palm with his thumb, relishing the slight twitch of her fingers. His blood sizzled at the point of contact. He waited for her to pull away, and was pleased when she curled her chilly fingers around his and relaxed back into her seat a little.

A moment later he was turning the keys again, parking the truck in her still-empty driveway. This time she let him help her out of the cab and made no objection when he walked her to the back door. She slipped the key into the lock, and led him into the kitchen, flipping the switch to illuminate the island. He reached out to take her hand, but she was already starting to rustle around the kitchen.

Joss leaned back against the island and watched her in bewildered silence. Nan pulled open the upright freezer, and pulled out a pint of hand packed peach ice cream from the co-op. She grabbed spoons from a drawer that she then gently bumped closed with her hip. She pulled a little bottle from the fridge and grabbed two mismatched juice tumblers from the dishwasher.

She handed him the spoons and tumblers, and headed for the stairs.

CHAPTER 15

Somewhere between meeting his eyes over his parents' table and taking his proffered hand in the cab of his truck, she'd made up her mind.

It was a mild enough night, perhaps one of the last ones they'd have for porch sitting before winter tucked in.

The moon was high and full, a gossamer film of clouds softening its edges. She wanted, more than anything, to sit with him, to kiss him again, under that moon. Even while her imagination spun soft, romantic stories, she was flipping through her mental inventory of the fridge. No cold bottles of beer, no good whiskey or gin for cocktails, but in the refrigerator, a half bottle of Muscat just waiting for the right occasion.

The peach ice cream had been a sudden inspiration. Sweet, cold perfection to balance the wine. Knowing in her bones that he would follow without being asked, she led him towards the back stairs.

She hesitated only briefly at the door to her apartment. Until now, this space had been a sanctuary for her. She hoped her instincts were correct allowing Joss in.

Beyond the living room, through the screen door, was her tiny porch. She curled into the threadbare love seat tucked in the corner.

She put the ice cream and wine down on the orange crate that served as a table and patted the seat.

"I hope you like peach?" she asked as he sat.

"I do." He never took his eyes off her face.

She handed him a spoon and opened the ice cream. She dug into the pint, savored the cool, creamy slide of it on her tongue. She handed the pint to Joss, shivering in anticipation when their fingers brushed.

While Joss had a spoonful of ice cream, Nan poured two fingers of the sweet wine in each of the tumblers. He set down his spoon, resting it upside down next to hers on the pint lid and took the glass she offered. She clinked her glass against his and raised it in a toast.

"To an unexpectedly lovely evening."

"It's not over yet." He sipped with her.

Joss leaned across the love seat, setting his glass down. His fingers were chilled from the glass when he touched her cheek. She felt herself holding her breath as he drew her lips up to his.

His mouth tasted of peaches and wine. She opened hers, offering herself to him, taking more from the kiss. His other hand stole around her, closing the remaining distance between them. He held her there for a moment, fingertips trailing along the exposed skin at her waist, before launching an assault on her senses.

She was aware of so much; the warmth of his breath, his feather-light touch on her skin, the cool of the evening air against her flushed cheeks, the urgency building between them. She heard her own hum of pleasure and the peeper frogs singing in the marsh. She wound her hand in the fabric of his shirt and pressed herself against him, thrilling at the contact.

She couldn't believe she'd thought they'd get through wine and...
ice cream!

She pulled back, breathless from the kiss. She rocked away from him slightly, moving to get up. He grasped her hand and tugged her back.

"I'm just going to stick the ice cream in the freezer," she said, voice uneven with desire. She got up and walked inside to tuck the ice cream in her mini-fridge freezer.

Joss was right there, paused in the screen door when she turned back. She laughed as he caught her up in his arms. She clung to his shoulders as he swung an arm under her knees.

Laughter dissolved into need when his mouth, hot and impatient, found hers.

"Which door?" he muttered against her lips.

She waved behind her towards an open door. He nipped hungrily at her jawline as he carried her across the room. He was trailing his mouth down her neck as he entered her bedroom.

His foot caught on the rug, and they toppled, giggling, onto her bed. He nudged a stray curl off of her cheek, the mirth in his eyes blurring into hunger.

He leaned in slowly to kiss her mouth, skimming a hand down to her hip. She wanted both to stop time and to rush ahead; to memorize the line of Joss's jaw and the exact shade of his gray eyes in the moonlit room, and to tear him out of his shirt and feel the skin she'd spent so much idle time thinking about.

Oh, she wanted, but settled for a rushed tugging.

He slid his hand up her belly, fingertips just brushing her breast. She gasped at the thrill that zinged through her, pooling warm in her gut.

The front hall door slammed shut, loudly enough to break the spell between them. Nan leaned over to look out into the dooryard. Elisha's rental car was parked next to Joss's truck, the engine fan still whirring in the quiet night.

Nan sat up, breaking the circle of Joss's embrace. She listened to the click of Elisha's heels on the stairs, and the sharp report of her bedroom door closing. The sound seemed to reverberate through the inn. She looked at Joss, her gaze pleading with him to understand that she wanted him, but not with another woman's hurt feelings in the building with them.

Joss took a long, steadying breath and sat up, putting a little more physical distance between the two of them as Nan straightened her clothes. He put a hand on hers.

"I guess I'd better go?" he said.

"Yeah." Her eyes spoke volumes to the contrary.

He kissed her swiftly, a kiss full of regret and promise, and stood up. Nan walked him down the stairs to the breezeway, and watched him cross the dooryard to his truck. The truck's engine sounded thunderous in the quiet night as he backed up, turned around, and pulled out onto the dark road, headed east towards Catmint Gap.

JOSS TOOK his time driving back up the mountain. The late hour and the fizz of lust in his blood made focusing on the winding road a chore more than a pleasure. He searched his mind for a project, anything to cool his racing pulse, but his thoughts slipped away west, back into the valley and the woman he'd only just left.

Inspiration was a funny thing, though. Smiling at their tumble onto the bed, he realized what was missing. The old double bed in Nan's room didn't suit her. Her apartment didn't reflect the woman nearly as much as the furnishings in the inn itself. With a clearer head and his mind's eye focused on the room and not the woman, he realized the hand-me-down Sears & Roebuck head- and footboards were all wrong for who she was.

The bed he'd envisioned for her bridal suite was perfect for her.

His imagination summoned the four posts and the open canopy—the pale birch glowing, a tung oil finish to bring out the warmth and grain. He'd done the drawings and ordered the stock. No footboard, and the headboard just a graceful crescent curve with a web of twisted branches from fallen saplings. The bed wouldn't require a fabric canopy, the form itself would lend a fairy tale quality.

Unfussy but magical, just like her.

Inspiration and desire pushed his ambition. Maybe a series of pieces after the bed, a line of Nan-inspired furniture; the craft guild would take them on consignment. He pushed sour thoughts of Seth and his SoHo gallery into the shadows where they belonged.

By the time he reached the cabin, he was riding a high of inspiration. He sat down at his drafting table and went back to work.

THE WORK WEEK came and went, full to brimming with the minutia of running the inn. Nan hoped for a chance to speak to Joss, but their work, despite its close proximity, kept them from more than yearning conversations and a string of mildly flirtatious texts.

Tuesday morning they met on the second floor landing. Nan was finishing up with Elisha's bathroom; Joss was on his way down from the third floor. His greeting was professional enough, but the heat in his eyes spoke of the passion they hadn't fully tasted yet. She savored the warmth of his smile even as she caught him up on a few necessities.

"I'm going to be installing new exterior locks." She fished in her pocket for a shiny silver key. "This won't work 'til the end of the day, but you'll need it in the morning."

He'd taken the key from her, turning it over between his thumb and forefinger. "Can I give you a hand with that?"

"No. I think I've got it." She watched him take a key ring out and slip the new key onto a ring alongside several others. "But I'll let you know if I hit a snag."

Midweek, feeling like a middle-schooler with a crush, she'd brought him a danish and a cup of coffee after her guests' breakfast service. "I wanted to see how it was coming along."

Joss powered down the saw and set down a length of fresh baseboard.

"Thank you." He wiped his dusty hands on his work pants and took the plate and mug from her. He sipped at the coffee, eyes closing with pleasure. "This is great. Have a look. I'm getting ready to install the baseboard and window trim today."

The walls and ceiling were freshly re-plastered, the new window installed. She drank in the smell of sawdust and curing plaster. "It'll be ready to paint soon."

"Don't forget to call me."

Her cheeks flamed, but the flush that bloomed on the back of his neck didn't go unnoticed. "I won't. Promise."

Her evenings were full of office work and uncertainty. The crackle in the air between them was real, but she knew so little about his habits. It seemed too early in whatever they had between them to intrude upon the solitude of his evenings with a phone call, and he often left while she was serving tea in the parlor, taking away her opportunity to ask him to stay for a meal or a last cup of coffee. She buried herself in mastering her social media accounts. She was determined to leverage free exposure wherever she could.

By the end of the week, she was determined to get Joss to herself. He seemed to sense her mood when he came through the kitchen midmorning.

"Good morning." He squinted slightly from the brilliant sunshine coming through the south-facing kitchen window.

She looked up from prepping ingredients for tea cookies, one hand holding a cracked eggshell.

"There's coffee. I can't…" She gestured helplessly at the carafe and mugs with her eggy hand.

"No, thanks. I have to stop by Katie's place on the way out to the barn. I'll spend some money at the bakery." He walked around the island, deliberately passing her and leaning in over her maple board. "What are you making?"

She batted him away with her dry hand. "*Financiers*. Kate gave me her recipe; she says I have to serve them at tea."

"Remind me to thank her for that," he said, his breath warm on her neck. "They're my favorite."

She turned, propriety falling away; she could smell the soap on his skin. "Who said you can have any?"

The click of Elisha's heels in the foyer erased Nan's playful smile. Elisha came into the kitchen, travel mug in hand. "Nan? I was hoping to get some coffee for the drive."

Nan wiped her still eggy fingers, embarrassed by Elisha and her flawlessly groomed self.

"Excuse me." Elisha's tone was knowing, her arched brow spoke eloquently. "I'll just help myself." She filled her mug, added a whisper of cream, and departed, an unfathomable expression playing across her face.

Joss leaned back against the opposite counter; Nan silently cursed her constant guest's timing.

"I'm sorry about that."

"Nothing to be sorry about," he replied.

Suddenly mindful of the mess, Nan tossed a broken eggshell in the dirty bowl to her right, and turned to wash her hands at the sink.

When she turned back, Joss was straightening the coffee carafe on its tray. "I should go," he said. "I'll talk to you later?"

Nan could only nod.

She'd assumed it would be easy to carve out a moment to talk to him, to establish some kind of equilibrium between their contractor-client relationship and the attraction that simmered beneath the surface of every glance, every brief conversation. But nearly a week had passed, she was expecting a full house over the weekend, and Kate was insisting she take Saturday evening to go to an art opening in Burlington. He'd said later, but she wasn't sure when exactly later would be.

CHAPTER 16

Kate wheeled into the driveway of the inn on Saturday, spraying gravel behind the tires of a flashy red coupe. The car's garnet paint glittered in the late afternoon sunlight. Nan could only assume it was Jack's, but did he know his kid sister was driving it? Kate left the keys in the ignition and emerged from the driver's side door. Her long legs unfolded like something from an Eighties music video, complete with impractical but sexy-as-hell blood-red stilettos. Heels which didn't slow Kate down as she maneuvered her way across the driveway carrying a huge canvas bag.

Nan watched her friend's approach with a grin. Kate was a force of nature on an off day; when she wanted to get attention, she was a cosmic event. Nan wondered if the population of Burlington was prepared.

Kate's dress was black, delicate straps opening into a deep vee; tiers of silk skimmed from an empire waist over her lean curves, falling dangerously high on her endless legs. She'd caught her chestnut hair back in a low, messy tail, and she wore chandelier earrings hung with red gems that brushed the tops of her mostly bare shoulders.

When Kate let herself into the apartment, Nan noted the smoky grey painted eyes and knew some poor flatlander was going to get knocked on his ass tonight.

Kate stopped dead in the middle of the room, her generous mouth open in an O of disappointed surprise. "I told you this was dressy, sugar plum, not a funeral!"

Nan put down the notes she was making for Amanda. "I wouldn't wear this to a funeral."

"Thank God, Frances. They'd mistake you for the corpse." Kate paused for dramatic effect, letting Nan's never-used given name hang in the air. "I'm glad I packed some things for you. Now, let's get you out of this...frock." She flicked at Nan's cap sleeves.

Kate bundled Nan out of her oft-worn black cocktail dress right where she stood. As the dress pooled around her feet, Kate appraised her with an old roommate's familiarity.

"The blue," she muttered, rummaging around in the bag she'd dragged upstairs. "Do you have that pair of skinny jeans I made you buy in Boston last spring? And a strapless bra?" she asked, not looking up, as she shook out a lustrous bit of sapphire blue fabric.

Nan watched the light play on the folds of fabric. It looked impossibly soft.

"What would you do without me? I mean, thank god we're the same shoe size. There's hope for you yet..." Kate was speaking more to herself than to Nan. "Go! Get the jeans, lady. We've still got to do hair and make up!"

"Kate, it's Burlington, not New York," Nan protested.

"Yeah, but the guy opening the gallery is a friend of my brother's. From New York." Kate was merciless. "Your go-to cocktail dress from five years ago will not do. We are taking no prisoners tonight. You've been working too hard. I've been working too hard." Her eyes twinkled. "Tonight we play hard." Kate tossed her the blue top. "Now go get dressed!"

In her bedroom, Nan pulled on the jeans–so deep an indigo they were almost black–and slipped the satiny top over her head.

She twirled for her reflection in the full length mirror. Kate was always right. The halter neckline and the subtle seaming suggested height she didn't have. The color brightened her face. The ensemble was admittedly far more chic than her dress.

She returned to the living room to find Kate missing.

"In here, sugar plum," Kate called from the bathroom. "There's a pair of ballet flats and a belt for you on the sofa, and a bracelet on the coffee table."

Nan accessorized and walked into the bathroom. Kate immediately sat her down on the toilet lid and tipped Nan's chin up. For a few minutes she dipped her hands in pots of hair product and fiddled with her brushes and palettes. Nan did as she was told, pouting and blinking on cue, finally taking the small bottle of bergamot oil scent that she favored from Kate's hand and touching it to her pulse points.

Kate cooed. "You are a masterpiece, my dear. Look."

Nan took herself in. Kate had given her unruly hair some sassy texture, had played up her mouth and long lashes. She looked like a mischievous pixie.

Kate was triumphant. "Now, let's go break some hearts!"

A few minutes out of town, as dairy farms and roadside shops flashed by, Nan asked the question she'd forgotten during the frenzied makeover. Enveloped in the buttery leather interior of the R8, Nan wondered aloud about where Kate had acquired the Audi.

"Does Jack have a new car?" Nan ran a hand along the dashboard. Kate's older brother loved cars, the faster the better.

"Yeah," Kate grinned and dropped the car into fifth gear. "He's riding up with a friend tonight, so he said I could borrow his sweet new ride."

Nan couldn't help but laugh. When Jack Pease arrived, mayhem ensued. Kate worshipped Jack, and her brother adored her back. Nan had lost track of the tales Kate had told about her brother, heartbreaker of Thornton Union High, and his playful mischief. His antics and conquests at Williams and Harvard Law read like Casanova's diary, and Nan herself had been along for a handful of his adventures in Cambridge and Boston.

She was curious just how close a friend Jack was bringing along tonight.

"Is he going to bring his friend by the inn? Or will I have to beg for five minutes of his time on this visit?"

Kate's expression was Sphinxlike.

"Much as I'm sure he's always secretly wanted you to beg for him, sugar plum, I think he'll make it over to see you on his own. He's ridiculously proud of you." Kate pushed the car a little harder; Nan swore she felt the car leave the ground as they topped the hill overlooking New Haven Junction. "Not to mention that, as your lawyer, he's got a vested interest."

Jack's car slipped through the cool twilight, Route 7 vanishing beneath the tires, with the sun dipping behind the Adirondacks in the West and bathing the Green Mountains in rosy, golden light. Lake Champlain glimmered in the sunset as they sped along the final miles into Burlington.

Kate parked the car in the mall garage, and the two of them walked the last two blocks of Church Street along the fairy-lit cobblestone street. The gallery was at the northern end of the pedestrian mall, and Kate paused to admire half a dozen boutique windows as they went.

Nan caught her best friend ogling a pair of emerald earrings and laughed. "All that drool's going to ruin your lipstick, Ms. Pease."

"Someday," Kate promised their reflection, "I am going to be in a position to splurge on something like these."

Nan saw the determination in Kate's reflected expression and hugged her best friend. "Someday we both are."

Joss hated suits. He did, however, know how to wear one. When a guy hung out with Jack Pease, he was more or less obliged to look good. Jack quite simply wore clothes well, and managed to appear as if it all happened by happy accident.

Jack's ease among the crowd in Seth Weston's new gallery was something Joss envied slightly. He'd never been at home in the fine art world. Something the three men knew well–and often avoided talking about.

Jack handled Seth's legal affairs in Boston and New York already; the new Burlington location's proximity to home offered him the opportunity for a few days of mixed business and pleasure. Joss simply welcomed the chance to spend time with his best friend without having to trek down to Boston or–god forbid–New York.

His feelings about seeing Seth were mixed, even with a few years' and a few hundred miles' distance. Though his disagreement with his former roommate and agent was firmly in the past, Joss still felt the sting of failure every time their paths crossed. He pushed the resentment aside. For the evening, they were all hanging out together, and such moments were rare.

Jack turned the conversation on him while he was woolgathering.

"Kate tells me you're working for our Nan." At Seth's questioning look, Jack clarified. "Another innocent coed whose horizons I've expanded."

Something ugly and jealous flared in Joss's chest even as he kept his expression carefully neutral. The idea of Jack expanding any of Nan's horizons made him want to punch his urbane pal in the gut. "Just what kind of horizons are we talking about?" His strained voice gave his interest away and he cursed the hot reaction.

Jack peered at him over the neck of a local beer. "Hey, relax."

Joss watched realization dawn in Jack's expression: a curious and smug turning up at the corner of his Brooks-Brothers-model features.

"I just meant she and Kate used to come down to Cambridge on breaks from culinary school while I was at Harvard. I showed them a good time. Not to say that I would have turned Nan down once upon a time, but she never asked." Jack set the beer down on the table behind them. "She's taken to treating me like an annoying older brother, and lately–even worse–like she's a client."

Joss's grip on his beer bottle relaxed. Seth waved a hand and slipped away to speak with another guest.

Jack raised an observant eyebrow. "She's not just a client for you, I see."

The jealous fire banked for the moment. Joss shook his head. "Not just a client."

Jack chuckled and laid a hand on Joss's shoulder. "A lot more than a client, if the look on your face is any indicator."

The gallery door opened just as Joss flashed his friend a go-to-hell look and took a long swallow of his beer. He swore the lights dimmed to a prima donna's follow spot. Kate's long legs ate up the distance to her brother's embrace. Every man in the room's gaze followed her like a laser, but Joss's eyes were all for the woman who accompanied her.

Gone were Nan's tidily casual clothes, the soft tendrils of hair framing her face. If Kate was spotlit, Nan was incandescent. Blue satin fell from her throat to the curve of her hip; her legs were lean in snug denim. Her eyes and lips those of a playful temptress.

Kate's alchemy, no doubt, but as Nan's eyes flicked from Jack's face to his, she smiled, and she was all Nan under the subtle glamour. He saw a flash of surprise, then approval, in her gaze, and flushed just a little.

Jack might have mentioned she'd be there with Kate.

Kate hooked an arm through her brother's, kissed Jack on the mouth with an affected smack of her lips. Jack caught Nan around her waist with his free arm and whispered something in her ear. Her eyes sparkled, and the green flame in Joss's heart flared.

Jack chastised Kate and Nan like the overbearing brother he was, releasing them. "You girls are drawing attention away from the art." He clinked his bottle with Joss's. "Come on, Joss. Let's find Seth, so he can be stunned by the two most gorgeous women in Vermont."

Nan grabbed Kate. "You said Jack was bringing a friend."

"You assumed I meant a woman," Kate replied with a wink. "I didn't want you fretting about this being some kind of double date, the fact that Jack's my brother notwithstanding."

"*Touché*," Nan muttered. "You tarted me up. He's going to think it was for him."

"It was. You can be mad at me later." Kate squeezed Nan's hand. "In the meantime, let's have some fun."

She turned to see Jack return with Joss and the gallery owner.

Jack introduced his friend. "Seth, you remember my sister, Kate? And this is Nan Grady. She's the owner of the Damselfly Inn in Thornton, a client and a dear friend."

Seth shook Nan's hand. "Seth Weston." It was a firm handshake, and Nan felt appraised like a painting. "Jack, you do know the loveliest women."

Nan glanced over Seth's shoulder at Joss, who stood to one side of the exchange, frowning slightly.

As Jack turned to his sister, Nan studied the gallery owner. Molly's half-told story of Joss's time in New York came to mind. She wondered if Seth was somehow connected. He was younger than she'd expected an art gallery owner to be. Seth couldn't be any older than Jack, but there was something weary in his eyes.

Eyes which traveled Kate's body in open admiration. "Kate, when was the last time I saw you?"

Kate gave Seth a frank, seductive smile. "Too long ago."

Jack motioned to Nan and Joss. "Let me introduce you two around. Kate and Seth can catch up."

A server passed with champagne flutes, and Joss snagged a fresh one for Nan. She was about to thank him when a handsome older man approached them. "Joss?"

Joss stopped. "Professor Sykes. Good to see you."

Jack propelled Nan into the heart of the party, leaving Joss to his small talk, invited himself into a conversation with a pair of red-haired twins. "Carolyn, Andrea?" The women kissed his cheeks. "I'm sorry to interrupt, but I want to introduce you to Nan Grady. She just opened the new inn in Thornton."

Jack ducked a playful swat from one of the twins, and explained that they ran a local children's charity.

With Jack at her elbow, she was deftly maneuvered around the room. She tried hard not to seek Joss out over the rim of her glass, but it was a losing battle. His dark suit highlighted the strong, lean lines of his body, and the gallery lighting picked up the gold in his dark hair. The deep indigo shirt he wore turned his gray eyes stormy.

She felt his gaze on her as the minutes passed. The hum of awareness he created in her blood competed with the heady rush of sparkling wine; she flowed through the party on a current of high spirits. The mix of business and pleasure was new and heady.

The only disappointment was that Joss seemed carried by an opposing tide, drawn around the room counter to her own journey of introductions and small talk.

The jazz trio returned from a break and started a set of Forties standards. A few couples took to the floor amongst the sculptures and started dancing. Nan wondered if Joss liked to dance.

Jack was introducing her to the man who'd waylaid Joss earlier, an art history professor from Thornton College. She shook off thoughts of Joss and took the man's outstretched hand.

"Jordan Sykes." He held her hand just a beat past the handshake.

"It's lovely to meet you." Nan blushed again, cursing her fair skin. Professor Sykes was a classic silver fox, right down to the charmingly predatory grin.

"Jack says you're the owner of the new inn on County Road."

"I am," she replied. The professor's entire attention was focused on her. She basked in his regard.

"I drive that way every day. The place looks great."

She didn't hear Kate come up behind her.

"Joss is certainly looking yummy tonight," Kate whispered, "and by the way he's been watching you, I'd venture to say he'd say the same about you." Kate flashed a guilty smile at the professor. "I'm so sorry, Professor, I have to steal this lovely lady from you for a moment."

Nan managed to stammer out a weak, "Excuse me," before Kate tugged her away.

JOSS WATCHED Kate steer Nan away from Jordan Sykes. Jordan was in many ways a mentor, but his former advisor was old enough to be Nan's father. Joss didn't want to be held responsible for his actions if Sykes held onto Nan's hand for any longer.

He'd left her to enjoy the party, to enjoy meeting the potentially important people, to mingle. He'd breathed through the impulse to interrupt every man who appreciated her sparkle, tried not act like a dog in a pissing contest, but she looked so damned good. He was on a knife edge all evening, a heartbeat from hauling her off and letting them have their way with one another in a back room.

The jazz trio segued into an easy, romantic version of *Moon River*, and he gave up. Joss crossed the room, heading Kate and Nan off. "Ladies," he said, eyes on Nan's. To his own ears, he sounded rough and unsteady.

"Nan?" He brushed a knuckle down her arm. "Dance with me?"

Nan's eyes flicked to the floor in the center of the room then back to his. Her face lit up, a reflection of his hope, his desire. She took his hand, and he led her into the heart of the room.

Joss drew her into his arms, closing one hand over hers against his chest, toying with the smooth hem of her blouse where it fell at the small of her back with the other. She laid her temple against his shoulder and sighed.

His earlier jealousy melted away on the saxophone solo.

They moved together, flowing to the warm, rhythmic music. Joss reveled in the heat of her skin under his questing fingers, and the feel of her nails grazing the tapering hair at the back of his neck. Joss inhaled the citrusy scent of her perfume, the herbal notes in her hair, her own underlying essence.

He let the pads of his fingers rest against the skin of her back, while the satin of her blouse gathered between his thumb and forefinger. She leaned up as if to speak to him, but said nothing. Her breath against the pulse under his jaw sent his heartbeat skipping.

He held her close, enjoying the sinuous flex and stretch of muscles as he led her through the music. He felt no hesitation from her. The knowledge heightened his awareness of their bodies moving together.

Joss understood he was making a public claim on her affections. He knew he was known for being shy of entanglements, but did she? She'd come into his arms willingly enough, but she couldn't know what the others in the room would assume about them.

Then her hand smoothed down the back of his neck, and she looked up at him from under her lashes.

There would be time for talking another evening.

When the music shifted out of the slow number, Nan drew back, still firmly in his arms, and smiled. "You dance as well as you negotiate a disaster area, Mr. Fuller." She leaned in to kiss him lightly on the mouth. "Thank you." As she led him toward the drinks table, Joss thought perhaps he was underestimating her.

Kate was waiting for them with Jack near the bar, a knowing smile playing on her face. Jack just looked bemused.

"You guys want to ditch the art crowd and get some food?" asked Kate. "I'm starved."

"Katie." Jack looked at his sister in wonder. "Are you always hungry?"

Nan seconded her friend. "I'm in."

Joss shrugged at Jack, "I think that about decides it. Pizza and beer?"

Five minutes later the four of them were headed back down Church Street in the cool of the evening. The avenue was vibrant. Nan felt buoyant. Church Street's eclectic mix of performers, eccentric locals, university students, and tourists never failed to delight her; sharing it with Joss made the lights sparkle more brightly.

Ahead of them, Kate looped an arm through her brother's. Like tall, long-legged demigods they strode towards the flatbread pizza hearth and brewery they'd chosen.

Joss hung back, seeking her hand, and matching his pace to hers.

They walked for a couple of blocks in comfortable silence, while the Peases put distance between them. The birches lining Church Street were strung with white lights, the cobblestones glittered with reflected light. Music and conversation spilled out of the bars and restaurants they passed.

They rounded the corner onto College Street and caught sight of Jack and Kate across City Hall Park, heading into the front doors of their destination.

Nan laughed ruefully. "I literally cannot keep up with those two."

Joss tugged her hand, pulling her around to face him. "You're beautiful."

Light, music, voices–everything faded. She could only blink at him in breathless wonder.

He leaned in and brushed her lips with his own. It was a feather-light kiss, just enough to make her understand that he was speaking the truth.

Still holding her hand, Joss led her across the street into the park.

CHAPTER 17

Nan's heart was racing, a thousand thoughts clogged her throat, and she had the unbearable sensation that this was all too lovely to be true. The warm pressure of Joss's calloused hand, his words, his kiss were evidence to the contrary. Still, in her secret heart, she was afraid to trust the evidence.

When they entered the restaurant, Kate and Jack were perched at a bar table, pint glasses already in front of them. There was no room for her fears and doubts in the warm, crowded restaurant.

"We wondered if Jack was going to have to bail you guys out for public indecency or something. Where've you been?" Kate laughed.

"Enjoying the evening. Not everyone strides over the landscape like you two," Joss replied smartly.

Nan shifted the conversation away from herself and Joss. "We're here now, Kate, so why don't you tell us all why you're not back at that gallery seducing Seth."

Jack nearly choked on his beer. Kate took a long swallow from hers.

"He always acts like he's interested," she began, "but there's a Big Hurt behind his eyes."

Jack and Joss exchanged a look. Nan wondered if Kate's assessment hit too close to the mark.

"Like that guy in Paris?" Nan asked, knowing the answer and looking for a distraction.

"What guy in Paris?" Jack's face was a grotesque mask of brotherly alarm.

Kate and Nan broke out in giggles.

"Sorry, Jack." Nan recovered her breath and looked at Jack sheepishly. "Kate lived like a nun while she was studying abroad."

Both women snorted with laughter.

Jack nodded sagely. "Much better."

The waitress came around to take their order; she gave Jack a less-than-subtle once over. "What can I get you all?"

Kate stifled a snicker.

"Another round of drinks," Jack said. "And?"

Joss deferred to Nan and Kate with a gesture. The girls exchanged a look, and Kate spoke. "The kalamata and rosemary pizza, with extra feta."

"Mmm." Nan's gaze met Joss's across the table. The pizza was her favorite, but her hunger had little to do with food.

The conversation ebbed and flowed over the pizza and drinks. The crowd thinned while they talked. When the waitress brought them the check and a reminder that the place was closing, Jack flipped open the folder and Joss pulled his wallet out.

"I've got it," Jack slipped bills into the folder and slid it away from Joss. He winked at Nan. "It's a business expense. I'm taking my client out, after all."

Nan couldn't help but smile. "I do like the sound of that."

Jack's phone pinged and he snuck a look at his messages, grimacing. "Katie, be careful with my car on the ride home, okay? And bring it by Mom and Dad's in the morning? I apparently need to be back in Boston by afternoon."

"Jack, it's too late for you to go back to Mom and Dad's place tonight." Kate looked at Nan with a wide, innocent smile as she spoke.

"Why don't you drive us back to my place in your car. You can have my couch. Joss won't mind taking Nan home."

Nan shot Kate a grateful look. With a wave, Kate led her brother out the door.

Joss's truck was parked on a nearby street. A thin cover of clouds veiled the sky, and despite the summery warmth of the afternoon, Nan could smell winter in the night air. They walked in silence. Nan was achingly aware of his closeness, but suddenly unsure. She wanted him, but she felt exposed by Kate's maneuvering as much as she was grateful.

Joss opened his truck door and brushed off the seat. Though it smelled of sawdust and machine oil, the cab was clean. It struck her as sweet, that he might think she cared about getting a little sawdust on her jeans.

Once she was settled in the cab of his truck, he turned on the stereo and adjusted the click wheel on an old iPod. "Do you like Ben Folds?"

"I do." Nan watched a pack of UVM students cross the road as they passed the Flynn Theater. "Kate and Jack and I saw him in Boston once."

"I sense a story." He drummed on the wheel along with the music, giving her an encouraging nod.

Ten years before, Jack had scored VIP seats to the show from a partner at the firm where he was working as a summer associate. He'd brought her and Kate and a few of his law school buddies. They had ended the night at an MIT frat house party on a Beacon Street roof deck, all because Kate met a guy at the club who didn't want to let her go right away. Nan could still smell that long-ago city air, kissed with salt from the harbor, heavy with exhaust fumes and cheap liquor.

Joss recalled diving into the river where it flowed past the Peases' house on New Year's Eve and nearly getting frostbite walking back because Kate and one of her friends had snuck down after them and stolen their clothes.

Nan confessed that Jack had waived his legal fees for three years as an investment in The Damselfly. Joss told her about crashing with the

Pease family the night he and his father argued over Joss not wanting to take over the farm.

"Was your dad very angry?" She couldn't imagine Walt Fuller even having a temper.

Joss's lip curled wryly. "I was a kid, and pissed off. The farm dictated every decision my parents ever made and I hated it. It was the only home I'd ever known and I didn't want it, and knowing that made me hate myself. I lashed out at them, said some awful things in front of my mom, and Pop told me to find somewhere else to stay that night if I hated their roof so much."

Nan's heart squeezed in her chest.

Joss blew out a breath. "I came back the next morning with flowers from Cora Pease's garden for my mom. Pop took a little more convincing, but I think he always understood better than he let on."

The easy conversation insulated them from the world outside Joss's pickup as they drove south and then turned west into the valley. When a Thornton fire engine passed them headed back to town, Nan pressed her palm against the glass

"Don't worry," Joss said. "There are a lot of places they could have been tonight."

When The Damselfly came into view, it was a shock to see a Thornton Police cruiser and the Fire Chief's SUV in the driveway and the kitchen lit up. Nan held her breath; Joss nudged the gas pedal and the truck leaped forward.

Nan was out of the car before Joss had killed the engine. She could hear Joss's footsteps catching up to her as she ran into the kitchen.

AMANDA, pale and shaking, sat at the farm table, twisting her hands. She saw Nan and jumped up, pressing a garbled apology into her shoulder while she clung like a child. While Nan hugged the sobbing girl, Joss nodded at Pete Lowry and the Fire Chief, both of whom had stood when Nan burst through the door.

Pete Lowry spoke to Nan as Amanda quieted. "Ms. Grady, this is Chief Samuels."

At Nan's mute nod, Chief Samuels explained. "Someone set fire to a shrub out front about an hour ago. One of your guests was awake reading in the front upstairs room. She saw the smoke and called 911. Miss Lloyd put it out with the garden hose; she's a quick thinker."

"I tried your cell, Nan," Amanda sniffled, "but it went to voicemail, and I didn't know what to say."

"Ms. Grady? Can we have a word with you? Somewhere quiet?" Pete asked Nan, who was disentangling herself from Amanda.

"Of course, Sergeant Lowry. We can talk in my office," Nan offered, and led the older man out of the kitchen.

Nan's exit left a gaping silence. Amanda stood for a moment more before sinking down into a chair at the table. She leaned on one hand, staring blankly out the picture window.

Joss broke the lull. "You okay?"

The girl brushed her hair back from her face. "I'm okay, it was just scary. I'm Amanda Lloyd." She stuck out a slim hand.

Her fingers were icy. "Joss Fuller. Can I pour you some coffee?"

"I'm not really a coffee drinker." Two pink spots appeared on her cheeks. "I like hot chocolate."

"I'm sure there's some around here." He couldn't begin to guess where, though.

"It's okay." Amanda dropped her chin into her cradled hands.

Joss peered out the front kitchen window at the blackened remains of the shrub in the yard. "Is the inn full tonight?"

"Almost," Amanda counted on her fingers. "Couples in Champlain and Mansfield, both on the back side of the house. The Morgans are in Addison, the front room overlooking the garden. Sergeant Lowry spoke to them, and they went back to bed. The Browns in Mansfield were pretty frightened." She looked at Joss with eyes filled with tears. "They said they're leaving first thing in the morning, and Professor McNair is in Newport this weekend."

The tears spilled over, and the young woman swiped at her eyes.

"Hey," Joss felt awkward and impossibly old. "It's over now."

Amanda blinked hard.

"I didn't see a car out there. Do you have a ride back to the College?" Joss asked.

"Sergeant Lowry said he could drive me back to my dorm. I usually drive myself, but my car was acting up, and I got a ride from my roommate. Nan was going to drive me home, but I," she stopped suddenly, and flushed with embarrassment. "I'm babbling," she finished.

"You've had a tough night. Let me run you back to the dorm," Joss offered.

"I'll get my bag," Amanda replied.

IN HER OFFICE, Nan offered Pete Lowry one of the two wing chairs in the bay window and sat down opposite him.

"So, aside from a roasted shrub, there was no serious property damage, and the ..." he consulted his notepad, "Morgans didn't see anything but the fire out the window. It doesn't leave a lot to go on."

Nan peered out into the pitch-dark night; what she hoped to see, she didn't know.

"I'm concerned, Ms. Grady." He shifted in the chair, leaning forward on his knee. "Three incidents, two of which could have caused physical harm to you or a guest. Are you sure you don't know anyone who's got a problem with you?"

Nan tried to imagine someone that angry with her. "If I think of anything, Sergeant, I'll be sure to let you know."

Lowry hefted himself up. "Do you mind if I speak with Joss before I go?"

"Sure. Let me go get him."

The empty kitchen took her by surprise. She doubled back through the foyer into the parlor, but neither Joss nor Amanda were there. She almost bumped into Pete Lowry on her way back to the office.

"Looks like Joss's truck's not in the yard. I'll call him tomorrow for a statement."

She was horrified by the helpless, disappointed tears that spilled over. "I guess he must have decided to get back to his place before it got too late. I'm sorry."

Sergeant Lowry pulled a handkerchief from his coat pocket. She took it gratefully, swiping away the tears.

"Lock up, now, Ms. Grady," he said gruffly. He paused to pull a card from his wallet. "You call me if you don't like being here on your own–and your guests don't count."

NAN WATCHED the cruiser drive away. Despite the guests upstairs, in the kitchen she did feel alone. She made a circuit around the first floor, checking the windows and the back patio door. She was sliding the chain into place on the front door when a pair of headlights sliced the darkness. Her heart was hammering in her chest when she finally understood that it was Joss's truck. She met him in the kitchen where he was setting a six-pack of the local brew on the kitchen island.

"Do you want one?" He tapped the cardboard carrier. "I stopped at the gas station near campus."

How could he have just left? How could she be so relieved that he was back?

The tears that had embarrassed her in front of Pete Lowry evaporated in the heat of anger. "Joss, it's been a long night. You're going to want to get home." She pushed the six-pack away. "You can take that with you."

His eyes narrowed. "Nan, I'll sleep in the parlor, but I have no intention of going anywhere tonight. For all we know, whoever did this is still out there."

"It was kids. A stupid prank." She knew she sounded shrill.

Temper flared in his eyes. "Don't be stupid, Nan. Someone puts a brick through a window, then tags your garage. Now arson, and you're going to tell me it's kids?" He slammed a hand down on the butcher block top. "Someone's targeting you."

"I'm being stupid? I can't let this scare me, Joss. I have to take care of things here. If I let this become some kind of bogeyman, I'll spend the rest of my life imagining noises in the garden and shadows outside the windows. What kind of life is that?"

Joss stood his ground. "None at all if the place burns down around you."

"If that happens," she snapped, "I won't have to worry about being afraid anymore." Her own vitriol surprised her. She was spoiling for a fight, any fight. He was convenient, and strong enough, she hoped, to take it, because she was beyond reining it in.

"Jesus, Nan!"

"Don't yell at me, Joss."

"I'm not yelling at you. I'm trying to get through to you." He prowled the kitchen, peering out into the darkness.

She didn't want to be coddled. She wanted to lash out at whoever was trying to hurt her. "What if that's not what I want?"

When he didn't reply, her anger flagged. "Look, it's late. You should go."

"The hell I'm going anywhere." Joss came around the table. "I'd be worried sick all night. Like I said, I'll stay in the parlor if I have to."

He took her by the shoulders, searching her eyes. She pressed her forehead against his chest. His body was tense, his heartbeat heavy. The temptation to give in to him, to let him handle things, was strong. Through the haze of her fury, she knew too that if he stayed, they would sleep together. She didn't want their first time to be like that.

She backed away. "Joss, go home."

He watched the window for a long moment. Then, without a word, he walked out into the night, the screen door banging like a gunshot. His truck roared to life and hauled out of the driveway, headlights cutting a bright swath in the darkness as it sped east.

CHAPTER 18

Four in the morning was an ugly hour even when Nan was well-rested and prepared for the day ahead.

Four o'clock that morning felt more like a circle of hell.

The earlier bravado she'd shown Joss carried her upstairs, with a sharp kitchen knife in one hand, but deserted her when the house settled into deep silence. Sleep danced just beyond her reach, weariness burned her eyes.

She'd spent the remainder of the night curled in a ball on her sofa in the darkness, with the ten inch, stainless steel blade glinting dully from the coffee table.

Nan felt rather than saw the light shift, and recognized that she should get up–start her day–instead of brooding alone in the dark. She stretched and rose, deciding a shower might help her perspective.

The scalding water steamed away some of the cobwebs. Scrubbing away the grime of being awake all night cleared her head. Clean and wrapped in one of the lush bath sheets she'd splurged on for the inn, however, she found herself defenseless against an onslaught of doubt and regret. Pink dawn lit the tree line out the window as she examined the toll the sleepless night had taken on her face.

She'd banished Joss–buried all her churning feelings for him and sent him out into the dark. It would have been so easy to hand him the reins, to let him stay and protect her. To let herself fall into the growing intimacy between them. It wouldn't have occurred to her to send him away until she'd found him gone, and doubted not so much him, but her own instincts.

She hadn't stopped to consider where he'd gone or why until the sick ball of fear had given way to halfway rational thought. Of course he'd offered Amanda a ride home. Of course he'd come back with an offering–a cold beer and his company.

Of course he'd insisted on staying.

Unbidden, memories of their slow dance the evening before surfaced. Less than twelve hours ago she'd been in his arms. Joss had stopped her, out of the blue, on a sidewalk, to tell her she was beautiful.

A hot stone of shame lodged in her throat. When his truck wasn't in the driveway, she'd assumed he'd left, and when he came back she acted like a child.

The tears she'd been holding at bay spilled over. Past being able to stop them, she sank to the floor of her bathroom and let them come.

CHAPTER 19

$\mathcal{N}$an felt as if a strong wind might blow her away as she went about her business that morning. She set the breakfast table for the Morgans, the Browns, and Frank and Debbie Roberts, the older couple staying in Champlain.

When none of them came down before nine, she poured herself a fifth cup of coffee and gave them the benefit of the doubt. It had been a long night for everyone.

When her guests finally did come down, Nan decided she preferred them safely up in their guest rooms.

Mr. and Mrs. Morgan were going home a day early.

"Paul has some work he really ought to be doing, and under the circumstances..." Susie Morgan's tone was cool and unapologetic. Paul Morgan wouldn't meet her eyes, but a dark stain of embarrassment rose up the back of his neck and onto the lobes of his ears.

Nan fought the urge to laugh, knowing tears would likely follow.

The Browns were off to meet friends at a nearby winery boasting a local varietal grape that was making headlines. Mr. Brown wanted to give her the number of a private investigator; his wife angled for gossip. Nan played it close to the vest, hoping to curb the spread of gossip. Mrs. Brown's haste to meet her friends suggested Nan's hopes were in vain.

It was Colonel Frank Roberts, U.S. Army, Retired, and his wife Debbie, who rescued her from her doubts.

"Damn shame," the Colonel said, tucking into a stack of buckwheat pancakes. "Though to be honest, I think that spot needed a rose, not a hydrangea."

"Frank!" Debbie Roberts rolled her eyes, and patted Nan's arm. "Don't pay him any attention. He's a terror. Never had an opinion he didn't share."

"An inn needs roses," Frank said with a playful smile.

Debbie blushed at her husband. "Oh, you." She patted the seat next to her at the table. "Nan, this man is a secret romantic. On leave from his first deployment–back when we were kids, he took me to this little B&B called The Rose Inn in Sherman Oaks. The owners were rose nuts. Potted roses everywhere, cut roses on every table, a greenhouse with prize-winning breeds, all tucked inside this walled-in property."

"Deb, she doesn't care about The Rose." Frank smiled at Nan when she freshened his coffee.

"Oh, no," Nan said. "I think I love it."

Debbie took the sugar bowl away from him after three spoonfuls. "You don't need that. Anyway, we barely left our room for three days, and now he just wants roses everywhere we go."

"Colonel, you are a romantic." Nan pretended to forget the sugar bowl when she tidied the coffee service.

"We're going back there in the spring. We're staying at The Rose, and Frank's indulging my favorite hobby–"

"Deb, she doesn't care about your *Garlic*."

Debbie rolled her eyes. "Sarlic. As if you didn't know it."

Frank set his silverware down. "She's been dragging me around to look at this statue for years. You make a solid breakfast, Miss Grady. Those folks who left early are missing out."

"Thank you, Colonel."

"It's Frank, and don't you let this whole thing get you down. You've got a nice place here." He stood, and pulled Debbie's chair out for her. His eyes twinkled. "It'll be even better with a rose bush or two. Deb and I are loyal to our favorite places. We'll be back in a year or two to check up on you."

The more Nan thought about it, the more she was certain Colonel Roberts was probably right. She did need more roses out front. And thinking about them took her mind off the desire to steal a moment and text Joss an apology.

He deserved better than a text. He deserved her full attention. Even if, deep in her secret heart, she hoped to hear from him first.

By lunch time, the urge to call Joss, to come up with some reason he should come down to the valley, was nearly overwhelming. Instead, she went out into the front yard to vent her frustration on the charred remains of her hydrangea. She was wrist deep in garden soil when the buttery purr of Jack's Audi slunk up the driveway. She didn't look up as the engine quieted and the door opened.

Only when the driver's shoes crunched on the gravel and his cheerful whistling identified him, did she turn her head.

Jack snickered. "That, pretty lady, is one ugly hat."

"Stuff it, Jack," she snapped. "I'm gardening. Gran always said ladies can wear ugly hats when they garden."

"Fine, kid. I'll take Katie's fresh toasted-coconut doughnuts to the Fullers'." The threat was mild, his wounded expression failing to mask his affection for her. "Molly actually appreciates my kind little gestures."

Nan set down the trowel she was still gripping like a weapon, and rocked back on her heels.

"I'm sorry, Jack," she apologized. "I had a long night."

"So, where's Joss, then?" Jack flashed a pirate grin.

"I haven't got a clue." She snapped a burnt branch off and tossed it in her wheelbarrow.

Jack eyed the shrub. "What happened?"

"It's a long story. Come on in." She stood, took the paper sack of doughnuts and led Jack inside to the kitchen. She busied herself with plates and coffee cups while Jack watched her with a baffled expression.

Jack wrapped his arms around her, squeezing gently. "What's going on?"

Her reply was a broken whisper. "Everything, Jack."

Jack pried the mugs from her hands. The comfort he offered soothed her rough edges.

"Hey." He pushed her hair away from her face. "Don't cry. I brought doughnuts."

Nan hugged him hard, a wobbly laugh escaping into his shirt. "I'm sorry. I'm a mess this morning. We got back last night to find Sergeant Lowry and the Fire Chief here. Someone set fire to one of the shrubs." At Jack's shocked expression, she held up a hand to stop him from interrupting.

"Everyone's fine. Joss wanted to stay so I wouldn't be alone. He even offered to sleep down here. And I sent him away. He was angry." She stared out the kitchen window at the charred remains of what had been a gorgeous sky-blue hydrangea. "Who would do this to me?"

"If I knew, they wouldn't be a problem for you anymore." Scowling, Jack put a plate on the table for each of them. "Sit," he instructed. "Eat."

Jack poured coffee. Nan broke her donut open, picking the coconut studded glaze off and nibbling. Kate's toasted coconut doughnuts were a rare treat. She only offered them on Sundays, and they usually sold out by about nine in the morning.

She let a wave of gratitude wash over her. Not everyone's attorney dropped in with rare Sunday morning pastries. Not everyone's attorney let them cry on his shoulder.

When she'd come to him for legal advice about starting the business, he'd offered not only to give her free counsel for a couple of years, but he'd found her a couple of investors for her down payment. Those funds, added to her modest savings, had tipped the scales when she'd gone to the bank for a mortgage and a loan.

Nan couldn't help wondering, in the companionable silence, if Jack was somehow disappointed that Joss wasn't with her. He'd seemed so sure when he arrived, that he would find his best friend there.

Jack reached into the fuchsia paper bag for a second doughnut. "Do you have guests today?"

Nan heard the careful neutrality in his voice. Afraid he was asking on behalf of his investors, her heart sank. "Two room's worth as of right now. The third one's asked for a refund and checked out without staying for breakfast." She pushed back at fatigue. "You sure you want to work *pro bono*, Jack? I think I need to face the idea that someone doesn't want me to be here."

"Whatever's going on? We'll figure it out." He swept a stray flake of coconut into his palm and dropped it on the plate.

"Too bad you can't fix the inn and my hydrangea," she sighed.

"Joss is going to want to do that for you."

Nan flattened donut crumbs against her plate. "We'll see."

"Listen," he began, in a tone Nan recognized as Older Brother Handing Down Wisdom, "Whatever argument you had last night, Katie and I both saw something else a few hours before. It'd be a shame for you to forget that. I'd guess that before the day's out, Joss is going to come around here looking to air out whatever was said. Give yourselves a chance, okay?"

Jack took their dishes to the sink.

Nan's heart swelled. She had chosen Kate–and by extension Jack– as her family; it was reassuring to know some of her choices were the absolute right ones. "Thanks. For the doughnuts and the lecture."

"You're always welcome to both." He offered her another desperately needed hug.

She clung to him for a moment, loathe to let go of a friend, then sucked in a breath and pushed away. "Now, I know you have to say goodbye to the Fullers before you head south, so get out of here," she said, squeezing his arm affectionately.

Jack kissed her cheek. "I love you, kid. I'll be back up in a couple weeks. Take care, okay?"

~

JOSS AWOKE DISORIENTED, in a pool of filtered sunlight. There were no curtains in the cabin; daylight was a hell of an effective alarm clock most days, but this morning was a notable exception. Pushing himself upright, he took stock of his shirt, tie, and trousers from last night hastily discarded on the floor.

He'd stormed in from his truck, furious with Nan's stubbornness and pissed off at himself for behaving like an asshole. After two fingers of bourbon and a beer chaser, he'd fallen into bed in his boxers and t-shirt.

He lay back down into the pillows, closing his eyes against the dull ache banging on his skull. A headache he certainly felt he'd earned. The whole night before had been a series of sucker punches.

Nan, looking like a fey creature at Seth's gallery opening, fitting easily into his arms on the dance floor. The building anticipation on the ride south on Route 7 and the abrupt shift to damage control at the inn.

His own caveman behavior.

He dragged himself from the bed, thoughts pounding against the backs of his eyes.

Complicated. He'd pushed. It hadn't been his place, but he'd felt compelled to protect her. She didn't know him well enough to know how deep that instinct ran in him. He'd learned chivalry at his mother's knee, and Nan brought it all up to the surface. A man protected the women he cared about.

And there it was. He cared about her. He was standing on the edge of falling in love with her. Complicated.

He scrubbed his hair with his hand, and rummaged through his fridge with the other. Nothing to do about the lack of food except head into town. Coffee at Sweet Pease was out of the question. Given what he knew of women and their best friends, his chances of not being skewered alive by Kate were slim-to-nil.

If he played his cards right, though, his mother would feed him.

Then he would go see Nan and apologize for being a Neanderthal. He knew he was rusty in the compromise department, but living on your own terms had a few drawbacks that way. He thought she was a woman who might understand that.

His phone rang. Jack's name came up on the screen. "Hey."

"I hope you're halfway down the mountain with a potted hydrangea," his friend said without preamble.

"Thanks for the advice, Casanova," Joss replied sarcastically. "What did Kate tell you?"

"Kate's up to her shoulders in the after-church crowd at the bakery. I know what I know from the source, buddy, and I'm telling you to get down there."

What the hell was Jack doing with Nan? "You talked to her?"

Jack's response was cool. "Take it easy. I went by to say goodbye and check on my client. I was hoping to get in a little good natured teasing. I found my fiercely independent little sister from another mister weeping in her coffee. I'm not saying it's all your fault, but I have a strong hunch you could put some of it right."

"Duly noted." Joss assessed his reflection in one of the sliding glass doors that led to his deck. "I guess I should take a shower and get in the truck, but where the hell am I going to find a potted hydrangea?"

Jack's answering laugh was smug. "I took the liberty of checking with Penny Coulson. She's got a few in stock."

"I owe you one, Pease."

"If I ever settle down, I'll collect." Jack's smugness was audible.

Joss grinned to himself. "I'm off the hook then."

"Oh, and probably not the moment to mention Drew's bachelor weekend, but it's definitely on."

"Right." He'd forgotten it. Completely. "Text me the details later. I've got a plant to pick up."

NAN'S PULSE sputtered when some time later Joss's truck rolled in; the columns of numbers on her computer screen swam out of focus. He climbed out of the truck in battered jeans and a polo shirt, a well-worn Thornton College cap on his head. His sunglasses concealed his expression, but Nan sensed tension in the set of his jaw.

He went to the kitchen door, knocked. She heard him nudge the screen door open, heard him call.

"Nan?"

She sat absolutely still. *He'd come to her.* Her heart wanted her to jump up, run to him, throw herself into his arms and weep. Pride held her in place.

The screen door banged closed. She heard his shoes on the gravel as he returned to the truck. Disappointment pushed pride aside as she watched him pull open the driver's side door, and she went to the front door.

She watched as Joss pulled the keys out of the ignition, left the driver's side door open, and went around to the bed of the pickup. He dropped the tailgate and jumped up into the bed to pull out a large cardboard box. Shifting the box to one arm, he hopped down and slammed the tailgate closed again. He scanned the windows over the garage, where her apartment windows were.

He wasn't leaving. Pride took a backseat.

Joss came toward her as she stepped out onto the porch. The breeze molded his shirt to his torso. He held the box easily, despite its size; she wondered at the contents. A step at a time, he moved through the dappled shadows on the driveway, never taking his eyes from her face.

When he reached the top of the stairs, he set the cardboard box down at her feet. Before she could ask what it was, he separated the folded flaps and pulled out a young hydrangea in a pot. He offered it to her with a boyish smile. "Since you're short one."

"Thank you." The words wobbled in her throat as she took the plant. He followed when she slipped past him to carry the new shrub down the stairs to its new place in the garden. The charred stalks of the dead hydrangea left black smudges on her fingertips when she touched it. The anger inherent in burning a garden still shocked her and a fresh wave of tears welled up. She reached to swipe away the moisture but Joss's hand caught her arm.

He pulled her into his arms. "I'm sorry."

Joss was warm and solid, smelling of soap and growing things. The fabric under her fingers was worn soft with washings. It was so easy to melt into him, to lean her worries against his strength. "I didn't want to send you away last night."

He kissed her, then. Slowly, deeply, wrapping his arms around her and pulling her up on her toes.

She locked her arms around his neck. She could feel the same need in him she'd felt the night before, but the jittery edge of fear was tempered. She'd been strong the night before; in the midday sun she let herself lean into him, let herself be strong with him.

Joss drew away, dropping a light kiss on her forehead as he lowered her down. His hands lifted to frame her face, and he touched his forehead to hers. "I didn't want to go."

There was an ashy smear on his neck from her finger. "Can you stay now? I could use some help getting this," she brushed the burnt shrub again, "out of the ground, so I can plant my new one."

"I can't think of anything else I'd rather do," he said. "Is there still a shovel in the garden shed out back?"

THEY PLANTED the new hydrangea under the midday sun. He stayed to help her move the compost in the wheelbarrow, worked alongside her while she pruned, weeded, and mulched.

Nan improvised a picnic snack on the front porch. Flushed, sweating, and grubby, they shared a plate of bread, cheese, and a pitcher of iced tea.

Nan settled into one of the two rockers on the porch.

Joss sat on the stairs, leaning back against the railing to take in the view of the marsh. The Adirondacks slipped hazily toward the southwestern horizon. "Jack said he was here earlier. You two go back farther than I figured."

"A ways, yeah." Nan thought back. "Kate dragged me along to visit him at Williams. I was terrified of him. He was so good-looking and charming, and everyone seemed to know him. I was lost."

Joss's eyes crinkled. "I didn't see a lot of him when we were in college. Just when he was home."

"And I never came here with Kate until much later. I was afraid to intrude on their family life."

Joss laughed out loud at that. "As if the Peases would consider a visit from Kate's friend an intrusion?"

Nan looked out over the marsh. "I didn't understand that. I was raised by grandparents who weren't demonstrative; I'm used to being on my own. Sometimes I'm not sure how to be around a family like that."

"Hey," Joss said gently, "if you're going to learn, Cora and John are amazing teachers. They were a second family to me my whole life."

"Did you need one?" Nan couldn't imagine needing more than Molly and Walt Fuller in your life.

"More than you know," Joss said lightly. Nan could hear the seriousness underneath. "My father and I butted heads a lot."

"I wish I'd had someone to butt heads with. I never dared disappoint my grandparents." She caught the sharp look Joss gave her. "No, not like that. They were kind. But disappointing them, after they took me in? I couldn't do it."

Joss was quiet a moment. "So, there was nothing between you and Jack?"

Nan turned to him. Something, not precisely anger, not exactly joy, flushed her cheeks. "Would it matter?"

He returned her glance, open and direct. "It would."

She kept her answer simple. "Nothing."

Birdsong and passing cars filled the silence. Clouds pushed at the sun. Joss finished his tea and went down onto the lawn.

He squinted up at the second floor. Nan knew without his saying that he was looking at the windows. "Am I losing my whole heating budget out these windows?"

"I won't lie. They're not the most efficient windows," Joss remarked dryly. "But they're not that bad, especially given how old they are. You should really have the storm windows put in before November, though. Chances are, they're in the basement."

She grinned with sweet relief. Storm windows, she could handle. "Friendly advice from my contractor?"

"I knew the couple who lived here. They were friendly with my grandparents when they ran the dairy. My father grew up with their kids. They took good care of this old place. And I took care of a lot of it when they got too old to do it alone."

He couldn't help himself, she thought. He had to take care of people.

Joss was still talking about the windows. "You may want to consider replacing the windows down the line. It'd be a big investment, though. I'd be happy to give you a quote." He leveled her with a playful expression. "As your contractor."

Nan caught the look, the shift in the tone of his voice. "My contractor," she repeated slowly, meeting his eyes.

"Is done for the day, and we never got to finish what we started last night." He climbed the porch stairs. "Last night had nothing to do with you being a client."

She ran a hand through her hair and twisted a stray lock in her fingers.

Joss reached down to take her hands, then pulled her up against him. "I hated leaving you."

He smoothed her hair away from her face, cupping her cheek in his palm, and pressed his lips to the corner of her mouth, kissing his way to the center, pausing when her lips parted beneath his. "Not that I mind making out on your lawn," he chuckled, "but it's probably better for business if I kiss you inside your house."

Nan glanced at the road, empty in both directions as far as she could see. "Oh, I don't know. I think we're safe for the moment."

They made it as far as the kitchen before Joss tugged her back into his arms. "Please tell me I don't have to leave again anytime soon."

Nan quashed the urge to explain to him why she'd needed to be on her own. Joss's mouth was deliciously insistent, scattering her concerns. She laid her fears aside and slipped into unhurried desire.

When his tea-tart lips left hers to travel her jaw and throat, her own moan of pleasure surprised her. With a growl of approval, Joss smoothed his hands under her top, tracing the band of her bra, teasing the curve of her breasts. When she pressed herself against him, filling his hands, he smiled against her mouth and angled to deepen the kiss. Nan contented herself with exploring the wonderful musculature under his tee shirt.

They kissed, hungrily but without rush, as the shadows lengthened on the floor.

As the sun began to dip below the skyline, they heard a car pull in. Nan drew away, looked down at her watch. "Oh, no," she said, looking up at Joss apologetically.

"In all the drama, I forgot I was meeting with Anneliese to talk group rates for a wedding she's trying to book. I promised her dinner, and that Chloe could come along."

"If it's okay with Anna," Joss offered, crossing the room to pick up his tools, "I can take Chloe over to the farm for an hour, so you two can have your meeting in peace. Mom would love to see Chloe, and you can invite me to stay for dinner."

Anneliese had pulled in and was closing her car door with one hip while she shifted a sleepy looking preschooler onto the other one. Nan caught her friend's curious expression at seeing Joss's truck in the driveway.

"Can I?" The teasing dispersed the lust that had crept in like fog. Nan started out the kitchen door to greet Anneliese.

Joss followed her out. "I didn't know you knew Anna and Chloe."

"I cold-called her when I was getting the inn ready this summer. She's turned out to be a great referral and I like her."

They all met near the garage door.

"Hey, Nan," Anneliese said, shifting her young daughter onto the other hip. She turned to Joss with a warm smile. "Hey, Cous."

Joss wrapped Anneliese and Chloe in a bear hug.

"Hey, Chlo," Joss said, ruffling the little girl's blond curls. "Think your Mama will let us go see Uncle Walt's cows while she talks to Miss Grady?"

Chloe's face lit up. She reached out for Joss, who settled her in the crook of his empty arm.

"We'll be back in an hour," he said to the two women, before dropping a casual kiss on Nan's lips and walking out the door.

Anneliese blinked, giving Nan a curious once-over. "Contractor or not, that was no business call."

Nan opened her mouth to protest.

"Save it," Anna admonished. "I think you're both great. Enjoy each other." She followed Nan into the parlor. They sat down opposite each other and Anna pulled out a few files. "This stuff should take about five minutes. Which leaves the other fifty-five for you to tell me what's going on with my cousin."

CHAPTER 20

At the edge of Nan's yard, Joss swung Chloe Thompson up onto his shoulders. The little girl giggled.

"Who are we gonna see today, Chlo?" he asked, crossing the yard.

Chloe scrunched up her face and counted on her fingers. "Lulu, Daisy, an' Baby Mae!"

Joss trotted for a few yards, mooing, enjoying her laughter and finding it strangely endearing when her plump fingers gripped his hair a little harder than was comfortable. As they approached the property line, Joss slowed and dropped his voice to a stage whisper.

"What do you think, Chlo? Are there bears in the woods?" he asked, ducking under a low branch and gripping her calves tight.

"No!" she shouted gleefully. "Monsters!"

"Monsters! Oh, no!" Joss feigned terror. "Protect me, Chloe! I'm afraid of monsters!"

She leaned down, pressed her soft cheek against the top of his head. "Don't worry," she said quietly. "There's not really monsters." She reached down and patted his unshaven cheek. "Scratchy," she murmured.

His heart turned over. They emerged on the other side of the trees, in full view of the dairy barn. "Should we go right to visit Lulu and

143

Daisy and Mae? Or should we go see if your Great Aunty Molly has cookies and milk for us?" He paused, sure Anna would probably frown on late afternoon cookies, but a little girl didn't get to visit Great Aunty Molly's kitchen every day.

"Cookies!" Chloe decided.

Molly met them at the door, arms open wide. "Come see me, pretty girl!"

Just as easily as she had gone to Joss, Chloe went into Molly's arms and planted a big kiss on her cheek. "Aunty Molly, do you have cookies?"

"For sweet little girls with kisses to share? Always." Molly shifted the child to her hip with a practiced slide.

Joss waited in the mud room for their return. Molly came back out with Chloe in tow, carrying a big chocolate chip cookie in her two hands. Molly handed Joss a sippy-cup half full of milk.

"What brings you over here with this charming young lady today?" Molly asked.

"I was over at the inn, helping Nan with her garden." Joss searched his mother's face for confirmation that she was up to date on the prior evening's events. He assumed Jack would have filled her in when he dropped by. "Anna came over for a meeting. I thought Chlo might be bored hanging out alone, so I volunteered to bring her to visit the girls."

Molly patted his cheek, echoing Chloe's earlier gesture. Joss's heart turned over again.

"You're a good man," his mother said. "Just bring the cup back in before you go back over."

Joss led Chloe across the yard toward the barn. It was a small word for a massive structure, long and rust red. Joss's great-grandfather had built it into the slope of the land, allowing for equipment storage underneath. Chloe made short work of her cookie and was dusting crumbs off her hands as they approached.

The door was open, and Joss could hear his father further down. "Pop!" he called. "You have company!"

His father ducked out of a stall. He saw Chloe and waved. "Come on down here, Miss. Someone wants to see you."

Chloe ran down the center aisle of the barn. Joss watched his gruff, quiet father light up as he scooped Chloe up and perched her on the door to Baby Mae's stall.

"She got big," Chloe was saying, eyes full of wonder, as Joss approached the stall. The Jersey heifer had indeed grown since Anna had brought Chloe out to the farm back in the spring. Then, the newborn calf had been wobbly kneed.

Mae still had her expressive brown eyes and gentle demeanor, though. The young cow came right over and nudged Chloe's hand. The preschooler beamed at Walt and Joss, delighted.

Walt tightened his grip around Chloe's middle as she leaned down to press her snub nose against the cow's muzzle.

"Old MacDonald had a farm. E-I-E-I-O!" she sang.

Joss supplied the next line. "And on that farm he had a cow."

"Mae!" Chloe added.

"E-I-E-I-O," they sang together.

"With a moo-moo here," Walt added, and the three of them launched into the rest of the song, allowing Chloe to choose the animals on the farm, each one more outlandish than the one before.

Sheep! Turkey! Bear! Monster! Giraffe! Dinosaur!

Watching his father singing silly songs, the deep lines of a life of hard work somehow eased by his obvious pleasure, Joss imagined him as a grandfather, imagined his mom as a Gramma. Molly and Walt and the dairy had always been a destination for the children in the family over the years, but Joss suddenly pictured it a little differently.

A little girl with wide, cognac-colored eyes and ruffled hair, or little boy, sturdy and gray-eyed, trailing their grandfather around the farm and bartering kisses for cookies with their grandmother.

"Mae's my fav'rite cow, Joss," Chloe said, turning and reaching for him.

"I know she is, but do you want to say hello to the rest of the ladies?" Joss asked.

"Can I come back an' say 'bye to Mae before we go see Mama?" she asked.

"Of course, sweetie," Joss replied.

Chloe scampered off down the aisle to investigate the stalls. There weren't too many in the barn at present; Joss could see the herd in the higher pasture, taking in the last of the sun. They'd start making their way back shortly, udders full and ready for milking.

"How're things, son?" Walt asked.

Joss kept his voice low and his eyes on his small cousin. "You heard from Jack what happened?"

"Any ideas who could have done something like that?" Walt leaned back against the stall door.

Joss shook his head; the whole thing baffled him. He was about to say so when Chloe screamed.

He and Walt ran through the barn to where Chloe stood, staring huge-eyed, at an open stall. Joss picked her up, and she looped her arms around his neck and buried her head against his chest. She smelled like hay and sunshine and the earthy, fermented smell of a small child. He settled her weight into the crook of his elbow. "What happened, Chlo?"

Walt was staring into the straw. "Who the hell are you?"

Joss turned to see a teenage girl huddled in the corner. Chloe had obviously startled her; she was filthy, hair matted with hay. The girl regarded them through narrowed eyes, but the imprint of her sleeve stood out in pink on her cheek, like a child who'd fallen asleep in the car.

With his free hand, Joss pulled his phone from his pocket and texted his mother.

The grubby young woman curled silently in on herself, but she never took her eyes from the two men barring her escape.

Molly came out to the barn a moment later, dressed for walking. "Come on, Chloe. Let's go back over to the inn and find your Mama." Molly leaned in close to Joss. "Pete Lowry's on his way over."

While he and his father stood guard, Joss watched his mother stroll with Chloe along the edge of the East pasture, skirting the trees, imagining a time when he might stroll with a small child of his own between these houses as the sun set on a chilly September afternoon.

Pete Lowry made good time, arriving at Fuller's Dairy about ten minutes after Molly's call. The girl remained sullen and silent, but she didn't struggle when Pete informed her he was taking her back to the station until they got hold of her mother.

"Mr. Fuller would be within his rights to press charges for trespassing," Sergeant Lowry warned her. He gently drew back the curtain of her lank fuchsia hair and made eye-contact. "Danny."

Her eyes flicked nervously from the officer, to Walt, and finally to Joss, before dropping back to rapt contemplation of her toes.

Walt spoke up. "That won't be necessary."

Joss spoke up. "Pete?"

The policeman didn't need for Joss to finish his thought. "Ayuh," was all he said. He led the girl towards his cruiser.

Walt contemplated the now empty stall. "She's Terri Beaudette's little girl."

Joss sifted through his memory, Teresa Beaudette had been a few years ahead of him at Thornton Union High. She'd gone to Burlington to get a nursing degree and come back while he was in New York– with her certifications, a little girl, and a naked ring finger. "Terri was working for the Swifts, wasn't she?"

Joss knew the answer even as he asked it.

"They were living in the apartment over the garage," Walt added. "Terri and her daughter. Not such a little girl anymore."

"Walt? Joss?" Molly's voice called. "I'm back."

Joss felt the inn–and the woman who ran it–tugging at him. "Pop, I–"

"Go on, now." A knowing smile played at the corners of Walt's mouth.

Joss found Nan and Anna in the kitchen.

Nan was at the island, her maple butcher block blanketed with a rainbow of chopped vegetables. A pot of water boiled merrily on the range.

Chloe saw Joss and beamed. "Joss!"

Anneliese sat at the table with her daughter on her lap.

"Did you have fun at the farm, Chlo?" Joss asked.

Chloe tilted her head back to talk to her mother. "Baby Mae got big, Mama."

"I bet she did. All babies do," Anna replied, smoothing the little girl's hair. There were questions in her eyes when she looked over Chloe's head at Joss.

Nan opened the fridge and pulled out sliced carrots and apples on a tiny stoneware plate. She uncovered a trio of baked chicken breasts, resting under foil on a plate, sliced off a bit, deftly cutting them into small bites and arranging them just so on the plate.

Watching her whip up a quick supper for Chloe, Joss was struck anew by the neatness of her movements. She never wasted a motion when it came to hospitality, but it never came across as rushed.

"Joss, can you grab her milk from the fridge?" she asked him.

He retrieved a glittery, pink cup from the refrigerator, crossed the kitchen, and took the small plate from Nan as he did, effectively drawn into the dance she did while she worked.

It was a good feeling.

While Chloe ate, Nan grated ginger and squeezed limes, whisking it into a small bowl.

"So, Joss," Anneliese said, supervising Chloe's dinner, "Nan told me you were in Burlington with Kate and Jack. Sounds like it was quite a night."

Joss snuck a glance at Nan, who studiously avoided his eyes. Her cheeks pinked deliciously.

Anneliese pushed a portion of the sliced chicken toward Chloe's fork. "How is Jack?"

Joss snagged a slice of bell pepper from the board. "You just missed him; he stopped by the farm on his way back to Boston. Something about a client meeting, which is probably code for dinner that costs more than my student loans for the year."

"Well." Anna's tone tipped into sarcasm. "Isn't he hot stuff."

"We should all get together the next time Jack's in town," Joss offered. "I bet Jack would love to see you. You haven't been around since–"

"Since I left town," she finished flatly.

Chloe was starting to fade, pushing her food around and leaning back against her mother. Nan suggested they take her upstairs to the apartment and set her up with a movie.

"We can bring dinner upstairs," she finished, draining chow mien noodles over the sink and tossing them into an oversized salad bowl.

Anneliese shot her a grateful look and bundled Chloe and her sippy-cup up.

"Do you mind grabbing a few beers from the fridge?" Nan asked Joss, cleaning up Chloe's plate. "I'll be up in a few minutes with dinner."

Joss opened Nan's fridge, grabbed a six-pack from the local brewery and followed Anna and Chloe up the stairs.

NAN FINISHED DICING THE CHICKEN, tossing everything together in salad bowl. She placed it on a big tray with bowls and flatware. She stood at the island a moment, looking at the tray, thinking of how easy it had been to include Joss in the dinner preparations, to say nothing of how it warmed her heart to see him come through the kitchen door with a kind word for his small cousin. They had barely known each other for more than a few weeks; after one unquestionably sexy dance and a few stolen kisses, she was letting her daydreams get away from her again.

She took a deep breath and picked up the tray.

Upstairs, she found Joss on her couch, flipping through *Yankee Magazine*. He heard her come in and stood up, laying the magazine down on the table.

Anna came out of Nan's room, closing the door softly.

"She's all snuggled up with Rapunzel and Eugene, but still talking about Baby Mae right to the end," Anneliese reported. "Thanks, Joss. That was such an incredibly sweet thing to do."

Joss nodded, "Really, it was no trouble. She's a cutie."

Anna shot Nan a raised eyebrow, gave her a little smile. Nan blushed.

Ignorant of the silent exchange between the two women, Joss took the tray from her and set it down alongside the magazine.

Joss opened beers for them while Nan dished up the salad. "So, Anna, how badly did you embarrass me while I was at the farm?"

"I haven't yet. And most of my stories are embarrassing for me, too."

Anneliese reminded Joss of the time they'd planned to hike a few miles of the Appalachian trail with Jack the summer after junior year. They'd ended up bailing early, and just sitting by the edge of Lake Pleiad, the boys getting tipsy on a six-pack of cheap beer and all three of them going skivvy dipping.

"God, you should have seen the look on your faces, Joss, when I stripped down to my underwear and jumped in!" Anneliese's face sparkled with remembered mischief.

"I thought Jack was going to have a heart attack," Joss remembered.

"You two didn't think I'd do it."

"Only in our dreams did we think girls were just going to get anywhere near naked and go swimming with us, and then when one did, she was my cousin," Joss replied. "We don't get into that kind of thing down here in the valley," he said for Nan's benefit, winking at Anneliese. "No matter who we asked, we could never get any other girls to go half-naked swimming with us," Joss finished ruefully.

"Don't believe a word he says, Nan," Anneliese taunted. "He and Jack could have had their pick of the girls in our high school. And they knew it."

"Jack knew it. I was always a little more skeptical," Joss corrected.

"He did know it, didn't he?"

Joss was already telling another story of their innocent teenaged misbehavior, but Nan thought she'd heard a slightly bitter note in Anna's voice when she'd mentioned Jack. She wondered idly if there was some history between them, and if Kate knew anything about it. She didn't want to cause discomfort for her friends.

When Anneliese looked at the clock on Nan's bookshelf, stood, and stretched, Nan was shocked at the easy passage of more than two hours. "I need to pack up my kiddo and head back to the homestead," she said. "Thanks for the dinner, Nan, and the girl talk."

"I'll walk you out, Anna," Joss offered, standing up.

"Anytime," Nan replied. "You should come out with Kate and me some night."

"Look out, Anna," Joss teased. "You run with Kate, you'll get a reputation."

"Maybe I need a new reputation," she said tartly, disappearing into Nan's room. She came back out a few moments later with Chloe draped over her.

Nan led the way downstairs into the breezeway. Joss followed Anneliese and sleeping Chloe out into the night, but not before he squeezed Nan's arm lightly. "I'll be right back."

Nan watched Joss close Anneliese's car door and turn to come back inside. She heard his steps on the driveway, his hands turning the doorknob. As the door opened, awkwardness flooded the room. So much had happened, so much had changed in the last twenty-four hours.

Her emotional storm and Joss's inextricable place at the eye of it washed over her as she stood there, waiting for him to open her door. There was so much they needed to talk about, and she had so little energy for any of it, not with the news from the farm earlier that evening, news she and Joss and Anneliese had tacitly chosen not to discuss.

There was an answering uncertainty in his face when he closed the door behind him and turned to face her. *So, he wasn't as sure of everything as he seemed.* The relief of it all ballooned inside her, releasing in a flood of helpless laughter. Better that than tears, she thought as she fought for composure.

Joss stared at her for a moment, standing there in the middle of the kitchen giggling like a loon, before he, too, gave in to laughter.

When the mirth wound down, when breath returned, he closed the space between them, and held on. She melted into him, curving herself against him. They rested there, the minutes ticking by, each of them loathe to change the mood.

"Her name is Danny Beaudette," Joss finally said, speaking against her temple. "I knew her mom a little when we were in high school. Terri. I just don't get it."

The name gave her pause. There was something vaguely familiar about it, but she couldn't recall what. "You really think this girl is the one who did all those awful things?"

"I don't know." His hands stroked the small of her back in rhythmic circles; she could have purred from the pleasure. "Pete seemed to think so, too. It's too big a coincidence to ignore, finding her there today."

She needed to think. The wonderful hypnosis of his hands scattered her thoughts, so she eased out of the circle of his embrace. "Joss, that was a lot of damage. What am I going to if it turns out to be some teenage girl?"

"She's a kid." His hands slowed and he leaned back. "She needs some discipline, but would you press charges?"

"She nearly set my home and business on fire. If she is behind all of it, she could have hurt Kate. Or it could have been a guest, and I could have lost everything in a lawsuit."

"She's a kid."

Joss didn't let go, but the connection between them was strained.

Nan blew out a breath. "What would you do? If it was your cabin, or your parents' barn?"

His expression clouded. She could almost see him working it out, resigning anger with convictions. He stepped back and pressed his palms into the counter.

"I'd make her work off the damage somehow. Community service or … I don't know. Something real, though. Something to keep her busy and make her realize the huge implications of what she did."

She could see it, the truth in it. He stood there in her kitchen with his arms at his sides with the simplest truth—and the entire population of a small Vermont college town–behind him. That was how he–and his family and their friends and the people who were the warp and weft of the community–would handle it.

She reached for his hand, lacing her fingers over his. "Let's see what Pete Lowry found out."

Joss touched her chin, tilting her face up to his in the dim light. "Let's."

Let's. A simple word, but a declaration of intent nonetheless. They would approach this together.

His lips skimmed hers, asking for more, but his phone rang, shattering the new tenderness in the room.

Frowning, he looked at the screen and answered the call. His responses were terse, and he ended the call with a heavy sigh. "Ellen's had a plumbing emergency. There's water flooding the new sections of the barn. I need to get out there and help her with damage control."

He cupped her cheek and kissed the corner of her mouth. "I'm sorry."

She leaned her head into his palm for a moment, savoring the contact. "I understand. Text me when you get home?"

"I will."

When he was gone, she carefully checked the locks, and turned on the floods. Teenage girl or not, she didn't want to invite any more trouble.

CHAPTER 21

$\mathcal{N}$an was still staring out into the inky night when headlights illuminated the driveway. Elisha cut the engine and crossed the dooryard, fishing in her Kate Spade tote for the front door key. Nan looked at the clock and realized that it was technically after hours.

She held her breath as Elisha's heels clacked across the foyer, pausing at the kitchen door.

Elisha came through in an oyster-colored suit, the jacket unbuttoned to reveal an emerald green camisole. She tottered on one foot and then the other, removing a pair of four-inch stiletto saddle pumps that probably cost more than room and board for the weekend.

"Was that Joss I saw leaving?"

Nan mentally shook off the lingering chemistry and pasted on a professional smile. "He was over to help me plant a new hydrangea." No need to mention he'd given it to her. "His cousin was here for a dinner meeting, so he stayed on."

Nan knew she sounded ridiculous trying to hide anything. Elisha wasn't a factor, and her presence was fast becoming as much a fixture at The Damselfly as Joss himself was.

Elisha pouted prettily. "I'm sorry I missed him. I won't keep you up, though." She plucked her heels from the floor and pushed the door.

"Elisha?" Nan stopped her before she was fully aware of what she was going to say. Elisha paused in the doorway. The invitation made itself. "Do you want a beer?"

When Elisha smiled and set down her shoes again, Nan wondered how anyone ever refused her anything. That smile alone was irresistible.

"I would love one."

Nan opened a pair of bottles from the fridge. When she reached for pint glasses, Elisha stopped her.

"Why dirty extra dishes?"

In the end, they split a six-pack of summer wheat ale, straight from the bottles. The discovery of Danny Beaudette in the Fullers' barn seemed very far away.

"I almost married him," Elisha said idly. She'd been describing the month she'd spent with her parents in Nairobi. "But mostly for the giraffes. And then my thesis advisor emailed me about something, and I had this epiphany…" She yawned expansively, causing Nan to do the same.

"I need to go to bed." The alcohol had taken the edge off; the conversation kept Nan in her seat. There was far more to Elisha than she'd imagined. "Three beers is probably my smart limit."

"I can't tell you the last time I had one beer, never mind three." Elisha lined the six bottles up between them. She'd shed the suit jacket and twisted her silky hair up off her neck with a silver hair stick. "Nor can I tell you the last time I stayed at a country inn that had more vandalism than my first apartment in New York."

"You probably didn't hear," Nan said, wobbling a bottle with her fingertip. "There was a teenage girl hiding out in the Fullers' barn today. And Sergeant Lowry figures she's our vandal."

"A teenage girl?" Elisha bit her lip. "That's a tough one, you know?"

"Yeah." Nan missed the twirling neck and the bottle clattered to the counter.

Elisha picked it up and returned it to the lineup. "What will you do? If it's true?"

"What would you do?" Nan watched Elisha expectantly.

The answer came swift and decisive. "I'd make her work off the damage. Here."

The same answer Joss had given, but for one small detail.

"Here?" As she asked the question, Nan knew it was the right answer. It was the thing someone who called Thornton home would do.

"No. On a chain gang." Elisha rolled her eyes, stood, stretched, and picked up her jacket from the back of her chair. "Thank you for the beer. Go to bed."

"Yes, Ma'am." Nan snapped a floppy salute.

Two days, a confession in an office at the courthouse, a meeting with a social worker, an uncountable number of phone calls, and one awkward meeting in neutral territory later, Nan was driving westbound out of town with 16-year-old Danny Beaudette in her passenger seat.

Nan had taken one look at the teen in her slouchy layers and combat boots, and wondered if she was out of her mind. "Will you be okay in those boots all day?"

"Yeah." First word.

Danny's tenacious reticence had ruffled her. Nan had struggled for a neutral topic. "You're a sophomore, right? How do you like Thornton Union?"

"S'fine." Had the contraction counted as one word, or two?

In the end, she'd let the radio fill the silence and had made a concerted effort not to sing along and embarrass herself further. When she'd stopped the car, Danny had peeled herself up off the seat and shuffled dully towards the kitchen door.

Elisha had been helping herself to a bowl of oatmeal from the crockpot. She'd raised a brow, but said nothing beyond, "Good morning."

Nan's cheeks had flamed when Danny simply looked at her before dropping into a chair at the big table. "Do you drink coffee, Danny? Maybe we can start there?"

"Sure."

Three words. So far, the young woman had graced her with three words since they'd met at the public library. Surely that was a beginning?

"Help yourself to breakfast, then we can go to my office and talk about how this is all going to work."

Danny gave her a sullen sideways glance, but got up with a loud scrape of chair legs on hardwood and filled a bowl and a mug. She liberally sugared both; something about the gesture made her seem younger than her years, and Nan resolved to find the silver lining in the situation.

Breakfast was an awkward affair, made even worse by Elisha's forcedly cheerful–and blatantly ignored–departure for the college campus. When Danny was done eating, Nan cleared the dishes. "Come on, let's get you started."

Nan was fairly certain, when she left Danny restocking the linen cabinets an hour later, that getting more than a grunt out of the girl was a major victory.

CHAPTER 22

While Danny and Nan circled one another like wary wild creatures, Joss was en route to The Damselfly, questioning where his head had been since he'd left Nan two evenings before. They exchanged a flurry of texts, some professional, some decidedly not, and he'd completely forgotten about the building inspection.

He'd arranged to meet Sarah Mason, the building inspector, for a final inspection of the Adirondack Suite's renovations. He'd planned the late-Saturday morning meeting hoping that Nan would be busy with weekend traffic, but that her guests would be out enjoying the valley. He hadn't wanted her to fret about it, but he hadn't meant to surprise her with it either.

He liked Sarah Mason. She'd come to town with her husband–an Italian language lecturer at the college, a few years before. With a background in urban planning and a contractor's license under her belt, she'd been a perfect fit for the Building Inspector's seat. Sarah knew how to pal around with the old guys, but she didn't take any crap from them. Joss liked her for her absolute professionalism, which was tempered with a dose of common sense.

Her truck was already parked at the inn when he arrived. Sarah sat in the cab, her feet dangling over the side while she spoke in rapid-fire Italian. She saw Joss and waved, rolling her eyes apologetically. Joss waited for her to finish, preferring that to going inside and facing the awkwardness festering between him and Nan.

Sarah finished her call. "Sorry, Paolo's sister called in a rant because we're not going to Florence for Christmas."

"We should all have your problems." Joss gestured toward the inn's front door with a wry smile. "Shall we?"

He led Sarah through the inn's front entry. The grand staircase was lit by a bar of late morning sunlight, swimming with golden dust motes. Nan's office stood open to the left. Open and empty. Through the wide opening into the parlor, Joss could see the afternoon's fire, already laid in the grate. The lemony scent of furniture polish mingled with the toasty aroma of well-seasoned maple cordwood.

Sarah sighed audibly. "This place is amazing."

Joss breathed in the homey aroma. Nan's instincts were excellent; she knew just how to seduce her guests. She didn't see it so clearly, but she knew just how to seduce him, too. "Wait 'til you see the third floor."

Sarah laughed. "Says the man who's remodeled it to the inspector who needs to sign off on the work."

He caught himself peering around corners as he and Sarah arrived at the second floor landing. Between Elisha and Nan, the inn was full of landmines this morning. When he reached the door to the Adirondack Suite, though, without seeing Nan, he began to wonder where she was. Her VW was parked in front of the garage. Elisha's rental was there, too, but he suspected she was out for her daily loop.

The door was cracked open, a clear alto voice singing the bridge to a pop song he only knew from the radio. He'd walked in on Nan singing before, but she usually tended towards a smokier delivery. Trying to avoid frightening her, he ushered Sarah noisily into the room. "Nan?"

The singing was coming from the bathroom. He tapped at the door as he pushed it open. The stringy dark ponytail and slouchy jeans didn't belong to Nan.

The young woman turned around, lips curled around the lyrics she'd been singing, but a harsh squeak was all that came out.

"What the hell are you doing here?" The door banged all the way open, and Joss winced at the thought of dented plaster.

Danny Beaudette pushed past Joss and stumbled into Sarah in an attempt to escape the small quarters of the en suite bath. Sarah steadied the girl, her forehead a knot of concern. "Joss?"

"I'm sorry." The apology was curt. "But what are you doing here?"

"I work here," Danny muttered. The words were barely audible. The fierce expression in her hazel eyes spoke far more loudly.

Leaving Danny and Sarah in the suite, Joss pounded down the two flights of stairs. After a cursory examination of the first floor, he called down to the cellar. No reply. She'd lost her mind, leaving that kid alone up there, putting a suspected vandal to work at the scene of the crime, right there with all of his tools and the freshly re-renovated room. He pushed through the empty kitchen and started up the stairs to her apartment.

He barged through her door to find her standing at the bookshelf, reading a postcard. She whirled on him.

"You scared me!"

"What the hell is Danny Beaudette doing cleaning the bathrooms?"

Surprise and anger flashed over her face. "What the hell are you doing bursting into my apartment uninvited?"

The rebuke registered, but he was still on the offensive. "I couldn't find you."

"So you assumed I was…what? Hacked to death?" Impatience, and something softer—*disappointment?*—filled her eyes. "I gave her the choice. Work off the cost of the repairs here, or work it off cleaning bedpans and washing floors at the rest home. She's a kid, Joss, a screwed up kid." Her expression drilled into his heart. "You reminded me of that."

Shame deflated his fear. "Yeah, I suggested you not press criminal charges. I figured some community service or, I don't know, something. But not here. Not alone half the time with you. She could have killed you."

Nan held out the card she was holding. "I don't think she meant to do more than chase me off. Not that it would have worked, but that's what I think. Look." She raised the card up slightly for him to read.

Joss flipped it over. It reminded him of trips to Hampton and Old Orchard as a kid, all the kitschy summer heat and noise.

Danny, it's not this pretty where we live now, but the beach is awesome. I miss you. Maybe you can come down here some time. It's warmer than Vermont anyway. Love, Ellie. Names and connections clicked like gears.

"How did you end up with this?"

Nan smiled wanly. "It came the day of the storm. I was going to take it to the post office; I figured it was addressed to the wrong house. And to a boy. Then lightning hit a tree, and I forgot all about it until this morning. I found it sorting through a pile of mail on the shelf. I still don't know why it came here, but I know now there's a connection."

"You're right. And it's pretty obvious." Joss gave the postcard back to Nan. "I should pay more attention when my mother gossips."

THEY WENT TOGETHER to find Danny and Sarah. Nan was puzzled by Joss's cryptic remark about his mother, but he seemed determined to bring the card up to Danny. The two were sitting in the window seat on the other side of the bridal suit from the damaged walls and ceiling. Sarah got up and met them near the doorway. Danny stared sullenly out the window.

"What was that all about?" Sarah kept her voice soft, but her concern wrinkled her face when she looked up at Joss. "You terrified that poor girl."

Joss blew out a breath. "I know." He carried the postcard to where Danny sat. "This is for you."

The teen took the postcard. Her smile briefly illuminated her face, before suspicion returned. "Where did you get this?"

Joss glanced back at Nan, who still stood with Sarah. "It came a few weeks ago, but Ms. Grady forgot to take it to the post office because of the storm and the chaos after. She just realized who it was meant for. She doesn't know who you are, Danny."

Sarah gave Nan a questioning look. Nan shook her head slightly, watching Joss and Danny. The girl just stared at Joss.

When Danny didn't volunteer, Joss filled in the information. "Danny lived here for a while before the Swifts left. Her mom, Terri, was Margaret Swift's live-in nurse."

Danny pulled her legs in against her chest and continued to stare determinedly out the window.

"I didn't put it together until I saw the card."

A guilt-flavored tenderness washed over Nan and she rushed over to the girl, dropping down on the window seat next to her. "Why didn't you say something?"

Joss replied for the girl, his tone kind. "Because it's hard, in a town like this, to admit you're affected by the cards life hands you."

Danny turned then, looking at Joss as if for the first time. She said nothing, but Nan sensed a softening in her.

Sarah, who'd watched the scene play out in silence, touched Joss's arm. "Why don't you and I have a look at the roof, while Nan and Danny take a moment."

Nan shot the building inspector a grateful look. She stood and dusted her palms against her pants. To Danny she said, "How about a coffee break?"

In the end, Nan made them tea, a fruity hibiscus blend she thought the girl might enjoy. She sweetened Danny's with a thick dollop of honey.

Facing the girl across her desk, she decided to ask the obvious question. "Why?"

"Dunno," Danny whispered. The break in her voice ruined the bravado she struggled for.

"So, Ellie? When did she move?"

Danny reached for the mug of tea, sniffing the fragrant steam before sipping. "When school ended."

"Have you talked to her at all?"

"No phone." Danny stared at the surface of her tea. "And they won't let us use the school computers for that stuff."

Nan's heart broke. To be sixteen, lose your home, and your best friend in one summer?

"Does Ellie have a phone or a computer? You can use mine to chat with her if you want."

Danny glanced up through the thick, mascara-blackened lashes that framed her eyes, daring Nan to change her mind.

"Go ahead." She powered up the laptop and closed the windows for her bookkeeping software. "At least send her an email?"

Nan pretended to catch up on some filing while the girl's fingers skimmed over the keyboard. From the joyful pinging, Nan guessed that Ellie was online. The softness she'd sensed in Danny returned. There were little snorting laughs and snappy clicks of nails against the keys, half-mouthed, one-sided conversations–the kind she herself had when she was texting Kate.

After Danny closed the laptop with a shy thank you, Nan set her young employee up with a gallon of paint, a roller, and instructions to put a coat of paint on the primed garage door before the guests arrived. Danny still hadn't spoken more than half a dozen sentences, but she slouched off to complete her chores without complaint. Her situation gave Nan a lot to think about while she set out tea, coffee, cookies, and fruit for her incoming guests.

An angry young woman, dependent upon another family for shelter, suddenly adrift. An idle summer because work was hard to come by in a small town for a girl with a large chip on her scruffy shoulder. Misplaced fury and terrible loneliness were a dangerous mix.

Nan spent a few moments entering Danny's hours into the spreadsheet of damages at a fair summer wage that all parties had agreed to. She had more than enough work to satisfy Danny's debt; she just hoped it was enough to burn through the young woman's rage and discontent.

Both Joss and Sarah Mason's trucks were gone, so Nan had no idea how the inspection had gone. She hoped for both of them that everything was signed off. She wanted to open the suite. He was needed elsewhere.

She wondered if he was serious about showing her Ellen Hill's barn. Even with the slight setback in the schedule that The Damselfly had caused, Joss seemed optimistic that they were going to wrap it up before the foliage turned.

She laughed to herself, leaving the spreadsheet to focus on setting the afternoon tea. From a troubled teen to a round barn in foliage season in a single train of thought–perhaps she really was settling into life in Thornton.

The crunch of gravel under tires drew her attention from the food and drink. A car with Rhode Island plates was parking under the maple tree.

Nan washed her hands and headed for the front porch to greet the first of her weekend guests.

THERE WERE moments when Nan knew with utter certainty that she had chosen the right career. Four couples checked in that afternoon, ranging from recently married twenty-somethings to the parents of a Thornton student. Four couples chatted in the parlor over snacks. Four couples ventured into town for dinner together and came back fast friends. Four couples were working their way through a few bottles of wine they'd brought back from dinner, enjoying the fairy lights Danny had strung once she was done with paint.

No matter how temporary the friendship, how different their visits to Thornton would be, those eight people would always have this night to remember, her place forever in their experience.

The night was mild, the sky broad and starry. Nan could hear the group's laughter floating over the property, along with the low melody of the music she'd turned on for them. She'd expected to be lonely, sitting on the front porch alone, a jelly jar of wine on the table next to her rocking chair, and a wool blanket over her shoulders.

Instead, she watched the steady glow of lights from the Fullers' farmhouse and enjoyed the quiet.

She'd driven Danny home at the end of the afternoon. It was a sobering ride out a road she didn't know to a worn-out, ranch-style house with a wide variety of vehicles and machinery occupying the dirt drive. A rangy dog peered at them from his chain, and a rangier man in greasy coveralls leered at her from behind the filter of his cigarette.

Danny must have noted her discomfort. "My Uncle Randy. This is his place. We're staying until…" Her explanation drifted off. Nan could fill in the rest. The young woman climbed out of the car. Nan watched her exchange a few terse words with the uncle, glancing over her shoulder at Nan's idling car, before waving Nan off with a raised hand and vanishing through a slamming screen door.

Now, watching the bats swoop over the marsh across County Road from the front door, Nan considered the difference in the girl's circumstances. She would be angry too, furious even, in Danny's shoes. Danny struck her as guarded to the point of being sullen–and deeply lonely–but not violent or destructive.

It didn't add up.

Her thoughts were interrupted by the slam of another screen door followed by an engine coming to life. Someone was leaving the Fullers'. Nan watched the headlights as the car backed out of their driveway and turned towards town, wondering if it was Joss making his way home after dinner with his parents. Her musings were answered when the truck–because it was a truck–pulled into her driveway.

She rose to greet him, leaving her jelly jar on the porch floor and holding the blanket with one hand. "Hi."

He smiled. A slow, easy smile that stretched all the way to those beautiful gray eyes. "Hey."

"Dinner with your parents?" It was small talk, she knew, but he tangled her thoughts.

"Yeah, and an early night. I've got to be at Ellen Hill's barn at seven tomorrow morning." He came up the steps and leaned against the railing. "But I was wondering if you could slip away for a few hours tomorrow afternoon. My cousin's son is the QB for the Thornton Union Hornets. It's a big game, and there's going to be a pretty epic tailgate."

Waiting for her answer under the porch light, his boyish charm was undeniable.

She would make the timing work. "I'd love to."

"I'm glad."

He reached for her hand, lifting her arm and twirling her to the floating strains of Miles Davis coming through the house. He caught her waist and snugged her body against his. She tucked her head under his chin and followed his lead, swaying together.

A peal of laughter rang out from the other side of the house. Joss slid his palms up her arms, raising gooseflesh, and she shivered. He kissed her, teasing out the promise smoldering between them—whose fulfillment she craved more than ever—then whispered against her lips.

"Very glad."

CHAPTER 23

*N*an pushed open the door to Mistle Thrush one minute after the shop opened.

Kate, through some magic of her own, was already inside, deep in conversation with Echo Turner, the shop's owner. Between them was a heap of fabric, a riot of color and texture.

The wind chimes above the door announced her arrival, and Kate and Echo turned.

"Here she is!"

Kate was across the shop to hug her before the soft-closing door clicked into place behind her. "I've already picked out three outfits. Echo let me in early."

Echo shrugged. "I can't deny Kate when she's got her Serious Shopping Face on."

Kate bundled three hangers and steered Nan towards the dressing room stalls. "We are crunched for time. I have to be back at the bakery about ten minutes ago, and Nan's got a picnic to be stunning at."

The first option was a French blue faux-wrap sundress which Kate decreed too long. Nan felt the pink and white striped maxi-skirt was too bright.

And then she tried on the last skirt.

Kate gasped. "Oh, sugar plum. Yes."

Nan looked at herself in the mirror. The skirt was perfect. White with bold red poppies splashed across the fabric. The snug waist and pleated flare gave the skirt a decidedly Fifties look. The hem was flirty, and showed her legs to their best advantage.

Kate took off the wedge sandals she was wearing and offered them to Nan. "Take these. And wear that black silk camisole, the one I covet."

Nan turned to her with wide eyes. "Kate, it's pajamas."

"Nan," Kate replied, "it's sexy as hell, and definitely not pajamas. At all."

Nan wasn't convinced. "Really? A silk cami at a tailgate?"

"You'll have to take my shoes, They're perfect." Kate nudged her out of the stall and waved at Echo.

Nan complied.

"And twirl." Kate and Echo inspected her as though she were a mannequin.

"Kate, if I take your shoes, what will you wear?"

Kate fished in her purse without missing a beat, pulling out a pair of folding ballet flats. "I'm always prepared for a shoe emergency."

Echo fluffed the skirt a little and smiled. "Absolutely the black tank. Sassy and unexpected, but still casual. Poor guy, he really doesn't stand a chance."

Kate grasped Nan's hands and squeezed. "He really, really doesn't."

The chimes announced a new customer. Kate's eyes narrowed when Elisha pushed her sunglasses up onto her forehead and beamed at them.

"Nan! Doing some shopping?"

Nan opened her shopping bag for Elisha to peer into. "A little."

Elisha sized her up. "I love that skirt, but I can't pull it off like you will."

Kate slipped in next to Nan, her posture defensive. "Joss is taking her tailgating later."

Nan let the blush come. There was nothing she could do to stop it. She was sure Elisha heard Kate's unspoken warning: *so steer clear.*

Elisha's eyes flashed steel in Kate's direction. "For a woman who's smart enough to run one of the best bakeries I've been in, you're fairly stupid if you think I'm some kind of threat. Joss and I have a common experience; we made out once ten years ago. And why would I waste my time on someone so obviously smitten with someone else?"

As quickly as the steel appeared, it was gone, and Elisha looked contrite. "I'm sorry, Nan. Excuse me."

Her exit left Nan, Kate, and Echo in stunned silence. *Smitten.* Despite the awkward encounter, Nan held Elisha's assessment close.

Kate took a deep breath. "I have to get back to the bakery, and apparently I need to catch up with Professor Barbie and apologize for behaving like a total bitch."

Nan squeezed Kate in a one-armed hug. "Yes, you do."

"Call me later!" Kate vanished out the door.

"Always a pleasure having you girls in the shop," Echo said with a small smile.

Nan mustered what remained of her dignity and headed back to the inn to get ready for her date.

Joss PULLED his truck into the inn's parking lot, left the keys in the ignition, and crossed the dooryard. He fought the urge to whistle; he couldn't remember the last time he'd so anticipated one of his young cousin's football games.

He walked into Nan's kitchen, tidy and gleaming, and paused.

Much like his parents' house, Nan's space appealed to him, welcomed him. Her trestle table shone, smelling faintly of furniture wax. A stainless steel carafe of coffee stood next to a pottery bowl of fruit on the countertop. He imagined himself sitting at the island, finishing a mug of coffee, maybe grabbing an apple for the road, before kissing Nan goodbye and heading to a job site.

Nan's voice interrupted his reverie. "Joss? Is that you?"

"On my way up."

He came to the top of the stairs with the last time he'd been into her apartment fresh in his mind. He rapped on the open door with his knuckles. As he entered the room, she was slipping her feet into a pair of black sandals. When she straightened, she took his breath away.

She wore a white skirt printed with bright red flowers. Like something from a Fifties film, it floated away from her hips and swirled around her calves. Her black top skimmed her body, and he fought the urge to draw his fingers down over the luminous skin of her shoulders.

She'd pinned up a few of the wavy tendrils that framed her face, and played up her long lashes and drawn-bow smile with cosmetics. The unexpected late-September heat and humidity had its perks.

"Let me get my bag, and I'll be ready to go," she said.

He felt like a teenager, awkward and overwhelmed by a girl in a pretty dress. She came back in with a canvas tote in hand.

"You're going to distract the boys from the game, looking like that."

"Is it too much?" she asked, self-consciously smoothing the skirt over her hips. "Kate found it for me at Mistle Thrush. I couldn't say no."

"You're perfect," he told her. His voice sounded thick in his own ears.

Nan closed the distance between them in three steps and stretched up to kiss him, sliding her arms around his shoulders. Joss angled his head and deepened the kiss, wrapping his arms around her, fingers splayed across her back, pulling her to him.

There was something new in her embrace, something effusive in the warmth of her kiss.

Nan arched against him, and let her bag fall to the floor. The way she smoothed her hands over his shoulders, tracing the flex of his muscles, she made him feel...beautiful, he supposed, though it wasn't the way he expected to feel. He gathered her into his arms and gave himself up to the passion that crackled between them.

She shuddered when his hands molded the swell of her hips, sighing audibly and melting into him.

Joss was drowning. The warmth of her, the heady blend of lust and tenderness he felt for her, threatened to pull him under. He wound his hand into her hair, cradling her head in one hand as the other strayed under the hem of the softly clinging top. He breathed her in like oxygen and let his heart lead.

When they came apart, each a little breathless, Nan let out a shaky laugh. Joss kissed her lips gently and bent to retrieve her bag from the floor.

"Shall we?"

In the kitchen, she pulled a large aluminum foil pan from the refrigerator. Balancing it on one arm, she took her bag from Joss, who grabbed the pan.

"What am I carrying?" he asked.

"My secret-weapon," she replied saucily. "Potato salad."

He stood back and let her walk out the door, appreciating the swish of her skirt as she did.

THE THORNTON HORNETS were hosting their arch rivals in an early season match-up, and the whole Fuller clan was out to support one of their own, cheer the home team, and eat. Well.

Adjacent to the bleachers, Molly and Walt had a tailgate picnic set up that promised to feed the entire crowd, including the opposition. Nan catalogued the family information Joss rattled off on the drive over.

"I'm going to need a spreadsheet to keep track of your family," she said.

Walt's older sister and her husband had made the drive north from Connecticut to see their grandson's game. Walt's middle brother had come down with his son and the son's girlfriend from somewhere in the Northeast Kingdom. Nan spotted Anneliese and Chloe in the crowd of family; she handed the pan of potato salad to Joss and waved.

Molly was in her element, marshaling troops of nieces and

nephews to set tables, unfold chairs, and haul coolers of food and drink out of the back of Walt's truck.

"Joss! Nan!" Molly called from her command position. "You're just in time," she continued as they approached. "Nan, see those two bearded mountain men at the fifty yard line? Walt's brother, Joe, and Joe's son, Aaron."

Nan laughed at the sight. Joe was tall and weathered, like Walt, but a grizzly, gray beard sprouted from his face like a storm cloud. Aaron was shorter; his beard was auburn in the sunlight, but no less frizzled than his father's.

"Go tell those two I need them setting up card tables over here, not harassing Ian's opposition," Molly finished, taking the pan of potato salad from Joss.

Joss started to follow her, but his mother pulled him back, gesturing to half a dozen more aluminum pans waiting in the bed of the truck.

"You're going to move these trays of ribs over under the canopy for me, young man. That girl can fend for herself."

While Joss started lugging trays, Nan saw Molly grab a plastic fork, pull open a corner of Nan's pan and treat herself to a sample, before returning to setting up the tailgate. Molly shot her an approving smile over her shoulder.

As Nan crossed in front of the bleachers, Chloe careened out from underneath, nearly crashing into her legs. Nan stopped short. The little girl skidded to a halt in front of her and smiled.

"Hi, Miss Nan!" Chloe laughed unapologetically, looking back her mom.

"Careful, Chlo." Anneliese stood, dusting her hands on her capris, and smiled at Nan. "You look gorgeous!"

"Thanks."

"How're you doing?" Anna asked, eyes full of concern.

Chloe patted Nan's leg. "Joss took me to see the cows."

Nan laughed, ruffling Chloe's hair. "I know."

She looked over at Joe and Aaron, standing like copies of one another, hands in their back pockets, on the fifty yard line, then back at Anna.

"I'm okay." She tried to convey to her friend that they could talk more later. Once little ears were otherwise occupied. "I'm supposed to get Joe and Aaron for Molly."

"Can I come?" chirped Chloe.

Nan looked at Anneliese, who nodded. "Sure, Chloe."

The little girl grabbed her hand and pulled her away. "Joe! Joe!" she cried as they ran, leaving her mother laughing.

By the end of the first quarter, Nan had been introduced to the whole Fuller family.

Walt's older sister, Patty, who looked like a Talbot's model, and her husband, Gary, told her about their daughter Ellen's romance with a Thornton student named Matt the summer she spent working at the dairy. A romance that led to Ellen and Matt's eventual marriage, their decision to live and work in Thornton, and their athletic brood.

Ian, at seventeen, was the starting quarterback for the football team. Sophie, at twelve, had aspirations of being the first female catcher for the Red Sox, and five-year-old Nick already knew more about World Cup soccer than Nan ever considered.

Joe invited Nan up to his cabin near the Canadian border, where he and Aaron ran guided snowmobile tours in the winter, and ran a disc golf course in the summer. Aaron's girlfriend, a soft-spoken photographer named Mariah, playfully assured her there was both running water and plumbing.

Chloe, who, by halftime, was lying on a blanket with her head in Nan's lap, told Nan about her uncle Pete, and how Auntie Molly made her chocolate milk when she visited the farm.

After the third quarter, Joss went to buy popsicles from the ice cream truck. The Hornets were down by a field goal. The game was too close for comfort; the home crowd was tense.

Molly settled herself next to Nan on the blanket. "If they aren't already, everyone in town's going to be speculating about you and Joss after today. I know it doesn't seem it, but not everyone here today is a Fuller."

Nan studied the whorl of hair at the crown of Chloe's head, heavy in her lap, for a moment before speaking.

"I'm okay with speculating, Molly. So long as it doesn't spoil what we've started." She watched Joss's mother's reaction closely. "I'm new to relationships that matter."

Molly chuckled. "You're a strong, smart girl, with a good heart—and a killer potato salad recipe. I don't think there's anything this town can dish out that you can't take."

Nan laughed. "It's all in the potato salad."

Molly started to push herself to standing, patting Nan's knee as she did. "Normally, I'd make Josiah drive a load of food and supplies back to the farm, but you two deserve some time to yourselves."

Nan watched Molly return to the heart of the tailgate with something like wonder in her heart.

CHAPTER 24

$\mathcal{I}$t was nearly sunset when she and Joss climbed into his truck. After the game, the whole Fuller family, the rest of the Hornets, and their families had all stayed for the tailgate. Nan felt buoyant after a warm welcome from nearly everyone the Fullers knew.

Joss seemed preoccupied as he started the engine.

He tapped the steering wheel in silence before turning to her. "Would you like to see my place in Catmint Gap?"

Nan laced her fingers over his on the gear shift. "I'd like that a lot."

She knew the road through Catmint Gap, as it was one of the routes she used to get to the interstate and points south, but while she'd always enjoyed the winding climb up to and over the spine of the Green Mountains, she'd never been off the main road. Joss's cabin was in wild country, bordering the State Forest, with ten minutes of rough dirt road after they left the turnoff.

"It belonged to some of my father's friends. It was a hunting cabin," Joss explained, as they came around the last curve in the road. "I bought it a few years ago. Been slowly renovating it ever since."

The logs on the exterior were dark with age and damp with lichen. The whole building seemed to grow right up out of the forest floor.

Joss cut the engine. "You're quiet. Is everything okay?"

She was. More than okay. She was overcome with the loveliness of the afternoon with his family and the surprising beauty of his home. She was intensely aware of the brilliant flare of attraction between them, a flame that she knew was burning steadier than she'd ever expected.

"I was taking it in," Nan replied. "How can you ever bear to leave it?"

"The kitchen is a little lacking, and the plumbing is rustic." He chuckled, dropping down out of the truck cab and heading around to open her door. "There are advantages to having a soft-hearted mother down in the valley."

The main room of the cabin was spare, but warm and masculine—much the way she thought of Joss: a pair of well-worn, mismatched leather couches and a maple coffee table anchored a huge, gently frayed braided rug. An impressive home theater system and a stone fireplace dominated the ends of the open cabin, with a bare-bones kitchenette in one corner. Joss crossed the room and pulled open a huge pair of navy blue, sail-cloth curtains to reveal the wall-to-wall glass that opened onto his deck. He opened one of the French doors and gestured for her to go ahead.

She stepped out, a little breathless, into the heart of the Green Mountains. The property fell off in a steep incline behind the house, and Joss's deck cantilevered out above the forest floor. He stepped out behind her.

"It's like flying," Nan gasped, her face glowing in delight.

Rose-gold fingers of sunset parted the trees, reaching down from the last edge of the already inky sky overhead. Joss slipped his arms around her waist and tasted the curve of her shoulder.

"I've been imagining you here, on this deck, since the night of the storm," he murmured against her skin, his mouth tracing the sweep of her neck.

Nan dropped her head back against his chest, and wrapped her hands over his. Joss rested his cheek against hers in the falling light, and the sun sank away. "Joss?"

"Mmm?" he replied, his mouth warm on her skin, his hands sliding over fabric to cup the swell of her breasts.

Nan turned in his arms. Her body was ablaze; the tenderness shared in the fading sunlight burned up as she pressed her body into his, the ashes of self-control blew away on her breath when she whispered his name.

He cradled her face between his palms and kissed her. His lips, hot and insistent, captivated. Nan slid her hands under his shirt, reveling in the shiver of muscle under her questing hands. She angled her head, drawing his tongue deeper into her mouth, meeting his passion with her own.

She was all sensation, the cool of evening air, the harmony of cricket song and her own hum of pleasure, the deck railing hard at her back, Joss's calloused hands against her softest flesh. The aching, greedy shimmer of desire along her skin.

Joss grasped her hands and pulled away. He held her eyes for a heartbeat; she answered his silent plea without hesitation. He led her back through the glass doors, up the narrow stairs to his bedroom.

His mouth teased the thudding pulse in her throat while his hands dragged at the zipper of her skirt. Nan threaded the worn leather of his belt back through the buckle, unfastened the buttons of his jeans, her own power thrilling through her as Joss sucked in a tortured breath. She nudged him away, tugged off her tank top. Joss dragged his Thornton Hornets shirt over his head and stepped out of his jeans as her skirt pooled on the floor. Desire trumped seduction as they hurriedly shed the rest of their clothing. Nan leaned back on the bed, reaching up to him.

For a heartbeat, she saw herself reflected in his eyes: the seductress, flushed, lean and curved, priestess and offering together. Delight coursed through her, and her own earlier words rose in her mind. *It's like flying.*

~

179

Joss took her hand in the half-light and drank in the sight of her. The curve of her hip, the stray curl of hair at her temple, the fire in her eyes answering his own as she drew him down. The punch of lust was swift and devastating.

Heat crackled between them as they devoured each other, skin hungry for contact. Joss gathered her up against him and rolled underneath her; she arched back as his hands closed over her breasts, moaned at his hardness pressed between them.

Joss reigned in the lust that threatened to ride roughshod over them both. He wanted to explore the curve of her breast under his fingertips, to savor her sigh as he drew the tight bud of her nipple into his mouth.

He'd seen something in her expression, some flicker as she reached for him, that rocked him. A mixture of certainty, seduction, and pure radiating joy, something exclusively connecting them in the moment, like nothing he'd ever had with a woman before. Joss knew that the future of his feelings for her had turned a corner, but the examination of those feelings would have to wait.

He skimmed his hands down her back until they rested at the swell of her bottom. Pausing, holding her still and close, he caught her gaze. "You're beautiful."

His words echoed those he spoke to her that evening in Burlington, never more true than now, poised on the edge of something so much more important than he'd predicted. She smiled that secret smile–older than the world–and stretched herself over him, kissing him until they were both breathless and needy.

"Joss," she whispered, taking his hand and guiding him to her slick heat.

He rolled her onto her back. She locked her legs around his waist, her fingers around his wrists. He took her in one urgent motion; buried himself in her. Their eyes locked in a heartbeat of stillness. Nan rocked against him, and they were climbing together, burning and tumbling and breaking apart together.

～

PEARLY LIGHT FILTERED into Joss's bedroom, painting dappled shadows across his sleeping form. Nan watched the easy rise and fall of his back for a moment before getting up to find the bathroom. It was chilly in the cabin, and the first thing she reached for was Joss's discarded Thornton Hornets shirt. She fished her phone from her purse to check the time.

It was time she got home.

She returned to find him awake, face wrinkled from sleep, waiting for her.

"Nice shirt."

She fidgeted with the hem where it skimmed her thighs. "Sorry, it was the first thing I grabbed."

"I mean it." He patted the bed and pulled back the comforter. "Come here."

"I'm sorry I woke you." She sat on the edge of the bed and leaned in to kiss him.

"I'm not." He kissed her nipple, nuzzling playfully through the cotton, reaching with the other hand to caress the length of her thigh.

"Joss," she began, her words drowning in a wave of pleasure. Her body spoke eloquently of how badly she wanted to stay with him, her words less so. "I want to stay."

"I really like this shirt on you," he whispered in her ear as he helped her pull it over her head.

"The inn–" Her words were lost. He was as ready as she was.

"I know," he said. "We'll be quick."

THEY WERE DRESSED and in Joss's truck on their way down the mountain by the time the first true sunlight reached up over the Adirondacks.

In the kitchen at The Damselfly, Nan started coffee and pulled out a tray of proofed pastries.

"This business never stops, does it?" Joss remarked, grabbing a seat at the island.

"No. It doesn't." She opened the fridge and pulled out butter and eggs. She set a frying pan on a burner and pulled a loaf of oat bread from the bread box. "If I'd been thinking last night, I wouldn't have let us fall asleep. I feel bad you're up so early."

"If I'd been thinking?" Joss reached across the island to take her hand. "I wouldn't have let us sleep at all." He stroked her palm with his thumb. "But it's worth being up early, especially if I get breakfast out of the deal."

"It's the least I can do after keeping you up half the night."

"That you did." He poured her a cup of coffee with a wicked twinkle in his eye that warmed her to her toes. "How do you take it?"

She answered without looking up from her pan. "Light and sweet."

"Yes, ma'am."

He caught her hand again passing the mug across the island, brushing her knuckles. "I like knowing how you take your coffee."

Elisha, wearing her running clothes and a knowing smile, found them finishing their breakfasts when she arrived downstairs in search of coffee. She eyed the omelet fixings over their joined hands.

Nan blushed furiously and yanked her hand back, but she couldn't banish the cozy intimacy between them.

"No yolks for me, Nan, if that's okay?" Elisha poured herself some coffee and perched next to Joss, leaning in slightly to make conversation. "You look bright-eyed for such an early start to the day."

Nan left the island and started separating out egg whites for Elisha's omelet, trying desperately to ignore the hot flush that crept up her neck. She kept an eye on Joss while she whipped the whites up with some salt and warmed her skillet.

Joss's voice sounded choked. "We passed rough inspection, so I want to get a jump on the finish work."

"A jump on the finish work, hmm?" Elisha sipped at her coffee, watchful gaze flicking between Nan and Joss.

Nan giggled silently as she folded herbs and a sprinkling of shaved parmesan into the omelet before flipping it over.

"Elisha?" Nan said, arranging her face into a neutral expression.

"I've got an intern working here in the afternoons for a few weeks. Don't be surprised if you see an unfamiliar face."

Elisha nodded; as Nan expected, she was unfazed by the news.

Joss downed the last of his coffee, and walked around the island to kiss her quickly. "Be careful."

She did her best with a look, while turning Elisha's eggs out onto a plate, to convey how unnecessary she thought his suggestion was. "I'll be fine."

When he was gone, Elisha set down her fork. "So, you're employing your vandal?"

Nan sat down across from her to nurse the coffee Joss had poured for her. "I am."

"Good for you. Make sure she gets exactly how her actions affected you, and maybe gain an ally?"

It was exactly what she was hoping: to bring the girl around to her side and offer her a bit of something to be proud of in the bargain.

"You're very perceptive."

Elisha smiled her inscrutable smile. "I have my moments."

Nan realized the professor wasn't talking about her high school intern anymore. Contrary to her first instincts, she felt she also had an ally in Elisha. "You really do."

CHAPTER 25

*J*oss was reluctant to tick off the last items on the punch list.

The suite was almost finished, and without it he would have less of an excuse to spend time with Nan.

There would be more tailgates, more dinners at the farm, more stolen evenings in Burlington, if he had anything to say about it.

He suspected he wasn't the only one in town with things to say about it.

He knew everyone in town was tracking their movements. You don't grow up in a place without understanding how a story travels. When he stopped at the lumber yard later, he fully expected to hear some good natured teasing about Nan.

Realizing he needed a different nail gun than the one currently on the third floor, Joss headed down to his truck. He heard her singing to herself over the din of her big, red stand mixer before he reached the first floor. He recognized the song from the KG Project's debut album. He stood there, outside the kitchen, for a moment listening to her rendition of Moira Kennedy's comeback single with a smile. He'd had a poster of the glam-rock queen on his wall in the Eighties. To hear

Nan singing her new songs was strangely satisfying, as if some part of his teenage fantasy was coming home again.

The machine stopped whirring, so he pushed through the door.

She was wrist-deep in dough, shoulder muscles rolling, her whole body engaged in the act of creating. They were similar in that way.

Had their hearts beat them to that realization?

Quietly, like a sunrise coming over the highest fir ridge above the cabin, she had slipped into his heart, far faster than he'd been prepared for. He'd always assumed loving someone would stretch him thin, but the truth was, he was beginning to crave the fullness he felt when he was with her.

Without his work at the inn, their schedules would work at cross purposes, and they'd have to steal time for each other. Weekends, typically his slow days, were her busiest, and that wasn't likely to change for her any time soon.

And speaking of weekends.

Her fingers spread out the flour on the countertop when he bent to kiss the back of her neck.

"Lovely," she murmured. "But I need to get these scones ready."

He leaned against the counter while she finished. Even distracted, she was swift and efficient; it was a pleasure to watch her. "I'm going to get to work in a minute, but I wanted to ask you something."

"Hmm?" she said, rolling the circle of dough flat.

"Next weekend, I'm going down to Boston."

Nan rinsed her hands under the tap, and reached for a towel. "To see Jack?"

"Yeah." He nodded. "Our buddy Drew is getting married in a couple of months."

"A bachelor party?" There was a knowing twinkle in her eye.

"Something like that." He stuffed his hands into his pockets.

"Will it be vintage Scotch and contraband Cubans? Or cruising for B.U. graduate students in the Ladder District?"

"Strippers and blow. Obviously."

She snorted at the deadpan. "So, who's Drew?"

"He lived next door to Jack and Katie when were kids."

Nan sliced the dough and placed wedges on a tray. She poured more coffee into her ceramic mug, raised the pot as an offering.

He shook his head. "We ran a little wild sometimes. In high school, the three of us," Joss admitted, "but Jack had his sights on Harvard and I was trying to get into Thornton, so we mostly kept our trouble under the radar." He handed Nan the cream pitcher. "Drew did everything faster, liked everything more dangerous, but god, he was fun to hang out with."

Nan took a swallow of his coffee, and pulled a face. He liked it less sweet, darker.

"He lit out of town when he graduated, a year ahead of us, and we didn't hear from him, except through his family, until about six months ago. He calls Jack out of the blue, at his office, to tell him he's getting married, asks Jack and me to be groomsmen. Next thing I know, I'm going to be in this crazy ranch wedding out in Montana next year, and Jack's planning a weekend in Boston for the three of us, Drew's kid brother, and the fiancées brother." Joss laughed. "My mom's convinced it's going to be like *The Hangover.*"

He hadn't expected her indulgent smile. "Sounds like it'll be a good time, though. Jack never does anything half-assed."

"No, he doesn't," said Joss. "Which, if you think about it, means trouble."

"You can handle it. You're a big boy," she chided, eyes sparkling.

Joss caught the flirt in her tone. "What I want to handle is you." He slid a hand down her hip.

She dodged his wandering hand. "I've got guests checking-in in a few hours and you've got a punch list to finish."

He dropped his hand away with a raised eyebrow.

"Oh, no," she said, stumbling over the words, "I didn't mean ..."

"Neither did I." He pulled her in close, kissed her hard. Left her breathless. "I've got to head out to Chimney Point to meet with the architect for a bit, but I'll be back here before I'm done for the day. The suite will be ready for paint by tonight."

Nan ran a hand through her hair. "Really?"

He couldn't help dropping a kiss on her nose. "Do you still want me to help?"

"Can you do a day this week?"

"I've got tomorrow free," he offered. "I'm not starting demolition on the Chimney Point project until Thursday."

"Tomorrow."

SHE LINGERED in his thoughts all day. He considered the inn, and how he was going to fit into Nan's life without the job tying them together. Guests, employees, the physical demands, and the constant need to be present. The logistics of dating an innkeeper were new ones for him.

He couldn't help thinking about the trouble with Danny Beaudette—and her recently added position on The Damselfly's staff. His misgivings about being away from Thornton at the end of the week grew the more he turned it over in his mind.

A stop by the dairy on his way back from Chimney Point gave Joss a chance to voice his concerns to his father. He found his father in the middle of a fence repair at the far end of the pasture that overlooked The Damselfly.

"Something doesn't add up. Angry kids sometimes do stupid things, but something bugs me about the whole thing."

"Beats me, Joss. Your mother and I didn't see a whole lot of her. Terri had a tough go of it the last couple of years. She had a good nursing job over in New York, but her folks got sick, and that brother of hers was never any good for help, so she had to quit and move up to their place out past Kiln Hollow. Seemed to me the job looking out for Meg Swift was a good one. Danny was probably better off here in the valley than stuck out there with her uncle."

"Am I being overbearing, worrying about Nan being alone with her over there?"

"Nope." Walt handed Joss his wire cutter and wiped his forehead with a faded bandanna. Joss knew, from the wry expression in Pop's eyes, he was going to get a dose of long-married wisdom. "As long as you're not actually being overbearing about it."

"Of course." Joss steadied a run of wire while his father fastened it.

"You know, your mother and I could always drop in, invite her over. We'll look out for her if it will help."

Joss dropped the wire cutters in his father's toolbox. "Thanks, Pop."

Between the dairy and The Damselfly, he made a call to another person whose help would ease his mind.

Kate answered on the fourth ring, cursing under her breath. "Hey, Joss."

"Hi Kate. You okay?"

"With the exception of the smear of vanilla bean custard on my screen, yes. What can I do for you?"

He heard a rustle and clang and wondered what treat-making he'd interrupted. "I know this sounds kind of like macho bullshit, but I'm worried about Nan all alone at the inn while I'm in Boston this coming weekend. She's decided to trust Danny, but I'm not sure this whole thing is over yet."

"Under the right circumstances, macho bullshit can be yummy." Kate sighed. "I think she's probably fine, but I get it. You want me to invite myself out there to stay?"

"Would you?"

"'Course."

"Thanks, Kate."

"It's no trouble. I like that you're looking out for her, but I have to go; I've got a pastry cream about to boil. If I fuck it up, I'll be up all night and out a fortune in Bourbon vanilla." Kate clicked off, and Joss slid his phone into his pocket.

Nan was closed up in her office, so he went straight upstairs with his mental checklist.

Two hours later, with the last of the items checked off, Joss cleaned up his tools in the fading late-afternoon light. The Adirondack Suite was done. His work at The Damselfly was done. He'd come back tomorrow and paint with her, but not on the clock.

More than a friend, but what exactly?

Needing a definition was new territory for him. New, and a little unnerving.

∼

NAN WAS in the hardware store when Kate called.

"Girls weekend!"

Nan tucked the phone between her shoulder and ear so she could compare paint chips. She might have told Joss she had the paint in reserve, but the temptation of new, perfect walls was too much to resist. "I've got a full house this weekend."

"Perfect. I'll come over after work on Friday. I'll bring snacks and nail polish and all the terrible Eighties rom-coms your grandparents wouldn't let you watch."

Dove Whisper was perfect for the room. Nan wondered how she'd missed it when she was repainting the room at the beginning of the summer. "No dates this weekend?"

"Not a one, and I miss you. It's such a tease; you finally live here, and I still never see you." Kate paused for a dramatic sigh. "So I'm coming over."

"I'll make sure to wash the futon sheets."

A manager called for a clerk over the intercom in the store.

"Where are you?" Kate asked.

"I'm at Robidoux's, looking at paint. Joss and I are going to paint the suite later."

"Listen to you, all casual. 'Joss and I,' like it's no big thing. I love it."

Nan pulled two gallons of paint from the shelf and carried them over to the mixing station. "Listen, Kate, I have to get the paint mixed. See you soon."

"Yes ma'am."

Nan pocketed her phone, and handed over the paint chip with an anticipatory smile.

CHAPTER 26

*I*t was only painting.

Nonetheless, Nan fidgeted with her hair, tucking stray strands from her temple while she regarded her reflection in the mirror over the parlor fireplace.

The painting supplies were upstairs; the new paint opened and mixed. She'd taped all the edges, sanded the rough spots, and wiped everything down with tack cloth. Her iPod was plugged in.

She'd made a playlist. Not sure what he'd consider painting music, she'd covered the basics of classic rock, with some blues and a smattering of her current favorites. She was one step away from a mixtape with hearts on the Side A sticker.

She'd decided on an old hoodie and some carpenter's pants that suited both paint splatters and her figure. A tray of Kate's chocolate-cherry cookie dough was in the oven and the timer on her phone was set to remind her not to burn them. There was iced tea in the fridge.

Her guests were on a drive up to Burlington, hoping to get lunch at the culinary school's restaurant on Church Street. She and Joss would have the inn to themselves.

She was anxious about it.

So many thoughts swirled in her heart. There was the ease with which their relationship had become intimate, his anxiety about Danny, her always looming concerns about her business, and the sense that Joss, despite his attention and obvious attraction, was still somewhat of a mystery to her.

Fussing at her reflection wasn't doing her any favors.

She sat on the staircase and twisted the ratty cuff of her sweatshirt, trying to dispel her twitchy energy.

"Nan?"

Nan had to laugh at the irony; she'd been so focused on trying to relax that she didn't hear him until he was already in the foyer. She felt her lips curve, felt how he lit her up.

"Hey."

"Hey, yourself." He leaned in and pressed a gentle kiss to her lips.

She smiled against his mouth. The kiss held for a beat, before they pulled apart, just a little breathless. Her anxiety retreated.

"Everything's all set upstairs," she said. "Come on up."

⁓

EVERYTHING WAS ALL SET, Joss noted. She'd prepped perfectly, right down to drop cloths and taped edges.

She was pretty as a picture in her cargos and hooded pullover. With her hair back in a bandanna, wearing an ancient pair of Chuck Taylors, she looked like a college co-ed. She was exactly the painting partner he'd pictured on the ride down from the Gap.

"How do you want to do this?" He hoped he was keeping the naked lust out of his voice. How many times had he been up here working, imagining getting her out of her clothes in this room?

"Well, you've obviously got the height advantage." She stood with her hands on her hips, gaze moving between him and the bare walls.

"How about I take the eaves to start. You can have the long-handled roller."

"Chivalrous, Mr. Fuller. I think that sounds fine."

Her playful tone wreaked havoc with his focus; Joss stuffed his hands in his pockets to avoid grabbing her and taking them both

192

down together in a paint-covered tangle. She turned, assembled her paint roller, and started pouring paint into trays.

Joss ducked into the bathroom to get the four-foot ladder he'd left there. When he came back, she was fully engaged in her painting. He let the music from her portable speakers fill the room up around them.

Nan broke the quiet after a few songs. "So, your mom stopped by a couple of weeks ago."

"She mentioned that. Said she brought over some of her strawberry preserves." He hummed appreciatively. "They're something else. She wins ribbons at the county fair, and around here, competition's fierce."

"She also brought me one of your pieces."

His mom hadn't mentioned that. Just as he hadn't ever mentioned that part of his life to Nan in a more than cursory way. He was suddenly unsure what to say, and that struck him as foolish.

"Did she?"

"A milking stool. She says you used to do more furniture, even sold some in New York." She stopped rolling, watching him with a curious expression.

"I'm glad you like it." He resumed his rolling, still uncomfortable with the metallic taste of failure rising in the back of his throat.

Her phone pinged. She left without a word and was back to work before the track on her iPod changed.

The rest of the walls went easily, if silently, and they met at a corner seam with the first coat complete.

Nan laid a hand on his arm. "I've got some of Kate's cookies and some iced tea downstairs. Want a break? It's nice out. We can have a snack on the patio."

He covered her hand with his and squeezed her fingertips. "Yeah."

While she was gone, Joss took a moment to shake off his mood. He didn't know why her casual inquiry about his work bothered him. He thought of an old Harry Chapin song about a dry cleaner who loved to sing, but his passion wasn't meant to be his profession.

That was how he felt about the furniture. Sure, he'd made some money from it, but he'd felt like a whore, standing in Seth's SoHo gallery, trying to sound like he cared about his *unique blend of magic and raw, pioneer aesthetic in the post-modern landscape*, or whatever bull-shit the art critics were spewing, while hipster dot-com CEOs who didn't know better bought it up because Seth said it was art.

The truth was that he made furniture because it satisfied a need.

He'd majored in visual arts partially to piss off his old man. It had worked. He'd been young and frustrated, and stupid about it. With the advantage of a decade's perspective, he saw that he was a little bit spoiled, being the only child, the only son of two very easygoing, loving, hardworking people. When he and his father had occasionally clashed over expectations and the future of the family farm, his failure to launch as an artist was the first time Joss had hit a road bump, and he'd handled it like a bratty kid.

He'd exploited a passion to prove a misguided point to his father.

When he'd come to his senses, he'd paid back every cent his parents had laid out for his education from the profits on the pieces he'd sold in New York and the commissions that had followed.

His continued student loan payments were his ongoing penance.

The whole thing had left a corner of his heart dusty and bitter. Now, when he felt the urge to craft something, he donated it, used it, or gave it to someone who'd use it before he considered selling it.

It just rubbed him the wrong way that his mother was bringing it up to Nan without letting him know. It was pure pride. He didn't want Nan thinking he'd given it up because he couldn't handle the big, bad world. The furniture fed his soul, but he didn't need it to feed his bank account.

He thought of the four-poster he'd envisioned here, thought of the bent wood design he was almost ready to start. The frame itself had been easy. What remained was the challenge, the pleasure of creating.

The only embellishment it would be missing would be Nan herself.

"Joss?" Her voice floated up the staircase.

"I'll be right down." It was time to come clean with her.

The open back door guided him to the back patio. It was an undeniably pretty spot. His parents' pastures stretched out between the inn and their house, and the shadow of the Adirondacks rose up along the western horizon.

Nan brought their snack out on a wicker tray, loaded with glasses, a pitcher of iced tea, and a plate of Sweet Pease's coveted chocolate-cherry cookies.

Nan set the tray down with mock gravitas. "These are from my private reserve."

"The honor is mine." Joss took the glass she poured with one hand while scooping up a warm cookie. "I didn't mean to kill the conversation upstairs."

She gave him a crooked half-smile. "It's okay."

"No. I was being ridiculous. I did–I do make furniture. How much did my mom tell you?"

"Just that you majored in visual arts, and that you've sold some of your work in New York. She said you got caught up in the contracting business and you don't do too much of the other anymore."

He let his brain register the gooey, warm cookie for a moment while he gathered his thoughts. "She right, but there's more to it."

"There always is," Nan laughed. "Not everyone is as singularly focused on their goals as I've been. You have a talent for furniture. You have a talent for home improvement. To me, bidding on a job seems less invasive, less personal, than putting a price tag on something from your heart. It doesn't mean the thing you love doing isn't valuable."

She looked into her tea glass, and took a long sip. Joss was stunned. Without a word of explanation, she'd come close to the very heart of it.

He reached out and wrapped a hand around hers, cool from the tea glass.

"You're only the second person who's really understood that," he said quietly.

"Who was the first?" Nan asked, immediately sorry that the question had come out.

"Jack." He held her hand for a moment. "Thank you for understanding."

They finished their snack, and Nan took the dishes into the kitchen. She met him back upstairs for the second coat. This time, they set to work on the same wall in companionable silence. It took them another hour to finish.

In between rolls of paint, Joss mentally finished the four poster. After his confessional moment with Nan, the siren song of a finished piece called to him. He felt itchy to get back to work on it, but again he wondered how Nan would receive such a gift. There was a prickly, stubborn streak in her, and now more than ever, taking care with her meant something to him.

They finished, and cleaned up the painting supplies. It didn't take long; they'd prepped well. He'd managed to splatter a bit on his painting clothes, but she barely had a drop on her. He touched a fingertip to the only drops he could see, a slight spray of pale gray freckling her forehead.

"If you ever decide to get out of the hospitality business, you could probably make a living painting, you know."

"Yeah. Nope." She shook her head slowly.

"A guy can always dream of a beautiful painter on site."

She looked away, but he saw the curve of a smile flirt around her lips. He'd flustered her.

"This look is hardly beautiful," she said in mock defiance.

He reached for her, tipping her chin up to face him.

"I think so," he said, smiling as he kissed her.

THERE WERE SEXIER PLACES, Nan supposed, than a drop-cloth-covered floor in a nearly empty room, but for the life of her she couldn't think of them, not with Joss's stubble scraping the soft skin under her jaw. Not with the steady heat of his body under her palms, and his kick drum heartbeat keeping time with hers.

Their kisses stretched like shadows, bodies moving together to the music in the room. Their hungry senses drove them closer together. They wove an achy, needy spell around one another, sinking to the floor in an awkward tangle of limbs.

She laughed when he grazed her ticklish knee; he caught the laughter up in a kiss and their teeth clicked. Fumbled buttons and zippers gave way to more urgent hands and lips, and their laughter turned breathless.

This was no mountain-cabin seduction. Half crawling, they made their way to a fabric draped chaise in the middle of the room. The thick muslin shifted under her knees when she moved over him, sliding her body along his when he laid back to make room for her. Desperate for release, they urged each other on, past caring about the cramped chaise or its stiff cushions.

Nan let the slight chill in the air cool the sweat on the back of her neck while she listened to Joss's pulse slow. His hands roamed her back, leaving warmth in their wake while they lingered in a haze of spent desire. The cool threatened to turn cold, and she snuggled against him, loathe to disturb the mood.

Still, he felt her slight shiver, and felt around on the floor for a discarded shirt–his–to drape over her. "Don't get up yet. I like us here, just like this."

"I'm not going anywhere." She spoke softly against his chest, confident he heard her in the lull between songs.

CHAPTER 27

*K*ate arrived Friday evening for her weekend at the inn with a month's supply of everything.

"I brought dinner!" She dropped a reusable bag from the co-op on the island.

"I'm almost done with my chores." Nan slung a kitchen towel over the oven door handle to dry.

"So I don't get to play *chatelaine*?" Kate sighed dramatically, dropped her oversized bag on a chair, and set about unpacking the food. "I'm starving. Are we going to disturb anyone if we have supper down here?"

"Nope, all my guests are out for the evening."

"Excellent!" Kate opened a box and sniffed deeply. "Where are the plates?"

Nan slid two plates between her friend and the food. "What's for dinner?"

"I called and asked Dee for a girls' night feast. We have Temple's finest mystery dinner in here. Fix yourself a plate." Kate pulled plastic containers out of the bag and handed them to Nan. "Can I open some wine?"

Nan had tumblers out before Kate finished the sentence. "There's an open bottle of Sauvignon Blanc in the fridge."

"You're going to have to dish, you know." Kate popped a coconut shrimp into her mouth.

Nan took a thoughtful sip of her wine. "I was afraid of that."

"Do Molly and Walt know?"

Nan gave her friend an arch look.

"Okay, right. Everyone in town knows." Kate was gleeful. "So, what do they think?"

"I haven't seen them since…"

"Since you had your way with him?" Kate waggled her eyebrows.

Nan blushed. "Yes."

"Oh, be proud of yourself!" Kate giggled. "I am."

"Yes!" Nan laughed.

Their giggles subsided. Nan scooped up some guacamole on a tortilla chip.

Kate watched her, wineglass poised at her lips. "You're in love with him." It wasn't a question.

Nan's laughter faded. She met her friend's eyes. "I am."

Kate raised her glass. "I'll drink to that."

They drank. Nan got up to refill their glasses. "Kate?"

"Mmm?"

"What are people saying?"

"Nothing," Kate replied too quickly.

"Kate."

Kate set her glass down firmly and circled Nan's wrists in her long, slim fingers. "The women who knew him when we were kids are just playing jealous. Most of them are already married and either expecting or mothering. They're just gossipy. You know, fake-mopey, 'I guess Joss was never going to go for a local girl after he went to the College.'"

"So they hate me."

"No, silly. Everyone who knows you, loves you." Kate released her. "And the truth is, most everyone in town loves Joss, and you've changed him. Just a few weeks since you two met, and he's different than he was." Kate stopped to gather her words. "He was always a nice guy. But not too nice. And he's been gorgeous since some time between freshman and sophomore year in high school."

"Really?" Nan asked.

"Really." Kate drained her glass. "I was in maybe eighth grade, or the summer before… and one day he came over to get Jack. They were going to hike one of the waterfalls, probably with some girl Jack was trying to make out with."

Nan snorted. Of course Jack was trying to make out with some girl.

Kate reached for the wine bottle. "I was making breakfast, I remember standing there with my hair in a braid and a bowl of cereal in my hands, and he let himself in the back door. I almost didn't recognize him even though I'd seen him the night before. He'd had dinner with us. But something struck me, and I was like, 'Wow.'"

She emptied the bottle between their glasses. "And then I remembered who I was thinking about and nearly dropped my cereal." Kate tilted her head, an adorable frown line forming between her eyes. "What was I talking about?"

"You were telling me that people think he's changed," Nan responded.

"Right. He seems …" Kate thought a moment. "Brighter. Like he's got a light on inside him." She reached across the table to touch Nan's hand. "So do you, sugar plum."

KATE FINISHED the top coat on Nan's left pinky toe with a flourish.

Nan stretched her feet. "Sunday afternoons should always include pedicures."

"Yes." Kate speared the last bite of egg and asparagus from a plate of cold quiche balanced on her leg. "Pedicures and quiche."

"You know, the way you eat, you should be the Four-Hundred Pound Woman, right?" Nan asked.

Kate nodded. "I am blessed."

Nan tossed a pillow at her.

"Watch the plate!" Kate laughed.

Nan reached over and took the plate to set down on the coffee table. "I'm glad you came over."

"Me, too. That man of yours is just full of great ideas."

Nan clunked the plate down on the table. "What?"

Kate's eyes went wide. "Nan, I..."

"You what?"

Kate capped the polish bottle. It hit the table top with a click. "Oh, whatever. Joss called me, mentioned that he was worried about you being alone. He may have suggested I invite myself over."

"Joss isn't my keeper." Nan snatched the polish bottle from the table to tap against her palm.

"No, he's not," Kate said, cutting Nan off. "He's a man, very likely a man in love, and he had the sense to realize you wouldn't like knowing you were being hovered over. So shoot him."

Nan collapsed into the sofa with a huff. "If only I knew how."

"If you want target practice, ask Jack. Who, for the record, had the same idea as Joss."

"He does know I'm not actually his sister, doesn't he?" Nan sighed. She was well and truly outnumbered.

"I'm not sure he does." Kate took back the polish bottle and dropped it into her nearby tote bag. "Look, be pissed off at me if you're feeling prickly about this, but don't be angry with Joss. I should have been honest with you."

Kate picked herself up off the floor and plunked down on the sofa next to Nan. She propped her shiny-toed feet up next to Nan's. "I have missed you, and I am glad I got to see you for most of a whole weekend."

Nan plucked at the hem of her tee-shirt. "I'm not angry."

Kate shot her a look.

"No, Kate. I'm not angry. Not at him, and not at you. Not really." She crossed her ankles and laid her head on Kate's shoulder. "I'm pissed that this thing I've worked so hard for is being attacked for reasons I can't understand, and I'm frustrated because I'm falling in love with a man who challenges my sense of independence."

"You know I firmly believe he's falling for you, too, and if I'm right, he loves your independence. He just needs to know you're safe. And maybe doesn't have a lot of practice being protective without being overbearing. It's just how he is."

Nan thumped her heel on the coffee table. "You shouldn't need to come over here."

Kate turned to Nan, all levity gone from her face. "Sugar plum, I'd say hi to Terri Beaudette at the co-op, but I'm still not sold on giving her daughter free access to this place. Not after what happened." Nan started to reply, but Kate cut her off. "No, I know. You want to do the noble thing, give the kid a chance. It's really decent of you."

"I'm not giving her free access, exactly. I'm here, and I'm not help-less. Or stupid."

"I'm just saying," Kate paused. "I was wary, too. I don't blame Joss at all."

Nan stared at her freshly painted toes.

Kate fluffed her ponytail. "We need to end the weekend on a high note. When the boys come home we should order a big bag of Golden Prawn take-out."

Nan grinned. It really was all about food with Kate. "Sounds perfect."

"So you're not mad?"

"Maybe a little." Nan let Kate sweat for a second before she smiled again.

"Good. Hold onto that," Kate said. "Just be mad at what happened, not at Joss and me. We love you."

"He hasn't said he loves me, Kate."

"He does."

"I haven't said I love him."

"To him you haven't," Kate reminded her.

"I don't need a man to take care of me, even one who might love me."

"But isn't it nice to know there's a man who does love you? And wants you safe when he comes back?"

"From male bonding and debauchery."

"In Boston. It's not like they've been in Vegas."

"You know full well your brother can find trouble anywhere he goes."

"*Touché*." Kate's phone vibrated against the table top just as Nan's phone jingled.

"The menfolk are in White River Junction," Kate said, checking her incoming text. "I'm going to take my stuff home and throw in a load of laundry." After searching Nan's apartment for her things, she shouldered her bag. "I'm serious about us all meeting up later tonight." She opened the door to the breezeway stairs. "Unless you and Joss have something else in mind."

"Kate!"

Kate's bawdy laugh was already fading down the stairs.

JACK'S CAR swung into the driveway an hour and a half later; the engine cut quickly, sighing easily as the fan kicked in. He and Joss unfolded themselves from the front seats, windblown from a chilly top-down ride over the mountain.

They crossed the driveway, laughing together, their long years of friendship palpable between them in the setting October sunshine. Nan watched them approach as she dried the dishes. She couldn't help but smile. Both of them tall, Joss hardy and strong, Jack lithe and urbane–they struck quite a pair.

She was drying her hands on a kitchen towel when they came in.

Joss swung her up in a warm, happy embrace. She inhaled the clean scent of the skin behind his ears and hugged him. He set her down, kissed her mouth softly.

Jack snuck in beside Joss. "Some for me?"

Nan reached for him, wrapping her arms around his waist and offering her cheek to be kissed.

"He gets the better deal," Jack said.

She stepped back, and Joss folded her against him with a casually possessive arm. She leaned into him, grinning like a fool. "How was Boston?"

"Boring," they replied together, mischief and mirth in their eyes.

Nan snorted. "I'm sure."

"How's my favorite innkeeper?" Jack took in the spotless-as-usual kitchen. "Do you have guests?"

"I do. They're out right now, I think."

"I talked to Kate on the way through town. She says we're having Chinese." He winked. "If Joss can keep his hands to himself that long."

"I think I can manage," said Joss, but he pulled Nan closer.

Jack's phone buzzed. "It's Kate." He checked the screen. "She's at Golden Prawn."

Joss whispered in Nan's ear. "I missed you."

Jack typed quickly and pocketed the slim phone. "She says, 'Ten minutes,' so we should see her in an hour or so."

"Okay, gentlemen." Nan hung her dish towel on the oven door. "I have some cleanup to finish. Grab a few beers, go on up to my apartment, and try not to get into trouble while I finish up here."

Jack and Joss headed up the stairs with a six-pack, and Nan made a mental note to bring a few more bottles upstairs. The men were still celebrating their bachelor weekend; if she and Kate wanted a beer, they'd best take care of themselves.

CHAPTER 28

$\mathcal{N}$an suspected Kate would be quicker than Jack gave her credit for. She ran through her mental checklist, pausing when she realized the afternoon tea spread was still in the parlor. It wouldn't take more than a couple of minutes to collect the dishes and clean up the leftovers. She grabbed a tray to carry everything, and pushed through the swinging door into the entryway.

A glassy ping, followed quickly by three more sharp pops surprised her, and she nearly dropped the tray.

She squeaked in distress when her foot came down on something small and jagged. While searching the floor for the offending object, she palmed the wall until she struck the light switch. When the light flipped on, she got a good look at the floor.

Puzzled, she reached down for a small metallic pellet on the bare floor. Turning it over between her fingers, she realized it was a spent air gun pellet. The long-forgotten ping of pellets on tin cans in her grandfather's back field rose from her memory like a ghost. A faint whistling caught her ear as she straightened, and she turned with a sinking heart toward the front door.

Her first reaction was grief, outrage that the warped antique glass in the front door, offering its charming, watery view of the marsh for a hundred years, was damaged. She forced herself to see that it could have been worse. Only a hole, precisely the size of the gunmetal grey piece of ammunition in her hand, let the cool air rush in.

She went to the front door, rushed out onto the shadowy porch. The valley was as silent as it ever was. Air moved over the marsh grass, birdsong and the mooing of dairy cows filled the air around her. In the spill of light from the foyer, she saw three more pellets on the porch floor boards.

Bending to pick them up, she had the crawling feeling that she was being watched, and realized that whoever shot her front door might still be out there. She retreated into the foyer and felt in her pocket for her phone.

She dialed Sergeant Lowry with steady fingers.

"Lowry," came a clipped voice.

"Sergeant? This is Nan Grady from the Damselfly Inn. I've had some more trouble here."

The cool tone warmed with concern. "What happened?"

She told him, briefly, what she'd seen, heard, found.

"You alone over there?"

Joss. Jack. No, she wasn't alone, but she'd forgotten them. She let the relief loosen her grip on the phone. A quick glance at the driveway confirmed that more than one of her guests was also on the property. "No."

"Anything hit besides the door?"

She hadn't even looked.

"I'll check that out when I get there." Lowry promised to keep a low profile for her guest's sake. "Tell Joss and Jack not to play heroes, okay?"

It was decent advice. They'd be angry, but for the moment, what they didn't know wouldn't hurt them. Abandoning caution, she made her way, still barefoot, across the pea stone driveway.

"Shit." The Mayers' Nissan had a tidy hole in the rear windshield. She inspected the remaining cars. Only one other was a victim of her mystery marksman. Anger flared up again. Of course it would be Jack's sexy, red Audi.

She was going to have to bring her friends up to speed.

Upstairs, Nan paused in the doorway. Jack and Joss were huddled over Jack's phone like a pair of teenagers, looking at what she could only assume were photos from their weekend.

"Something funny?" She struggled to keep the fear and anger from her voice.

Jack slid the phone into his pocket with an exaggerated look of horror. "What happens in Boston …"

"Yes. Well." Nan's struggle with her emotions was a losing one. Her chin trembled.

"Hey." Joss jumped up and crossed the room to her. "What's the matter?"

She took a deep breath and told them about pellet in the front hall. She watched their twin stormy expressions and was reminded of how much she loved her circle of friends. Her family.

"Whoever it was hit one of my guests' cars." She steeled herself. "And your Audi, Jack."

Jack swore roundly and peered out the window. "I leave that car parked on Commonwealth Ave and no one touches it. Fifteen minutes at an inn in rural Vermont and someone shoots out my tail light?"

"Christ." Joss hadn't moved or spoken until then.

Nan couldn't take it; the ugly tears came fast and hard. Joss reached for her and she stumbled into his embrace, weeping messily into his shirt. Joss only held her, rubbing small circles on her back. Neither man spoke. When the sobs subsided, she sniffled a little and swiped the wetness from her cheeks. "I just got off the phone with Sergeant Lowry. He's on his way over."

She was interrupted by the slide and thump of Kate's van door closing in the driveway.

Moments later, there was Kate, coming through the apartment door, two brown paper bags of take-out in her arms. She looked them over, a small frown wrinkling her brow. She glanced from Joss to her brother. "What did you two do?"

"Kate …" Jack paused as the cruiser pulled in behind his car.

Sergeant Lowry inspected the cars in the driveway, pausing at

Jack's cracked light and the hole in the Mayers' windshield. The doorbell rang, and Nan started downstairs. Joss started to follow her. Kate and Jack brought up the rear, but she held them back.

"I need to handle this." She waved at the take-out bags. "Save me some crab rangoons, okay?"

She left them there and went down to speak with the Sergeant alone.

⁓

WHEN NAN CAME BACK UPSTAIRS, Jack was on the phone in her bedroom, Kate was closing up take-out boxes, and Joss was peering out the porch door into his parents' pastures behind the house.

Joss turned when she walked in. "What did Pete say?"

"He took a look at some crushed marsh grass on his way over. He told me that those pellets are ten bucks for thousands anywhere you can get ammunition."

Jack came through the doorway with another curse. "So, pretty much everywhere?"

"He said I need to leave the floodlights on at night and call my insurance company." Nan flopped on her sofa. "He told me he would file a report, but unless I wanted him to bring Danny in again, he wasn't very optimistic."

"Nan," Jack asked softly, pocketing his phone and returning to the living room. "Is this place worth all of this?"

Her eyes narrowed. "Of course it is."

"Jack!" Kate wheeled on her brother.

"No, Katie, wait." He looked at Nan expectantly. "I think it's a valid question."

Her answer came easily. "Jack, this is my dream. I've been working towards this since I got out of high school. Like hell I'm going to give it up because someone doesn't like me here."

Jack smiled. "Good. Now I know you've got the fight in you."

Joss put a hand on his best friend's shoulder. "Jack?"

"What?"

"You're an asshole."

Jack laughed out loud. "And I get paid the big bucks for it."

Nan was still considering Jack's comment about the fight in her. "Did you think I didn't?"

Kate fixed her brother with a venomous expression. "He doesn't know you like I do."

"Listen," Nan said to all of them. "I know the three of you were only looking out for me, but I wish you'd given me a say about this weekend."

Joss started to speak.

"Let me finish. Jack, you're sweet to feel bad for taking Joss away." She caught a dirty look between the Pease siblings and arched a brow in Jack's direction. "We tell each other everything." She took a deep breath. "I want to be included. I don't want to feel like a victim."

Jack was quick to reassure. "No one thinks of you like that."

"Good." Nan turned to Joss.

"Katie," Jack interrupted, "let's go grab some dessert."

The Peases were gone before she could properly gather her thoughts.

Joss took the defensive. "Nan, I didn't mean –"

"I know, but you can't do that." She took a step towards him. "You can't treat me like a helpless female. I'm not."

"I know –"

"Do you, though?" She had to tip her head back to hold his gaze. "We don't know everything about one another. Yet."

"I don't think of you like that."

She put a tentative hand on his arm. Even the light touch reminded her of the easy physicality between them. "Tell me you're worried, ask me to take care of myself. Let me know what's going on in your head."

"You want to know what's in my head?"

She felt the temper in him when he hauled her up against him and crushed his lips to hers. The kiss was hard, possessive. She grabbed a handful of his shirt to pull him closer.

His eyes were hot when he pulled away. "I missed you like hell, and I worried myself sick all weekend. Even knowing Kate was here."

"We're coming back!" Kate called up the stairs.

Jack sighed. "This conversation isn't done."

Kate was carrying a plastic storage container full of cookies.

Jack followed with bottled water for everyone. "Am I crazy to think maybe Danny Beaudette isn't telling us everything?" He dropped into Nan's ancient leather chair.

"Jack and I have decided it isn't really about Nan," Kate said, perching on the arm of the chair. "The attacks have all been on the building. The property. Not Nan herself."

"Joss figured out the connection there." Nan leaned into Joss, who wrapped an arm around her and pulled them both down onto the sofa.

Jack grabbed a cookie from the bag. "Were you planning on sharing that with the rest of the team?"

She and Joss filled Kate and Jack in on the story of Terri Beaudette's stint as Meg Swift's nurse.

"I didn't know that. I'm losing my touch." Kate handed out cookies. "I can't imagine anyone hating you enough to do this, though. Even a pissed off kid." She bit into a cookie and giggled. "Except that girl you soaked with cold chicken stock coming out of the walk-in that time. What was her name?"

Nan laughed. "Laurie O'Dell." She relaxed into Joss; his hands, idly stroking her arms, lulled her.

Kate nudged Jack with her foot. "I think we've all had enough excitement for tonight. Come along, brother dear. Time to go."

"Of course," he said, unfolding himself from the chair. "Good night, you two." He followed his sister out the door and down the stairs.

THE RESPECTIVE ROAR and purr of the Pease siblings' engines vanished into the night. Nan snuggled into Joss's shoulder, grateful for the low light and the distraction of closeness. There were serious things which needed saying.

To begin, she chose levity. "How are you going to get home?"

"I left my truck at the farm and took the bus to Boston, since Jack was planning to drive north afterwards."

"You really were worried about me?"

"I was frantic. Jack told me I was a pain in the ass."

"What did Drew say?" Nan asked, turning to him, curling her legs up against his.

"Drew said –" Joss didn't finish.

"Whatever Drew said, it wasn't nothing," Nan said with a small laugh.

"Tell me about Laurie O'Dell."

"So, Drew's comments were too salty for idle conversation?"

"No." Joss kissed her forehead, "I just want to hear the story of a girl covered in chicken stock."

"You're changing the subject," Nan clarified, "but I'll tell you anyway."

She realized, as she thought back to her culinary school years, that she and Joss hadn't had this part of courting yet. The simple exchanges of history. From the first moment they'd met, their lives had been on fast forward.

"Laurie O'Dell lived across the hall from us at NECI. She was pretty, competitive, ambitious. Kate hated her."

"I can see how that might happen."

Nan felt Joss's chuckle. "She hated Kate. And somewhere along the way, she decided to hate me, too. Only I didn't have Kate's self-confidence, her brass. I was an easy mark."

"You're no one's easy mark." Joss quiet words in her ear warmed her.

"Kate would find ways to piss her off, just little things, and even better if it was to her own benefit. Or mine. Or ours. It made Laurie crazy." Nan smiled to herself. "And then, there was Brig."

Joss raised a brow.

"Brigham Cash." She let the unlikely name sink in. "I know, but he liked me. And Laurie liked him. Laurie saw him kissing me goodnight outside our door, and spent the rest of the semester trying to sabotage my degree."

Joss was quiet.

"Laurie was crazy. I'm fairly certain she was trying to trap me in the walk-in after class. I was pulling a pot of chilled stock to separate it out for freezing, and she followed me. She turned out the light and was starting to close the door, so I *tripped* and splashed her with stock. She screamed and our instructor came in from the classroom. I had to clean the whole mess up for being clumsy and wasteful, but Laurie got the message."

Joss's fingers were laced with hers, his body close, but she felt his thoughts moving away.

"Joss?"

"Yeah?"

"What is it?"

He squeezed her fingers gently. "It's ridiculous."

"What?"

"I hate that guy," he said. "Just for kissing you."

Nan pulled him down, gave him her mouth. She let him taste the woman to banish the thought of the girl she'd been. He responded with a tenderness that surprised her. When the need for breath separated them, she laid her head again on his shoulder. "Don't you want to know what happened?"

"No."

"Oh, you do." She whispered low and conspiratorially in his ear. "They were both picked for a choice externship at a golf resort in Scottsdale."

"And they rode off together into the sunset?"

"He rode off into the sunset," she giggled, "with a caddy named Sean."

Joss rolled his eyes, but his smile came more easily.

He combed through the hair at the nape of her neck; she felt the casual touch to her fingertips. "I promise I won't leave you out of discussions about your safety, Nan, but you have to promise me you'll take this seriously. This guy shot at your home, your business, while you were here."

"I will. I do," she said. "I don't want you worrying."

"I will worry." He tipped her chin up and touched his lips to hers. "I love you, Nan."

He gathered her against him, cradling her against his chest. She drank in his heartbeat, the lingering smell of wind in his hair from the top-down drive over the mountain with Jack.

Nan knew the words she wanted to say, but found them trapped under so many emotions, buried thick in desire and uncertainty. She pressed her lips to the pulse under his jaw, felt it quicken. His hands drifted, sought the hem of her shirt. Pushing up to her knees, she unbuttoned the first two buttons of his shirt.

Nan straddled his lap, sitting back a little to trace her finger from the hollow of his shoulder to the place where the shirt remained fastened.

He held still while she slipped the rest of his shirt buttons from their holes. Only his hands and their questing pressure on her hips betrayed his tension. Nan smoothed back the fabric, baring Joss's chest. Her hands moved over the flat expanse of his stomach; when his muscles shivered, she laid an open-mouthed kiss on his nipple, grazing the sensitive skin with her teeth. She watched his lips part, heard the air slip past. When his eyes drifted shut, power surged up from the recently woken heart of her. Warmth and desire blended in a passionate alchemy.

She wanted to plunder, to lay a course and navigate by the stars that were their bodies.

As smoothly as she could manage, she tugged her shirt over her head. His eyes were open–heated–when she tossed it aside. Those still hands suddenly moved over her to palm her breasts. Her own nipples pushed at her bra. She arched her back, filling his hands, and reached for his buckle.

He stroked her bra straps from her shoulders, leaving them loose over her arms, and slipped his hands between fabric and flesh. Even what little lace remained between them was too much. She reached behind her and flicked apart the catch, letting the garment fall away. He rolled her nipples between his fingertips and she moaned.

"You should see yourself," Joss's voice was hoarse. "You're incredible."

She ran her hands over her body, pausing to lace her fingers with his over her breasts. "This feels incredible."

He pulled her down for a kiss, lips impatient, cruising over hers, seeking the warmth of her mouth, but she slithered away down his body, lowering herself to the floor between his knees. He watched her, lust and questions in his hooded expression, but shifted to accommodate her unspoken direction. She opened his zipper, almost painfully aware of the rasp of metal teeth.

His fingers curled into the upholstery when, with a boldness she hadn't been sure she possessed, she took him into her mouth, teasing with tongue and lips. Her name was a beggar's prayer into the air around them, suddenly thick with the scent of desire. She heard his ragged words, felt his body strung tight. His obvious need surged through her like wine in the blood.

Nan wriggled out of her jeans, leaving them puddled on the floor and rose to kiss him, his taste on her lips. He searched her eyes, found permission and a plea there. Somewhere between a sigh and a cry, her pleasure found a voice when he grasped her hips and filled her.

She moved over him, taking his hands as they found their rhythm together. His gaze never left hers, not until her head fell back and she gave up her control. He let her lead, let her find her release before his, bringing her in close for a tender kiss before he was lost, too.

It was a few moments before Joss broke the panting silence. He caught her up in his arms and rolled them both down into the couch, keeping her tucked against his shoulder. "I missed you."

The feelings she couldn't quite verbalize swelled in her chest. "I missed you, too." She spoke to the place over his heart where her hand rested. "Can you stay tonight?"

CHAPTER 29

"The last time anyone shot anything at my car, I was living on a shady block in Hoboken." Stan Mayer was in a full blown snit about the damage to his car.

His wife was frantically patting his arm, and nodding at Nan. "That was before Hoboken was somewhere young people wanted to live."

Stan brushed his wife's hand away. "Jane, hush."

Stan's dismissal of his wife irked Nan, but she kept her face carefully neutral. "I can assure you, Mr. Mayer, that if you stop at the auto glass shop in Rutland on your way back to Short Hills, they'll replace the glass. I'll take care of it."

"Yes, Ms. Grady. You will." Having secured his new window, Stan Mayer left her office in a huff, snapping his wife to heel. "Jane!"

Nan was still contemplating the Mayers' departure when another voice outside her office iced the blood in her veins.

"I know, I should have listened, when you told me there was something about broken windows and a fire in the police log." One of the Zimmers twins–interchangeably lovely and interchangeably mean thirty-somethings on a nostalgia tour.

"Yeah, I know. I didn't Google first."

A pause, and then the juicy stage whisper of malicious gossip. "Thank goodness my car was fine, but the couple in the room at the end of the hall had a window shot out." Another pause.

"Oh, I'll be leaving a review when we get home. I mean, the place is beautiful, but when we booked, we were certainly not expecting a crime scene."

There was just enough time for Nan to arrange her face back into its mask of polite interest before a Zimmers sister knocked on the office door. "Can I help you?"

"My sister's on her way down with her things, and we're going to try to make that winery tour before we get to the antique show." She peered over Nan's desk at the laptop monitor. "So, if you could print out our invoice?"

With a click, Nan brought up their reservation; with a sigh she took twenty percent off their bill before hitting print. The sister in front of her scanned the numbers with shrewd eyes and smiled wolfishly before dropping a platinum card on the blotter between them. Nan bit back a reply and swiped the card.

The Zimmers sisters settling their well-toned behinds in their black Porsche SUV was the best thing she'd seen all morning.

The relief didn't last long. She could just barely afford the glass repair for Stan Mayer. Another insurance claim would only hurt her rates. The booking software showed gaping holes where she'd fervently hoped, and certainly planned, to have leaf peeping guests. Comping nights, declining reservations, and unexpected costs were sending her bottom line careening into the red.

She closed her eyes, pressing her fingers into her temples to recapture the ease of waking up in her bed to Joss's kiss instead of an alarm. He'd needed to run to his parents' to grab some tools from the supply he kept on the farm before heading out to Ellen Hill's barn, a project he kept hinting she drop by to see. Nan had drifted in half-sleep for a while after he left, watching the light fill the room with drowsy eyes. Her waking-dreams were idealistic visions of picnics in nearly-restored barns, of a lean, weathered farm-woman with a sharp wit who liked her immediately, who saw without asking the connection between her and Joss.

The ugliness of the numbers continued to intrude. She had no idea what to do about the possibility of failure. While rationally she knew it was always an option, and the odds called it the winning one, she'd never accepted that she might actually fail. She'd wanted The Damselfly for so long and with such fierce, single-minded focus, that there were no alternatives to hand.

Nan opened her internet browser and typed into the search bar: hotel management jobs. She clicked *Return* with her eyes shut. Her eyes opened to a listing on the NECI job boards from one of her former instructors: a woman who now owned, it seemed, a successful inn near Bar Harbor, Maine. A woman who was looking to hire a manager.

She opened a new email, pasted in the contact address from the listing, and closed it again as quickly. Failure would not be an option. She would get to the bottom of the vandalism; she would refocus her energy on making The Damselfly the destination she knew it could be. Her place in Thornton wasn't going to be given up so easily.

Noting the time, Nan realized she needed to fetch her reluctant intern, failing inn or no. She closed the Google search tab and put the idea out of her head.

NAN LET her VW idle outside Thornton Union High, hearing the shrilling that meant classes were concluded for the day. It took a few moments, but Danny slunk out the front doors in a pod of similarly grungy kids. A tall boy in slashed denim and a band tee slung a knobby arm over Danny's shoulders. Nan couldn't help but notice that when Danny saw her waiting, the girl shrugged out of the boy's reach.

Danny's face, speaking to the young man with her chin upturned, was hopeful. Her body was strung tight. The boy, for all his slouchy posturing, radiated anger. Nan tried to push more sinister thoughts from her head. It only took a moment for Danny to separate herself from her cohort. She climbed into Nan's passenger seat without so much as a hello. Nan slipped the car into first gear and drove away from the school in silence.

She took the back way around behind the college, her eyes taking in the turning foliage while she searched for the right way to ask a troubled young girl if she'd been playing sniper in the darkness not twenty-four hours before.

"Danny?" Nan's voice faltered slightly after the long quiet stretch.

The girl muttered into the book bag she clutched to her chest. "Yeah?"

Nan gripped the wheel hard. "Someone shot at the cars in my parking lot and at my front door last night."

The girl's head whipped around, her eyes wide. "What?"

Nan caught it in the moment she glanced over at her passenger: a flicker of understanding mingled with very real surprise on Danny's face. She kept her tone as light as she could. "A pellet gun. No one was hurt. But there was some damage." She paused to let that sink in. "And I lost some business. It's pretty serious."

Danny sank further into the seat. She spoke into her lap. "I didn't, I swear."

Nan held her tongue, waiting for more from Danny. She could feel some kind of confession thickening the air, but she couldn't imagine this young woman was the one who'd pulled the trigger. Despite the chill in the afternoon air, Nan was tempted to put the windows down to dissipate the tension.

When Danny spoke again, it wasn't the answer Nan was expecting. "I don't know anything about it."

"Okay." Nan didn't want to push the girl away. Despite everything, there was a protective affection blooming in her chest. She wanted to get to the bottom of Danny Beaudette's troubles and help her heal.

Drawing a long, slow breath, Nan put aside her concerns. "I want to get some bulbs in this afternoon. How do you feel about gardening?"

CHAPTER 30

The following morning, Nan and Amanda spent their hours housekeeping, readying the inn for their only booking. While Amanda gave the public rooms on the first floor a thorough dusting, Nan worked her way through the guest rooms on the second floor.

She had her earbuds in her ears, likely embarrassing Amanda by crooning along with *Cracklin' Rosie*. She had to laugh, imagining Amanda's horror, as she vacuumed and stripped the beds.

Her phone buzzed in the pocket of her jeans. She paused Neil Diamond and answered the call without looking. "Damselfly Inn, this is Nan Grady."

Joss's voice spoke into her ears, laughing and intimate. "You are adorable when you're singing."

She whirled around, feather duster and phone in hand, to see Joss in the doorway. With an embarrassed giggle, she pulled her earbuds out.

He put his phone away. "I knocked." He crossed the room, kissed her purposefully. "You didn't hear me, but I figured you'd have your phone."

Nan looped her arms around his neck. "Hi."

"I can't stay, and I know I'm supposed to bring dinner and a movie tonight," he said, dropping another kiss on her lips, "but I wanted to find out if you could get away for a few hours on Wednesday afternoon."

Nan did some quick mental schedule shuffling. "I can. Unless someone walks in, I'll be empty midweek through Friday afternoon, and Amanda is usually here on Wednesdays after her morning classes. She can keep an eye on things."

"Will she be okay by herself?" Joss asked, worry pulling a crease on his brow.

"I think so," Nan said carefully. She hated that this extra caution shadowed her every decision. "I told her she could bring her hockey player boyfriend over if they could behave themselves."

"I don't know how anyone behaves themselves in this place." Joss hugged her closer, kissing a trail along her jaw, nipping her earlobe. She purred her pleasure.

"A fine example I'm setting," she said, stretching up and taking his face between her palms. She kissed him, softly, but with no less purpose. She wound her hands into his hair, down his neck, across the breadth of his shoulders. She shivered as his hands slipped down her back and over the curve of her hips.

His mouth tasted of mint, with the underlying sweetness of hazelnuts and coffee. He smelled of sunshine and sawdust. He'd been at work already.

Breathless, she pulled away. He bent to recapture her mouth, but she set her hands on his chest with gentle sternness. "I have work to do."

"Me, too." Joss smiled against her mouth. "But I'd rather kiss you."

Nan felt a girlish giddiness. She stepped back to avoid giving in. "Where are we going on Wednesday?"

"It's a surprise." Joss's smile was mysterious. "I'll pick you up around one."

∾

WHATEVER SHE MIGHT SAY about Danny Beaudette, Nan could see the girl had a knack for plants. Truthfully, it made the whole incident with the burned shrub feel wrong, somehow. After learning the basics of bulbs on her last visit, Danny quietly took charge of planting seven dozen. The magnificent haul came from a new friend of Nan's—an old friend of the Swifts who was redesigning her gardens had offered her the lot. Just in time for fall planting.

Several times during the afternoon, Nan had peered out the windows, watching Danny carefully consider placement, sorting the bulbs and arranging them in some pattern Nan was unable to discern from a distance.

When, on her next day at The Damselfly, Danny asked Nan if she could do more gardening, Nan sent her out to thin the hosta on the back side of the house.

"Find a shady place to plant the ones you dig up, and remember: when they come up next year, they'll need space."

An hour later, Danny came to find Nan. She'd tentatively placed all the halved hosta around a Japanese maple just off the terrace. It was a good choice. The house shaded the yard there; the ring of hosta would bring the slim tree with its deep purple-blue leaves that much closer to the terrace.

If she added a pair of Adirondack chairs and a small table nearby, it would become an extension of the patio.

"Miss Grady?" Danny stood in front of her, hands in the pockets of her loose-fitting jeans, rocking on the heels of her boots.

"I'm sorry, I got ahead of myself. That sounds perfect." Nan shook the pillow she was holding into its case. "I'll come down in a minute and help with the watering and cleaning up."

Danny's cheeks rose, a shy hint of what Nan suspected was a gorgeous smile.

The new hosta bed was already in by the time Nan got down to the back yard. Danny had alternated a dusky, blue-green variety with a bright green and white one. The contrasting colors and shapes already looked at home beneath the tree.

"You can be in charge of the gardens for the rest of your time here," Nan said, impressed with Danny's work.

Danny lit up like summer vacation. "Really?"

"Really. I'll drag the hose over so we can get them watered."

Danny followed, taking the hose and unwinding it while Nan connected it and turned on the water.

"You're good with the plants and flowers."

Danny leaned in close, soaking the newly transplanted roots. "My friend—Ellie, her mom had amazing gardens, and we were always outside. She used to talk all the time, about everything. I kind of listened. It was interesting, all the stuff she just knew about how to grow all those flowers together like that."

They finished the watering, and Danny helped Nan wind the hose and stow the gardening supplies in the garage. Nan did her best to ignore the guilty flush on Danny's cheeks when they passed the newly painted garage door.

She set out the early evening tea and offered some to Danny, who took a glass of cold, sweet tea and a muffin into the kitchen. While she ate, she asked Nan about the blueberry bushes that formed a natural fence at the edge of the yard that faced the Fullers' north pastures.

"I know nothing about them, except that they produced enough this year for some jam and frozen blueberries for baking," Nan admitted. "Do you want to see if there's anything we need to do to care for them?"

"Mrs. Swift let me eat them off the bush when we lived here. They're so good."

A terse honk interrupted their conversation. Terri Beaudette's knocked-around Celica rattled impatiently in the driveway. Without a word, Danny grabbed her book bag from the front hall, and slouched out to the car.

No hint of the interesting, engaged young woman Nan had been speaking with remained.

～

Joss found Nan on her deck, wrapped in a knit afghan, with a book, when he arrived with pizza and beer. He stopped at the doorway and drank in the sight of her. "Hey."

She patted the cushion next to her. "It was too nice out here to stay inside, and I had a free half hour."

"You work so hard." He dropped down beside her.

"I love it."

"I know." He set the pizza and the six-pack on the milk crate table and lifted the box lid. "You hungry?"

"Is that from Fantastic Pizza?"

"Where else?"

"You can crack one of those open for me, too," she said, gesturing with her slice at the six-pack. "I earned it. I got Danny to open up a little today." She blotted the cheese with a flimsy napkin from the stack wedged into the pizza box. "It feels like progress."

Joss nodded. "I asked around. Terri's been picking up some extra per diem shifts at the clinic here in town, but she's supporting her old man and her kid brother as well as Danny."

Nan inhaled sharply at the thought of four adults and a teenage girl all crammed into that little house out on Kiln Road. "I'd be angry, too," she said wonderingly. "I really didn't like the look of the uncle."

"Yeah, he's not a very happy guy. It got me thinking about who might really be behind all of this." Joss set his pizza down. "Which brings me to my next point."

She waited while he searched for the words.

"I don't like leaving you here alone if there's even a chance this guy's involved," he said. "Hell, I don't like leaving you here alone at all."

"Joss –"

"Wait. I know. You can handle it. But I wish you didn't have to. And I worry." He stopped, watching the sun as the last of the light sank away over the Adirondacks. "What if I stayed here?"

She was silent.

"I know the timing's off. We're just starting out."

She picked at the label on her bottle.

"But I'd feel better knowing I was here with you."

"I understand what you're saying, and there's a huge part of me that wants to let you stay." He saw the answer in her eyes before she spoke. "But I share my home with strangers all the time, and I can't have some guest with a different definition of propriety telling the world that the innkeeper at The Damselfly has got some guy shacking up –" She stopped and twisted the bottleneck, only to have to wipe her hands, damp from condensation, on the blanket, still wrapped around her shoulders. Her cheeks flamed. "I didn't mean –"

Joss stood and stepped towards the railing. Her words bounced around behind his eyes. *Some guy.* He didn't really believe that was how she felt, but it stung nonetheless. He loved her.

He thought she loved him, but she hadn't said the words.

"Joss," she whispered, slipping her arms around him and laying her head against his back. "Let's not argue about this now. I promise you, I'll be careful." She tightened her arms around him. "And I promise, if something more happens–anything–I'll ask you to stay."

"I guess I'll have to live with that." He answered without turning.

He felt her warm breath through the fabric of his shirt, felt a shiver roll through her. The mild day had given way to an evening smelling of snow. He thought of her afghan, discarded on the loveseat. "You're cold. We should go in."

"Any chance you still want to watch a movie?"

"No," he said, "I don't really."

"Oh," she said, dropping her arms. The evening air filled the space where she'd been.

"I don't want to watch a movie." He took her hand and spun her around, pulling her back. She crashed into him, but he caught her snug against him. She grabbed his shoulders, clung to him when her feet left the floor.

The kiss was brutal. Here he demanded what she wouldn't promise him, and she gave it to him. Gave herself into his keeping, his protection while he ravaged her. He held her as he tugged the screen open, pushed against the door. Her lips parted and he took her mouth.

This time he knew the way to her bed, and he fell heavily, bringing her down with him. His hands streaked down her torso, hooked in the waistband of her jeans and tugged. She sat up, unzipping the denim and sliding her hips free.

Joss pushed up against the mattress, rolling her under him and pulling her free from the jeans as she tugged her shirt off. He slipped his hands under the satin of her bra, his thumbs brushing her nipples as she arched up under him.

He dropped to his knees next to the bed. He kissed a path from her ankle to her knee. His hands smoothed up her thighs; his lips followed, finding her all heat and sweetness.

She cried out when he found her center.

Up and up again, he sent her flying. He shed his clothes and came down on the bed next to her, and when he kissed her again, he was drunk on the warm, languid feel of her stretched out alongside him.

He traced the outline of her body, trailed kisses across her breasts.

"Joss," she breathed, reaching for him. "Please."

She wrapped her legs around him, drawing him to her, and when they began to move together, he gave himself into her keeping.

THE NEXT DAY, with the memory of Joss's kisses lingering, and the promise of a lunch date taunting, Nan took a critical look at her closet.

Her wardrobe was in dire straits. She reached for her lifeline via text: *fashion SOS.*

When Kate wheeled in after work, Nan had emptied half her closet into an empty laundry basket. She sat on the floor with her head between her knees. "I have nothing to wear."

"I know, sugar plum," Kate agreed, surveying the damage. "But you don't usually indulge in fashion emergencies."

"No." Nan sighed, looking up through her hair. "You usually create them for me."

Kate shrugged a shoulder. "*Touché.* What brought this on?"

"Joss is taking me out to lunch tomorrow."

Kate put up a hand. "Say no more." She dug into her voluminous bag. Without looking up, she shook out a few tops and dumped a bag of bracelets and scarves out onto Nan's rug.

"Go put on your charcoal straight-leg trousers, the ones I made you buy at Mistle Thrush."

Nan fetched the pants in question from the lone hanging rack in her closet, stripped out of her khakis and tugged them on. She shucked off her tee shirt and, at Kate's direction, raised her arms, allowing Kate to drop an emerald green shell over her arms.

"I'm taller, but you've got more boobs, and I was right, it does work!"

Nan pulled herself up straight. The fabric felt amazing on her skin.

Kate was eyeing her critically. "You'll wear something pretty under this, right?"

Nan tied the sash and adjusted the neckline. She leaned over and pulled two bras from her top drawer, dangling them for Kate's inspection. "The lavender, do you think? Or the cream?"

"The cream," Kate said with a nod. "Save the lavender for when you really want to knock his socks off."

"Well, then." Nan dropped the pair of undergarments back into the drawer, fighting off a blush.

Kate slipped a set of slim, silver bangles over her wrist, and peered hopefully into Nan's closet. "Now, shoes!"

CHAPTER 31

Wednesday morning turned out to be a frustrating one. Nan spent half the morning fiddling with the reservation software, and the other half down an internet rabbit hole researching salvaged glass for her damaged front door. When Amanda cruised in at twelve-thirty, she gave up, cursing herself for wasting time she might have spent making an effort on her appearance. It wasn't every weekday afternoon that she had a date.

"I'm headed out for a few hours. It should be pretty quiet. Feel free to use the wifi when you're in the office, and be sure to take a handset with you when you're doing the rooms."

"Sure." Amanda was already stowing her book bag. Mid-terms would be in full swing in a week or two.

"Amanda?" Nan asked, remembering her earlier conversation with Joss.

"Yes?" Amanda answered without looking up.

"Is your boyfriend coming by to keep you company?"

"He was going to come by after his lab," she said. "Is that still okay?"

"It's fine." Nan resisted the urge to wink. "Just keep it professional."

The younger woman made an embarrassed show of rummaging through her backpack, then heaving a stack of textbooks onto the desk.

Joss pulled in at ten to one. Nan was fidgeting with the bow she'd tied in the sash of Kate's emerald blouse. When he stepped down from the cab of the truck, Nan was relieved to see that he'd traded his customary carpenter's pants and henley for dark washed denim and a sky blue button-down, and traded his work boots for Doc Martens. At least she was neither over nor under dressed for whatever Joss had planned.

She dashed down the stairs to the kitchen to meet him at the door.

Joss slipped an arm around her waist, pulled her close and kissed her. "I may never bring you back."

"Keep talking like that, and I'll never want to come back."

Once they were one the road, he connected his .mp3 player to the sound system, and a warm voice tumbled out over rich guitar.

"Did you know I like Grant Lee Phillips?" she asked, a smile playing across her lips.

"I hoped you might."

He slowed to wave to his father, passing them on the way home to the farm, then continued into town, a comfortable lack of conversation filling the cab of his truck while the music washed over them. He skipped the state highway and headed east on a local road.

"Are you going to tell me where you're taking me?" Curiosity had finally gotten the best of her.

"It's not really that big of a deal." He picked up a numbered state route and drove north. "I made lunch reservations for us in Bristol, and then I thought maybe we'd drive over into Waitsfield. I just wanted to spend an afternoon with you."

An electric thrill skittered up Nan's spine, spreading warmth out through her limbs. She reached across the cab of the truck and covered his hand with hers on the gear shift.

She watched the forest thicken as they drove up into the foothills of the Green Mountains. In all the years since she'd first come to

Vermont as a culinary student, she'd never ceased being amazed by these woods and mountains. Bristol, nestled into the shoulder of the mountains, was charming, and lunch at the intimate dining room Joss had chosen got her thinking about what she could do with her own, albeit smaller, space.

The restaurant was a rambling farmhouse snugged into a bend in Baldwin Creek. Surrounded by barns, gardens and greenhouses, sheltered by the evergreen forest and General Stark's Mountain at its back. A low fire banished the autumn chill; the menu was inspired by local game and the hardy vegetables growing steps away. Nan was enchanted.

"You know, you have me at a disadvantage," he said over the entrées.

Nan paused, a forkful of young spinach and roasted pumpkin salad on her fork. "How so?"

"My best friend is your lawyer, my parents are your neighbors, your best friend grew up with me. You've heard all of my stories." His lips turned up sheepishly.

She laughed. "I haven't heard half of them, and we both know it."

"Really, though," he countered. "I don't know any of yours."

Nan sipped from a tall glass of crisp hard cider. "I don't have any."

"Tell me about your grandparents."

She rearranged her silverware on her plate. "My mother broke their hearts," she said softly, looking up to meet his eyes. If her sudden candor surprised him, it didn't show. "I'm three years older now than she was when she died."

Joss listened, waited.

"My grandparents were private people. My mom was their second baby, and a late one. The first one, a boy, died. I'm not sure my mom ever knew that, though. I didn't even find out until after they died." She twisted the stem of her wineglass in between two fingers. "They took us both in after my father took off, and when my mom died they kept me. Gran was quiet about everything, but fierce in a way."

Joss laid his hand over hers on the table. "You get that from her."

"Do you really see me like that?"

He squeezed gently. "I really do."

Nan slipped her hand away and refolded her napkin in her lap. "When she passed away, my grandfather only lasted two weeks without her."

"I was twenty-two. They left me everything. Their home, the money they'd carefully saved over all their years together. I sold their house. That's how I managed to buy the Swifts' place." Another sip of her cider loosened the memories where they stuck in her throat. "Sometimes, I wonder if they would be hurt that I took it all and banked it against having something of my own. Then I remember that they knew what I wanted, and they were never sentimental people." She took a breath and gave him a wry smile. "That was probably more than you wanted to hear, right?"

"I want to hear whatever you want to tell me."

His earnest reply soothed the ache of old grief.

The waiter came to clear their dishes and offer them dessert menus.

Joss's response was quick. "Just the check."

Nan eyed the old-fashioned dessert cart poised just inside the dining room door. "No dessert?"

Joss looked like a kid in front of Kate's cupcake case. "I've got that covered."

"Really?"

"Definitely."

THERE WAS ONLY another month before taking the mountain road over to Mad River Glen might require snow chains, so Joss took advantage and headed northeast and up towards the pass. When, once down in Warren Village, Nan asked if they could go into a craft boutique she'd always been curious about, Joss stopped, but he seemed reluctant to follow her inside.

He lingered at the doorway, but the woman behind the counter came out to greet them with wide open arms. "Joss Fuller!"

"Linda." He hugged her, reluctance melting away. "You look younger every year."

"Flatterer," she chided, but her eyes sparkled.

"Lin, this is Nan Grady. Nan bought the Swifts' place—the big old Victorian next door to my parents' farm. She's running it as a B&B."

Linda had the lean lines of a skier or a swimmer. Nan figured she probably hiked and practiced yoga, too. Linda also had kind eyes that Nan understood saw far more than just Joss's new neighbor.

"Hi, Linda. It's nice to meet you."

"Linda's a potter." Joss finished the introductions. "She taught me what little I know about it, and sponsored me when I wanted to join the crafters co-op here as a woodworker."

Linda laid a maternal hand on Joss's arm. "He was a junior at Thornton back then. Some of the others thought he was too young, but I loved his work." She picked up a small turned-wood bowl near the register, jingling the change and keys within. "I still do."

Joss looked wistfully at the little bowl. Nan ran a finger along the burled edge. She looked at Joss in wonder.

"You two look around," Linda said with a less-than-subtle nod at the jewelry displays. "Let me know if you need anything."

Nan splurged and bought herself a small watercolor—a snow-dusted cornfield, harvested stalks stubbling and shadowing the white, with the moon-frosted mountains filling an imagined night sky. Joss's gentle teasing over her agonized decision curled around her like an embrace.

From her position at the front of the store, Linda the potter looked on. Nan felt that gaze to the roots of her hair.

Fifteen miles north, they sat on the tailgate of Joss's truck, paper cups of hot, spiced cider and the remains of fresh cider doughnuts on a flattened paper bag between them.

"Best dessert ever," Nan leaned across the picnic and kissed him. "Thank you."

Joss caught her chin, holding the kiss between them like a promise. "Best dessert ever."

Nan rested her head against his arm for a moment, enjoying the flow of tourists in and out of the cider mill. "Linda adores you."

"She's great."

"I really do want to know more about you." Nan tilted her head, leaning forward to look him in the eye. "It's like your superhero alter-ego, this side of you who makes beautiful objects and rubs noses with potters and agents and dealers."

Joss turned, crumpling the bag and tossing it into a nearby trash can. "It's just something about me that most people know. It's old news," he said. "Let's head back, and I'll tell you anything you want to know on the ride home."

THEY CHASED the setting sun over the mountains, sinking into the valley along with the last trails of fuchsia sunlight. The woods and streams, farmland, and village centers blurred past. The cab of Joss's truck took on the closeness of a confessional.

Contrary to his offering, Nan didn't ask him anything. She sang along with his music and watched the scenery. He made an impulse decision to take the interstate up to South Burlington. Selfishly, he wanted to keep her for a little longer, and the more monotonous road would give his mind a little more space to tell her a story.

"You know that moment, the one where everything is going to be perfect?" He spoke over the fading guitar notes of a favorite song.

He saw in her face that she did know.

"Ten minutes before you walked into my inn for the first time." She spoke without thinking; he knew that. Knowledge didn't stop a tiny stab of disappointment. Swallowing a clever remark, he opened up the door to his rarely-spoken-of time in New York.

It was Patrick who welcomed him to the co-opted warehouse space in a forgotten, industrial corner of Brooklyn where the artists were

congregating. It was a vast, neglected space, but there was life spark-
ing–literally– in the haphazardly divided areas of the hangar-sized
space. A fused-metal jeweler waved from behind a welding mask; she
had bells in her dreadlocked hair. A shared kiln serviced several potters
and ceramics artists. A large-format, self-described "collagist" occupied
one somewhat brightly lit corner, and a makeshift wood shop another.

Patrick slapped a notebook nailed to the wall. "This is our best
attempt at a schedule. Pencil your hours in. Don't be an asshole about
it." From where Joss stood, "don't be an asshole" pretty much summed
up the slapdash bylaws of the small commune. So, he shook Patrick's
hand and forked over his rent for the month. He rode the F train from
Brooklyn to Jack and Seth's loft with a head full of designs and ideas
for reclaiming material.

Seth Weston had introduced him to Patrick; Jack had introduced
him to Seth. Seth was a friend from Williams, someone Jack had run
with during his Harvard law school years, while Seth dropped out of
his paid internship at a venture capitalist firm to manage a Newbury
Street gallery and try his hand at representing artists.

When Jack landed at the Midtown offices of Kearney-Mulligan,
Seth packed up and headed to Manhattan with him; he'd lost someone
close to him, he'd been in need of a change. Jack's effortless success
had supported them both, after a fashion. Jack kept one of Joss's foot-
stools in his bedroom; Seth had seen potential.

Joss had been dazzled by the future Seth painted for him. Galleries
vying for his work, Upper East Side ladies slumming it to snatch up
his latest piece, extravagant openings, high ticket prices, riding the
tide of artisan everything to uncharted success.

For a while, he told Nan, it all came true. He found a couple of
jobs–set-building for a non-Equity theater company, working the
door at a club–and spent the rest of his time sourcing material for
pieces and toiling away in the shared space in Brooklyn.

He didn't tell her about his brief affair with the dreadlocked
jeweler or the early-days thrill of having underage girls flashing him
to get into the club. It had all gone sour in his memory. Seth brokered

a deal, got him gallery space, arranged an opening. For a few months, it seemed as if he was on his way.

It wasn't an easy thing to discover you were a flash in the pan.

After a while the commissions slowed, the sales dried up, the gallery space was handed to the next starving wonder. Warehouse rent was harder to come up with, and he spent too much time trying not to pick fights with his loft-mates. Jack, professional dispute moderator that he was, told him to go home for a week and cool off.

He did go home and cool off. Six weeks later he drove down, packed his things, and left his keys. His last stop was in Brooklyn to pick up the tools in his locker at the warehouse.

They were passing through Vergennes, fifteen minutes from The Damselfly, when he laid open that last dark corner of his past. "I wasn't proud of it, giving up." He couldn't look at her, couldn't bear to see pity in her bourbon eyes.

"You didn't." It wasn't a platitude. He heard her conviction and waited for the rest. She shifted in her seat. He snuck a glance at her profile in the slanted sun. "You're still making art. Just not according to someone else's rules. And you're saving round barns and innkeepers in distress."

"Thank you." He wasn't sure she had it all right, but the weight of it was gone. She knew. "Speaking of your distress, did you ever talk to Danny about the other night?"

"She says she didn't do it."

Joss slowed to make the turn that would cut over and behind the college and bring them to the inn past his parents' farm. "And that's it?"

"I'm not a prosecutor," she snapped. "Someone has to be kind to this girl. And –"

"Yeah, I know. It was my idea." He kept his eyes on the road. "Except it wasn't my idea."

"I was going to say that I don't think it was her, but I think she might know who it was, and pressing her too hard might not be the right thing to do just yet."

"Okay, but please –" He reached out to brush her cheek. "Be careful."

∾

HIS VOICE WAS hoarse when he asked her to take care. She thought at first it was emotion, but realized it was more that he was talked-out. Nan had tumbled headlong into his story, walking the streets of New York with him. The loft shared with a younger Jack, a younger Seth. She'd smelled solder and sawdust in the artists' commune in Brooklyn. Her heart had squeezed at his departure. Her own pride understood how much that perceived failure had cost him.

Pride was a prickly thing. She'd had the perfect opportunity to mention to him that things were falling apart. That bookings were down, that guests were leaving unhappy, that the lost weeks of reservations were going to end up being the least of her worries. Holding back from him felt like lying, somehow, but she couldn't push the words past her lips.

Twilight was coming on when Joss parked the truck outside the inn. "I never meant to unload all of that on you."

She scooted as close to him as the truck's center console would allow and reached up to lay her palm on his faintly scratchy cheek. "Lunch was incredible, the whole afternoon was amazing." She pressed her lips to his. "Thank you."

He combed his fingers into her hair, angling their mouths and teasing her lips with his tongue. Nan cursed the barriers between them and the mountain of work waiting in her office. It would be so easy to surrender to the spicy sweetness lingering in their mouths, to take him upstairs and let him wipe all the worry from her mind.

Joss caught her glance at the waiting inn. "Can I walk you in?"

Nan shook off her regret. He didn't need her baggage. "Better not. Once you're over the threshold, I don't think I could resist dragging you upstairs."

He nuzzled the soft skin below her ear. She felt more than heard his words. "I'm definitely walking you in."

"I'll be okay between here and the door."

Joss's response came on a frustrated growl. "I don't know if I will."

She kissed him again, playfully nipping his bottom lip. "I'll make it up to you. Promise."

He waited in the cab of the truck until she was inside. She waved from the kitchen window, watching him drive away with her heart still riding shotgun.

CHAPTER 32

*M*ake it up to him she did.

She was hardly a blushing virgin, but lovers had been few and far between. More often than not, her fantasies outstripped the actual men in her life. The power she felt, being with Joss, beckoned to her. The idea that her fantasies might be closer to reality was a sweet one.

Save the lavender for when you really want to knock his socks off, Kate had said.

They'd teased one another occasionally about their contractor-client relationship, and she'd had more than a few risqué thoughts about him while he was on the job. Maybe it was time she trusted him enough to act on those fantasies.

Several days later she called him on a morning he'd told her would be fairly light, a morning her own schedule wasn't too full, swallowing back butterflies and hoping her deception would be well-taken.

She dressed carefully, a slim skirt and crisp blouse.

"I've got maybe fifteen minutes before I have to head into town. Cora Pease wants to redo her master bathroom," he was saying, head stuck under her bathroom sink, looking for the leak she'd asked him about on the phone.

"If I can't get it taken care of, I'll put a call in to my plumber. He'll sort you out."

Not exactly what she had in mind. "Joss?"

"Mmm?"

She dropped her voice to a throaty stage whisper. "I might have been wrong about the sink."

She was three buttons into undoing her blouse when he backed out from under the sink. Under the crisp white cotton, she revealed a fantasy of lilac lace to not only Joss, but her own reflection in the bathroom mirror. Her color was high, her eyes wicked.

"I –" He stood, started toward her, but she put out a hand to stop him. Holding him with her gaze, she slowly slipped the fourth button undone, the fifth, parting the cloth, running her hands up the column of her throat.

She closed her eyes and shivered. Stretched her shoulders, let her hands drift to the valley between her breasts. Ran delicate fingertips across the scalloped lace, pulled the plackets of her blouse away, slipped the sleeves down her arms.

No sooner had the cotton ghosted to the floor, she reached behind her back.

THE RASP of her zipper clawed at Joss's self-control.

Watching as she slid her hands down her belly, beneath the gray wool of the slim skirt, was nearly his undoing.

She stepped out of the skirt, gingerly. Dark gabardine pooled on the honey-toned plank floors.

She glowed with purpose and pleasure, delighting in the tight, hungry set of his jaw, his obvious desire. Gently, she toed off her ballet flats, pushed a stray curl from her cheekbone and took a small step towards him, invitation clear in her eyes.

He gathered her back against the counter, hitching her legs up around his hips, burying his hands in her hair, tipping her head back to take her mouth. She met him there, aching, greedy, hands grasping, tugging at the clothes that separated them.

He had no thoughts for finesse, only the hard need to claim her, fill her, possess her. Barely free of his jeans, he slipped her panties aside, found her hot and slick. Grasping her hips, he drove into her. She clung to him, chased his storm, let it overtake her, before settling, wrapped around him, her lower back pressed into the beige laminate.

He touched his forehead to hers, willing his heart to slow, his lungs to draw breath.

"Jesus, woman. Do you have any idea what you do to me?"

She kissed him then, tenderly, smiling against his mouth, and slid down his body, until her toes touched the wood floor.

"I think I have a fair idea," she said, stepping away to retrieve her blouse and skirt. Joss pulled himself together, the familiar zipping and buckling grounding him again. Before she could busy herself with dressing, he reached for her hand.

He traced the pale vein on the inside of her wrist with a finger, pulled her close, skimmed his free hand from her hip, up her spine, to cradle her head. Held her there against his heart for a moment, before pressing his lips to hers.

"I'll see you later," he promised.

HE WASN'T able to take his mind off Nan all day. The sight of her, aglow with mischief and pleasure, loitered at the edge of his vision. He replayed the scene in his head, her slim fingers on her buttons, the feel of her in his hands, the heat, her playful laughter. A day of meetings, phone calls, and paperwork nearly drove him mad.

What he craved was a day of hard physical labor, framing, flooring, siding, anything to tamp down the desire to drive back into the valley and have his way with her, guests at the inn be damned.

By quitting time he was hell bent on getting to her. He dialed her number as he drove west past Thornton College.

"You mentioned guests checking in when we talked earlier this morning, before…" he trailed off, caught up again in the vision of her.

"I do have a party of six in three rooms through the weekend. They checked in about an hour ago. I'm on my way in to serve tea."

He bit back disappointment, but a plan was already forming.

"I'm on my way out to the farm. I have a few things to take care of, but I need you. Please tell me you want me to come over for dinner?"

She didn't hesitate. "I'll be as free as I ever am after I clean up the tea service. What do you have in mind?"

"You, naked in your bed, with nothing between us but what's necessary."

He could almost hear the heat in her cheeks through the phone.

"I meant for dinner."

He laughed then; two could play at the teasing game. She would think about him, ache for him like he had for her all day. "So did I."

CHAPTER 33

$\mathcal{N}$an did think about him. She couldn't have avoided it if she'd tried.

His soft, teasing voice before he'd disconnected the call echoed in her ears. Her guests, a trio of couples whose sons were roommates at the college, were eager to tour the remodeled Adirondack Suite. She indulged their curiosity, mustering all her charm for the couple with an older daughter who was planning a spring wedding.

She showed them Joss's handiwork, remembering the morning he'd folded towels with her. She answered their questions about her contractor, picturing him after the rainstorm the night they'd met.

They took a brochure and Anneliese's card; she gave them a few recommendations for dinner with their college student children. She tidied the parlor and washed the dishes. She relished her quiet turn-down ritual: folded-back coverlets, a pair of Sweet Pease truffles in Kate's signature shocking-pink box on the nightstand, a stir of the lavender and clove potpourri to scent the room, and she was done.

She turned on the exterior lights and locked the kitchen door. She hadn't yet heard from Joss, so she fixed a plate of leftovers to take upstairs. She would return to lock the front door once her guests were back. She hated making her guests unlock the front door unless they were out very late.

Joss would be there with her by then. A shiver of pleasure ran down her spine.

Their brief encounter in the bathroom that morning had left her buoyed all day. Even all these hours later, there was still a bounce in her step as she climbed the stairs to her apartment. Enacting a fantasy, playing the courtesan, had given her a new piece of herself to examine, and she liked it.

She opened the door and nearly dropped the plate she was carrying. Her coffee table was pushed against the wall, a tartan blanket spread out on the rug in its place.

Her pillar candles were lit in the center, a bottle of wine open next to two tumblers.

Joss was standing by the rolling cart that served as the counter in her kitchenette, unwrapping plates which looked like Molly Fuller's china.

He left the tinfoil, skirted the picnic blanket, took the plate from her hands and set it aside on the bookshelf near the door.

He pulled her close, welcomed her with a kiss. The buoyancy she'd felt all day blossomed into joy. She threw her arms around him and kissed him.

"In case you're mad that I snuck in –" Joss pulled away, smiling. "I brought dinner, courtesy of my mom. She really does like you."

Nan reached for his tee-shirt. "Will it hold, do you think?"

The half-moon was bright through the windows when they eventually sat down together on the tartan blanket. Nan regarded the guttering candles with a wary eye. "We probably should have blown those out, you know. Burning the inn down empty would be bad enough, but I have guests tonight."

Joss's low laugh made her blush. She speared a glazed baby carrot from her plate, waved her fork at him in mocking reprimand. "Don't you dare laugh at me!"

"You started this whole thing with your little performance this morning." He slid his palm up her bare calf.

Laughter and easy intimacy seasoned the meal. They shared a bottle of wine Nan had been holding onto for a few months. Joss packed the dishes up in his mother's picnic basket while Nan blew out the candles. She turned to find him watching her, holding the basket by its handle, an unspoken question in his eyes. She took the basket and set it down next to his feet. Taking his hand, she led him into her bedroom.

CHAPTER 34

$\mathcal{N}$an was in the garden shed, lost in a new favorite song through her headphones, when Danny found her.

"Nan?" Danny was turning a sweat-dampened curl of hair around her fingers, shifting her weight from side to side.

Nan took her headphones out, letting them hang from her palm. "What's up?"

"Do you have some of the white paint for the porch railing? In the garage?"

"I do." Nan tried to think of a spot that needed touching up and came up short. "Why?"

Danny sucked in a huge breath; the words came out in a nervous rush. "I scraped it up with the steel rake while I was turning the soil for those parade roses you wanted me to put in."

"Oh. Okay." Nan knew the exterior trim paint was around, but where?

Danny kept talking, confessing the full extent of her self-perceived transgressions. "I leaned the rake end up against the railing, and I was moving the wheelbarrow and I tripped on the rake handle like an idiot –"

"It's okay." Nan stopped the young woman mid-ramble. "Really. Are you alright?"

Relief flooded Danny's features. "Yeah, just embarrassed. I'll repaint it."

"Another time. Really, Danny, don't worry about it."

"Okay." Danny dropped the hank of hair she'd wound into a fat ringlet. "I'm going to take the roots and weeds around to the compost pile." She looked hopefully at Nan. "I wanted to cut some flowers for the guest rooms, if that's okay, then my mom should be around to pick me up."

"That's a lovely idea. Go on."

Danny dashed around the side of the house. Nan watched her go, a new kind of pride welling up. Danny's monosyllabic reticence and bored-teen shuffle were nearly gone, at least at the inn. In only a few weeks, Danny was opening up and finding real talent and interest.

Nan, seeing the changes in Danny, wondered if in the end it wasn't worth all the trouble she'd caused.

~

JOSS DROPPED by the inn after a long day of punch list work on a kitchen remodel. The view of Lake Champlain from the house in Charlotte almost made up for the client's inability to be satisfied with anything.

The kitchen was dark, but there were lights on in Nan's office, so he let himself in through the front door.

His phone pinged. The parlor was empty, so he took a seat on the bay window seat to cope with the kitchen designer's frantic texts about last-minute changes to the cabinet hardware.

It took a flurry of texts full of web links and photos to reassure the designer. Joss pocketed his phone with a definite yearning for Nan.

Through the bay window, he saw his father maneuvering the tractor into the equipment barn. A glance through the trees that separated the properties showed his mother on the deck watching her husband finish the day's work. Years of familiarity told him she'd probably slip her feet into a spare pair of boots and join him for the evening milking.

The farm had always been his place, even when he'd turned his back on it; his cabin was a refuge he'd made for himself. Nan, and by extension The Damselfly, had quickly become a haven for him.

He wanted home.

He wanted to make a home with her, to come home to Nan, to be her home. He wanted whatever their version of his parents' familiar dance was. All of it. Growing up steeped in love and a deep sense of place, it should have been obvious to him, but it had taken Nan to make it real.

The front door slammed. Joss was expecting to find Nan in the foyer, but he nearly collided with Elisha, just back from a run. Not a good one, from the look of it.

"Joss!" Even sweaty and crabby, she was impressive.

"Elisha." He stepped back from her obvious irritation. "I didn't mean to startle you. Everything okay?"

"Just one of those days, I guess. Started out well enough." She gathered her platinum ponytail back in one hand and smoothed the ends. "My agent called. My publisher is offering me a follow-up contract. I'm going to meet some colleagues for a celebratory drink in town, but I thought I'd get in a run first."

Joss leaned against the door to Nan's office while Elisha talked through her anger.

"So, I got this amazing new training watch, and I'd set it on the porch railing to calibrate while I was stretching. I headed out on a new route, figuring I'd put the supposedly high-sensitivity GPS through its paces on the back roads, only I must have forgotten to put it on–I was distracted, thinking about the book."

Joss thought about some of the back roads in the valley; she could have gotten herself good and lost.

"I finally got myself back here, thinking I'd find the watch on the porch where I must have left it, but it's gone, and I looked upstairs and in my car, just in case I'm crazy and put it there." She puffed a sigh, fluttering the loose tendrils of hair around her face.

"Anyway, it's vanished. I'm late. I'm exhausted."

"I'll keep an eye out for it while I'm here," Joss offered.

Elisha managed a tiny smile. "Thanks, Joss. I'm going to check the kitchen before I shower."

She pushed through the kitchen door. Joss decided to go take a look at the third floor, maybe see if he could find Nan, since she hadn't surfaced.

As he rounded the landing on the second floor, Joss nearly collided with yet another woman who wasn't Nan.

Danny was closing the door to the guest room closest to the landing, and she dropped Nan's ring of master keys in surprise.

"S'ry." Danny muttered, bending to retrieve the keys.

When she stood, her gaze moved between Joss and the stairwell behind him. She dropped the keys into one of her cargo pockets.

Joss wondered what she'd been doing in the guest room.

Elisha jogged up the stairs, still looking cross, and passed them on her way to her room.

Shame tickled the back of his neck for being suspicious, but still he wondered. A missing piece of pricey running equipment, and a kid with a dishonest streak creeping around the guest rooms unattended.

"Actually, Danny, you might know." He struggled to keep his voice level, but innocent until proven guilty was hard to hold onto when this teenage girl could be a threat to Nan. "Ms. McNair is missing her running watch. Have you seen it?"

Danny's eyes widened and her cheeks flushed. "I haven't seen it." Her voice wobbled slightly through the defiant mutter that was her trademark.

Joss tried to see through her shocked expression. Was she an accomplished thief and liar, as well as a vandal? Shame pricked harder at his silent accusations–after all, he'd been the one to plant the idea of clemency in Nan's head, but he couldn't shake the feeling that all was not as it seemed with Danny Beaudette.

"Are you sure? Ms. McNair nearly got lost out in the valley, and she's concerned about it going missing."

"I haven't seen it, okay?" Danny snapped at him and sidled around his roadblock, but Nan started up at the bottom of the stairs and headed her off.

"What's going on?"

"I didn't take the stupid watch." Danny swiped at her eyes and pelted down the stairs, heavy boots stomping the treads as she went.

~

"DANNY?" Nan watched her vanish down the back all toward the terrace.

Joss was glowering after her, perched at the top of the stairs like a knight at the watch.

Nan started up the stairs toward him. "What's going on?"

"I asked her about Elisha's missing watch, and she bolted."

Nan took in the grim set of his mouth and his pocketed hands. He was upset about more than the missing watch.

She'd run into Elisha in the kitchen and heard the tale of the misplaced GPS. She had a theory about it, but she'd wanted to ask Danny about the timing before she took on what might be a significant retrieval project.

"How did you ask her, Joss? She's more or less terrified of everyone as far as I can tell, despite all her bluster."

He drew in a breath. "I didn't yell, I just asked her, pointed out that it was missing and that Elisha could have gotten lost in the valley without it, never mind that it probably cost the earth."

"Elisha," Nan chided, "is a grown woman, and I very much doubt she was in any real danger for an hour out in the valley."

Color crept up Joss's neck. "She could have gotten lost or hurt."

"She could have gotten lost or hurt even wearing a GPS around here."

"Look, Nan." Joss stepped back from her. "That kid isn't telling you everything. I can't trust her like you seem to, and while I don't want to see her in court, I don't like her being here all the time either."

The repeat argument was starting to grate on her nerves. "I can –"

He cut her off. "I know, you can take care of yourself."

Nan stepped back. His snide delivery felt like a slap. "When you say it like that, I have a hard time believing you. For the record, I'm not, nor frankly is Elisha, some damsel in distress."

"Hey…"

Nan felt it, the rare urge to really let off steam. There was a brief warning flash in her heart–*Stop! He doesn't know you well enough yet!*–but the words poured out anyway.

"Do you know why I was coming up here?"

He said nothing; he barely moved a muscle, but his expression was watchful. If he heard warnings of his own, she was past caring.

"I came up here to ask Danny about something that happened while she was weeding the front gardens. She came to me asking for paint, feeling terrible because she'd scratched the porch trim with a rake. I told her not to worry about it, that we'd take care of it another time, and she left me go to empty the wheelbarrow into the compost heap."

Her anger pushed her past him, and she paced the second floor hallway.

"Then I hear from Elisha about her new watch, GPS thing, vanishing from the porch railing, and I think, huh, maybe it was there while Danny was weeding, and it got knocked into the compost pile?"

He stood stock still, taking her tirade in silence.

"I figured it was worth checking before I decided to get hip deep in three months' worth of hot green-waste, because it might be right on top of the heap, if that's where it ended up, or Danny might have done the right thing and turned the pile.

"Now I have to go find her and apologize for your accusations before I can find out from her if she thinks maybe some three-hundred-dollar fitness gadget is buried in my future garden mulch." She was about to rein herself in when a half-remembered conversation with him surfaced from the night the door was shot at. *This guy shot at your home …* "And whatever happened to the guy who shot out my windows. Somewhere in your gut, you know there's more to this than just Danny."

Her temper flared so rarely that the long-winded speech left her shaky and a little breathless. She let her words hang in the hallway between them while she pulled herself together.

Joss spoke first. "Do you really think that about me? That I have some kind of misguided White Knight complex?"

As was often the case, the fight went out of Nan as quickly as her temper had flashed over. "Sometimes, yes."

She watched as he shuttered himself from her. It was as clear as watching someone physically close up the windows.

"I'm sorry you feel that way."

She thought about going to him, about softening the blow from her anger with the affection that came so easily between them, but the thought of Danny–messy, complicated, fragile Danny–taking refuge from his unspoken accusations somewhere on the property, held her where she was.

"I need to find her." She willed him to open up to her again, just for a moment. "I hope you'll still be here after I do."

<h1 style="text-align:center">CHAPTER 35</h1>

ometimes, yes.

Joss wondered how she did that–packed more hurt into two words than an entire one-sided argument.

She had no idea, none, how deeply he worried for her, how deeply she'd burrowed into his heart. The thought of anyone doing so much as giving her a difficult hour was unacceptable.

It stung his pride, to have his concern dismissed as some kind of delusion of grandeur. He looked out for her because he loved her.

A car in the driveway, followed by a metallic slam and then the slap of the wooden screen at the kitchen door, broke his train of thought.

He saw the aging Celica pull out, saw Nan standing on the pea stone driveway, and knew that Danny had gone home with her mother. Time to swallow his pride and make things right with Nan.

He stepped out onto the front porch a moment later to the growly sound of Nan shifting through the gears on her way east on County Road.

As soon as she was gone, another car pulled in, a sedan with out-of-state tags.

A couple climbed out of the car, twining their fingers together as soon as they reached one another. From the expectant pleasure on their faces, he took them to be guests.

To further complicate matters, Elisha came out the front door behind him, pushing some kind of giant pin into her gleaming twist of platinum hair.

She hadn't been kidding about going out. She looked every inch the part: deep purple dress wrapped around her tall, ruthlessly fit body, high heels, impressive sparkle on her fingers, at her ears.

"Everything okay?"

From the look on her face, she'd heard some of their argument on the landing. Joss chose to ignore it.

The couple approached them, starry-eyed as they took in The Damselfly in all its early autumn glory.

"Miss Grady?" The man directed his inquiry at Elisha.

Elisha smiled indulgently at him when he stepped back to let the woman walk up the steps first.

He towered over all of them, whip thin, with charmingly mussed hair and eyes reserved only for the black-haired sprite of a woman at his side.

He reached out for Elisha's glittering, polished hand. "Chris Todd, and this is Cara Takami. We're here to tour the rooms?"

Shit. She'd had an appointment.

Elisha opened the front door, and was already expertly guiding them inside before he could figure out what to do.

"I'm Elisha McNair. Ms. Grady had to step out, but I'd be happy to show you the inn. You're going to love the Adirondack Suite. The recent remodels have…"

Elisha's voice trailed off as the trio ascended the stairs.

He stood on the porch, feeling utterly useless. The frustration itched; he knew the best way to scratch it would be to put in a few hours on a project.

The drawings for Nan's four poster were back up at the cabin. It wasn't likely he was going to be needed at The Damselfly anytime soon. Better to head up to Catmint Gap and get some work done.

Better still to make right what he could before he left.

The compost pile was behind the garden shed in the far corner of the yard where lawn gave way to scraggly brush or pasture, depending on the direction. Nan kept it corralled with a tall plastic ring, and a short-handled pitchfork stood guard in her absence.

Ignoring the trident sentinel, Joss dug into the compost bare-handed, praying there wasn't anything too fresh under the weeds and garden trimmings. It took him less than four minutes to wrap his hand around the flexible band of the GPS unit.

He carried it inside cupped in his palm like an injured bird.

From the sounds of it, Elisha was still up on the third floor with the wedding couple. He stopped to wash his hands and wipe down the GPS, and then climbed three shame-filled flights to return it to its owner.

When he later caught himself watching the inn in his rearview mirror, he pushed back his regret and drove on. He and Nan weren't going to see eye to eye on the subject of Danny Beaudette.

One thought crept into his heart as he drove: *what else wouldn't they see eye to eye on?*

NAN PULLED her car in behind Terri Beaudette's at the house on Kiln Road. Terri started to approach, but Danny stopped her mother. Nan left the windows up to give the mother and daughter some privacy. When Terri shrugged and went inside the house, Nan stepped out of the car.

Danny assumed the defensive. "I didn't take anything."

"I know you didn't."

"I didn't –" Danny stopped short when Nan's words sank in. "You do?"

"Yeah." Nan leaned against the hood of her car. "I wanted to find you, to ask you if it could've fallen into the wheelbarrow and ended up in the compost. But you were gone."

Danny blinked at her. Nan saw the child she'd only recently stopped being.

Danny wrapped her arms around her chest. "I guess. Yeah."

Nan saw a chink in Danny's armor. "I'm going to be honest with you, Danny. I don't think someone who's as good with my gardens as you are would have torched a flowering shrub. I just don't buy it."

Danny's eyes dropped. She shuffled her toes in the dirt driveway.

Nan pressed on. "If you didn't do that, I have a hard time believing you tagged my garage or broke my windows. You might not trust me, and you're sure as hell angry at someone, but you didn't do those things."

Danny looked back at her, really looked at her, and the plea in her expression nearly broke Nan's heart.

"You don't even have to tell me who it was, but tell me I'm right. Tell me it wasn't you."

"It wasn't …" Danny struggled, gripping the sleeves of her shirt, hugging herself hard and staring at a point just over Nan's shoulder.

Nan could feel her heart in her throat.

"It wasn't anyone else." Danny glared at Nan, but the defiance was shaded with what Nan thought was fear. "It was me. I did all that stuff because I was pissed off about moving back here."

Nan clenched her fingers. She'd been so sure, so certain that Danny was going to admit there was more to the story.

"I have to go inside. My mom needs me."

Danny spun on her heel and vanished into the house.

When Nan got back in the car, she realized with a start that she'd completely forgotten the newlyweds who were coming for a tour.

Her tires spit up dust and small stones as she whipped the car into reverse. She heard a rock ding Terri Beaudette's car and winced. One more inadvertent thing she'd done to hurt them.

CARA AND CHRIS were just finishing their tour with tea and brownies in the kitchen when Nan came in. Elisha was telling them all about

the town. They seemed dazzled by her, and Nan wondered once again if she should consider Elisha as her spokeswoman.

Elisha seamlessly turned them over to Nan and departed. Nan got the feeling the other woman was running late. Another nacreous layer on the pearl of shame in her belly.

In the end, they were an easy sell. They were enchanted by the inn, and enthusiastic about reserving it for the bridal party. Their optimism banished a fraction of Nan's unease about the inn's continued success. Not everyone, it seemed, was turned off by recent events.

She promised to put together an estimate that included a small rehearsal dinner on the property. It was past time to take that leap. She showed them to their car, wishing them a safe journey north to stay with friends who lived near Burlington.

The inn waited in the dark, empty and grim.

Joss and his truck were noticeably absent when she'd pulled into the driveway. His stubborn insistence that Danny was hiding something rang true, but she couldn't get past the way he refused to trust her instincts. It was a fissure in their growing intimacy.

Her tirade looped and echoed behind her eyes. She wasn't sure which upset her more, Joss or her own vitriol.

She needed Kate, who answered on the first ring. "Hey sugar plum. What's up?"

"Can you come over tonight?"

Kate missed nothing. "Are you okay?"

Nan kicked the gravel at her feet. It was childish, but it made her feel better to lash out at something. "No."

"Is it ice cream-worthy?"

"Peanut butter-fudge swirl worthy," Nan said, a smile creeping along her lips.

"I'll be right over–Damn!" Kate swore.

"What?"

"I'm supposed to meet with Anna in ten minutes about doing a wedding cake portfolio for her clients."

The creeping smile curved more fully. She had girlfriends. "If she can stay out late, invite her along."

"Is this about Joss?" Kate asked. "They're related, remember."

Nan considered a moment. "Maybe she can shed some light?"

"Uh-oh," Kate said. "I'll see you later. With peanut-butter fudge swirl and Anneliese, if she can make it."

CHAPTER 36

$\mathscr{A}$nneliese arrived first, knocking twice on the kitchen door.

Nan was tossing a few stray pieces of laundry into her hamper and straightening the apartment. Anything to pass the time instead of fretting about Joss and Danny. She followed the knocking downstairs.

"You don't have to knock." She hugged Anneliese hard. Her friend's hair smelled like Kate's bakery. "You're not a guest."

"Am I allowed to ask why we're convening, or do we have to wait for Kate?"

Nan laughed grimly. "Everything's going to hell in a handbasket."

"Kate had better get here soon." Anneliese followed her upstairs with a sigh.

No sooner had they closed the door, than Kate's van flew into the driveway. The engine clunked into park, and Kate hopped out. Anneliese watched out the window as Kate unloaded a pastry box and a wine-tote.

Anneliese watched, impressed. "Is she always prepared for a horde of starving Marines?"

"She wasn't like this growing up?" Nan asked.

"She was Jack's annoying, then annoyingly pretty, little sister when we were growing up. By the time I was old enough to have seen her as a friend, I was gone. There were… poor choices, then Chad, and Chloe…" She paused. "When I came home, she was already running Sweet Pease."

Kate pushed through the door, depositing a bottle of wine and the pastry box on the table. "We're drinking white tonight, girls. I left the rest of the bottles in your wine fridge."

"What's in the box?" Nan asked, grabbing three jelly jars from the cabinet over her sink.

"Banana chocolate chip muffins, and some prosciutto and brie panini." Kate opened the box. "We cannot live on ice cream alone."

Anneliese took the jelly jars from Nan and started unwrapping the neck of the wine bottle. The look she gave Kate was pure awe. "I seriously can't wait to start sending my clients to you."

"So you two had a good meeting?" Nan asked, setting down some mismatched flea-market china on her coffee table.

Kate and Anneliese exchanged a knowing look as Anneliese sat on the sofa. "Sugar plum," Kate said, folding herself into the chair, "Anna and I didn't come here to discuss our meeting. What happened?"

Nan took a drink of her wine and sat next to Anneliese. "Now that I've dragged you both over here, it seems silly."

"Assuming my cousin's been an idiot," Anneliese smiled, "which despite excellent genes, is possible due to his inherent maleness, what did he do?"

It took a few jars of wine to get through the entire saga of Elisha's GPS, the argument, and her impulsive trip out to Kiln Road. Joss's absence when she returned rounded out the tale.

"So he was being an idiot," Anneliese confirmed.

"What did he say when you called him on it?" Kate pulled a sandwich from the box.

"I didn't. I was so hurt and …" Nan cast around for the right word and came up short. "Pissed. Which isn't really justification for behaving like a shrew."

"Nan," Kate said gently.

"No, I was–I am–angry." Nan peeled the wrapper from a muffin.

Kate took the wrapper from her and tossed it in the paper bag with the rest of the trash. "And when you get angry, you get defensive and weepy."

"Definitely defensive this time," Nan admitted. "But not weepy. I have that in my favor anyway. If I call him, though, I'll probably cry. And I haven't heard from him since I got back."

"Should I call Jack?" Kate asked.

"God, no," Nan said, "this is already too much like eighth grade."

Kate snickered.

"But with better kissing," Anneliese reminded her.

Kate's snicker became a full blown laugh, and Anneliese giggled.

"Much better kissing," Nan admitted, succumbing to the laughter until it fizzled out.

"Sugar plum, you know Joss." Kate looked to Anneliese for backup. "And we've seen the two of you together. You'll work it out."

"I know," Nan said. "I know he loves me."

"Wait!" Kate said, straightening in her chair, "Did he say it?"

"Are we sixteen?" Nan asked.

"We are if you didn't tell me he said, 'I love you!'" Kate exclaimed.

"He did," Nan said with a half-sad smile. "I'm not that brave."

"You will be, though." Kate sighed. "I think this calls for a second bottle of wine."

Anneliese was quiet.

Nan turned to her. "I'm sorry, Anna," she said. "This conversation can't be easy for you."

"I ran away with the wrong guy. I was infatuated with him," she said slowly, "and he cared for me; just not enough. When I met Chad, I fell for a fairy tale that never existed. I loved him, and he loved having me on his arm." She took a deep breath and rubbed at her wrist. "When he stopped loving that, he took it out on me."

Kate got up to go downstairs for the wine. As she passed Anneliese, she squeezed her shoulder. Nan and Anneliese were quiet for a moment.

"Nan," Anneliese said, "this is just a bump in the road. You know that, right?"

"I do," Nan said. "I lost my perspective earlier." She reached out for Anneliese's hand. "I needed my girlfriends to help me find it again."

"Thanks," Anneliese replied.

Kate came back in with two bottles. She let the neck of the already open one hover over Anneliese's glass. "What do you think?"

"Wish I could," said Anneliese, "but I have to get myself home. I can't leave my parents on their own with Chloe all night."

"Right. One more glass for me, then, since I'm fully intending to stay here tonight." Kate poured Nan's and her own from the open bottle. "But first, we figure out how you're going to fix things with Joss."

"I'm going to call him in the morning," Nan said.

"You could call him tonight." Anneliese grinned. "Then you wouldn't be alone when we left."

Kate raised her glass. "I do like the way you think."

"It's coming back to me." Anneliese smiled.

"So you'll call him in the morning? Tell him you need to talk it through with him. And that you're not wearing underwear?" Kate clarified.

Nan chucked a nearby throw pillow. Anneliese giggled.

"Oh, that's right," Kate teased, swigging the last of the wine in her glass, "you'd rather take them off for him."

Anneliese's giggles turned to full-blown laughter. In the end, Anneliese went home to her daughter, and Kate curled up next to Nan in her double bed.

Kate rose early with her and left to open the bakery. "Come by later this morning. I'll feed you a sandwich and you can tell me all about make up sex with Joss."

Nan could only stare at her best friend's retreating backside.

～

NAN'S PHONE felt heavy in her pocket all morning, but she let the hours tick by without making the call she'd promised to Kate. She wanted to talk to Joss, to smooth things over, to assure herself they were okay, but she kept hoping he would be the one to wave the white flag.

It would be easy to soothe both of their ruffled feathers, but she sensed in her bones that this was an important thing, this disagreement.

Elisha breezed through in the morning, swallowing scalding coffee and passing on cinnamon-almond buckwheat muffins.

Nan stopped her. "Thanks for saving me last night."

Elisha gave her the all-knowing half-smile. "It was nothing. And Joss found the GPS in the compost bin, after all."

Nan bit down the snapped reply that threatened. "Did he?"

Elisha avoided Nan's simmering temper, and departed.

When lunch time arrived without any word from him, Nan drove herself into town to take Kate up on the sandwich.

Sweet Pease was never empty, but midday was a particularly busy time at the bakery. Kate did a brisk business in sandwiches from the time the morning coffee crowd dispersed until the afternoon snackers came in. Kate employed a counter and register crew so she could focus on recipes and wedding cakes and the running of the business; they looked harried today. Nan took pity and kept her order simple.

"I'll take it to go," she said with a head tilt in the direction of the kitchen, "and visit the boss."

Kate was working in what Nan thought of as the Wedding Cake Lab. She was wearing her signature fuchsia chef's jacket and her hair ruthlessly scraped back and caught up in a baker's cap. Kate bit her upper lip when she was concentrating, and today there was a rosy flush of irritation over her mouth. In front of her was a rigged contraption of upside-down cake pans and plastic wrap on a rotating cake stand. She was tracing a filigree of icing over the plastic, a lacy web of curls with floral echoes. A piece of ivory lace in a clear plastic sleeve was pinned to the cork board behind the workstation, along with a photograph of a bouquet and another of an antique diamond solitaire ring.

Nan waited until Kate reached a pause in the tracery. "Hey, you."

Kate set her pastry bag down and pressed her sugar-dusted fingers into the small of her back. "Is it lunch time already?" She glanced at the clock on the opposite wall. "I guess it is."

Nan held up her paper bag. "I got you a sandwich."

Kate pursed her lips, but her eyes sparkled. "You didn't just buy me a sandwich from my own shop?"

Nan set the bag down. "I did, but you're buying the drinks."

When Kate came back with two bottles of sparkling water, she was in interrogation mode. "Did you call him?"

Nan shook her head, swallowing a mouthful of vineyard-style chicken salad on oatmeal bread.

Kate opened a water and pushed it across the counter to Nan. "Did he call you?" When Nan didn't reply, Kate changed the subject. "Okay." Kate wiped a smear of mayo from the corner of her mouth. "Remember how I told Robbie to ask Deirdre out, that night at Temple?"

Nan did remember. Kate had a gift for everyone's love life but her own. "Yeah?"

"He's started spending a lot less time crying at the bar." Kate was triumphant. "I am a matchmaking genius."

"What about you?" Nan asked. She made a show of casually packing her trash up in the bag. "Did that guy from the distributor ever call?"

"He called. I brushed him off." When Nan raised an inquiring eyebrow, Kate elaborated. "I don't need to waste time on a guy who's already on the road. My business is already enough of a demanding relationship."

Nan was unconvinced, but it was time to get back to work. Work, and being indecisive about calling Joss. "I've got some other errands; I should head out."

Kate shot a look at the tiers of icing drying in the Lab. "I should get back to that, but I'll walk you out."

Nan hugged Kate, comforted by the familiar smell of shampoo and flour that clung to the friend who was her anchor. "No need. I can find the front door."

"Nan?"

"Yeah?"

"Call him."

CHAPTER 37

$\mathcal{J}$oss was in his workshop on the farm, sweating out his mad. He chose to ignore the fact that he was strenuously hand-sanding a bedpost that was part of a gift for the very woman who'd made him so angry.

It made a sick kind of sense to hole up in plain sight of her home and work himself numb on the bed project. He'd deliberately parked out of sight of the inn, but he couldn't resist the view of the yellow Victorian down the road. When Nan had climbed into her VW and headed for town, he'd seen her go.

The pieces of the bed frame were nearly finished. It was one of his best. He knew that the same way he knew now that Nan was meant for him. That it was made for her wasn't lost on him–the delicate design coaxed from birch wood, strong and flexible. All qualities he found so appealing in the woman herself.

His muscles knew the motion of hand finishing, leaving his mind free to wander over their exchange the previous afternoon.

He played and replayed their conversation. He knew he'd jumped to conclusions; he knew he was being unreasonable. His own culpability was more than half the mad.

And that knowledge was the rest of the mad, if he was being honest. It wasn't Nan he was angry at at all.

The crazy part of it was, if he let himself be honest, he was proud of her, and pleased by the way she'd taken Danny in. The pleasure and the pride were tainted with mistrust. Not for Nan or her motives, but for Danny's.

She was hiding something, and Joss didn't like waiting for the other shoe to drop.

He was in danger of over-sanding. He ran a tack cloth over the wood, leaving it gleaming and free from dust. The pale birch would soak up the satiny finish. It would look like spun gold in the morning light of Nan's bedroom.

Shrugging off the frustration, he moved the post to the far wall where its companions rested. If he got started with the staining, it would only be another week before he could decide the bed's fate.

Assuming that, in a week, he knew what direction his and Nan's fate was heading in.

NAN GOT BACK to the inn with no time to spare before afternoon tea. Phoning Joss would have to wait.

After the scones, fruit, tea and coffee were laid out in the parlor, she collapsed in her desk chair. Her phone mocked her. What was she planning on saying to him?

Hi, Joss. I'm sorry I wailed at you like a harpy, but you are acting like a caveman, and I'm not interested in being dragged around by my hair?

Hey, Joss. Let's pretend that argument never happened, but let it erode our new relationship before it's really begun?

A delicate cough at the doorway roused her. Shame flushed her cheeks. "Yes, Mrs. Postiglione?"

"I'm so sorry to disturb you, but can you recommend somewhere we could get a quick meal tonight? Our son's recital isn't until eight o'clock and he warned us there isn't much open later."

Nan arranged her face into a politely helpful mask. "Temple, on

Main Street. Tell your server you're a guest and they'll take ten percent off the bill, and if the roast pork is on the menu, I highly recommend it."

When her guest was gone, she picked up her phone, pulling up Joss's number.

The inn's landline rang. Her insurance agent calling to check on the repairs. With a sigh, Nan set her cellphone aside and resolved to call Joss later.

When a dozen small things had stolen what remained of her evening, Nan gave up on trying to fix what she and Joss had broken. She was too tired for patience and tears. The insurance agent's call was followed by an inquiry about the bridal suite which resulted in a flurry of emails to Anneliese and Kate about referrals and cakes. Kate told her she needed to start considering hosting the actual weddings, and a quick search of zoning and codes led to a frustrating series of messages to three Town Hall offices.

Three new reservations appeared in the system for November, and Nan began to hope again that she'd been wrong to consider failure. Her optimism was interrupted by another knock at the office door.

The other guests were interested in local breweries and wineries. Nan had pulled up tour information for several, and sent them off to a popular wine and tapas bar on the way up to Burlington. A possible booking turned into a long conversation about the crime rate in the Champlain Valley; Nan summoned her deepest reserve of patience to assure them the vandalism they'd heard about on Yelp was an isolated event.

A throbbing headache sent her upstairs in search of Advil, and her bed was too tempting to turn away from.

She fell asleep in her clothes, stretched out diagonally on her bed as darkness thickened over the valley.

Staining went longer than Joss planned; night hung heavily over the farm when he finished cleaning his space. He thought about calling a truce and dropping by the inn, but the flood lights were the only illumination he could see. Nan's office and apartment windows were dark, the kitchen unlit, the guests tucked in for the night.

They'd certainly gone longer than twenty-four hours without talking before, but not with this kind of tension between them.

Again, Joss was struck by how fast they'd gone from strangers to so tightly wound together. The bonds between them tugged as he slipped his truck into fifth gear and left the valley behind, and he knew it would be a long night.

CHAPTER 38

$\mathcal{N}$an awoke disoriented from a dream of jingling keys and broken glass. The headache was gone, but she felt hollow, as if the painkillers had carved the headache from her skull in her sleep.

The clock on her bedside table screamed an indecent hour.

The dream lingered in the corner of her eye for a moment, but sleep tugged her lids closed.

When she slipped her arm around a stray pillow, she wished like hell it was Joss's solid warmth there beside her, and promised herself she would call him in the morning.

Joss woke to his phone jangling. He felt his day of sanding and staining in every muscle. After stumbling across his room in the dark, he fumbled the phone and swore when it hit the floor. Face up, he could see *Mom* flashing up at him from the screen. His heart leapt into his throat.

"Mom?"

His mother's voice, terse and low, filled his ear. "Josiah, there's been an accident. A car clipped the oak tree at the end of the driveway and flipped over. There's so much smoke, we can't tell if anyone…. Oh, Joss… We think it's Nan's car."

"What?" It was three A.M. It couldn't be Nan's car.

"I sent your father outside and I called 911, but–"

"I'm on my way."

It was the longest twenty-minute ride of his life; he knew he'd risked his own skin taking the switchbacks on the mountain road at those speeds, but fear and grim determination steadied his hands on the wheel.

It took a lot to truly rattle his mother, and she'd been well and truly rattled. A thousand awful scenarios filled his imagination, all improbable, none with a good ending.

He blew through downtown Thornton praying the police force was either sleeping or already on their way out to the farm. When he cleared the last stand of trees where County Road curved and dropped into the heart of the valley, he could see the farm from a mile away, emergency lights like a flashing beacon drawing him home.

He slowed a fraction as he passed the inn, noting with a breaking heart that Nan's car wasn't parked as usual in front of the garage door. A small cluster of people stood together under the porch light, keeping a distant vigil on the scene unfolding down the road, but Nan's windows were ominously dark.

Joss left his truck down the road a bit and skirted the emergency vehicles. The smoke had cleared, but the car still rested on its roof, headlights shining drunkenly into the trunk of the oak tree. His parents' driveway sparkled with shattered glass, and blue and red light splashed across the farmhouse and barn.

He staggered to a stop when one of the firefighters put an arm out to hold him back. The crew was peeling Nan's car open like a tuna can. The words female and non-responsive drummed in his skull.

He'd let her stew. He hadn't called.

Her phone.

He was pulling up her number when his mother came up beside him.

"Anything?" His mother's face was lined with sleep and worry.

He shook his head while the phone rang and rang. When it went to voicemail, he disconnected the call with shaking fingers.

THE SECOND TIME NAN WOKE, it was the insistent ringing of her phone in the nightstand drawer. A riot of emergency lights danced through her open windows, shocking her fully awake.

She rose, realizing with some embarrassment that she'd fallen asleep in her clothes, and went to the window. Through the screen of trees between the inn and the Fullers' yard, she could make out the two fire trucks, an ambulance, and a trio of police cruisers.

Voices outside alerted her to the presence of more than a few people, far closer than the dairy down the road. She barely stopped to slip her bare feet into her clogs before running downstairs to find out what was going on. Downstairs, her guests were congregated under the front porch light, peering through the trees.

Nan joined them, stepping through the small crowd to stand on the steps. "What's going on? I somehow slept through it."

Elisha leaned out over the rail. "Looks like a car wreck. I heard it, sounded like a trash truck dropped a dumpster. Maybe twenty-five minutes ago? We've all been out –"

Nan was halfway across the driveway, headed for the narrow path through the trees that connected their yards, before Elisha finished. She made her way towards Molly and Walt's house through the darkness, heart in her throat.

The front fender of the car was visible between the emergency vehicles, upside down on the grass in front of the wide oak tree that marked the entry to Fullers' Dairy. The EMTs were working on extracting the passenger from the car, while a police officer stood watch over a young man huddled under a blanket.

She squinted at the car through the flashing emergency lights. Her Volkswagen was the same model, the same color. Her blood ran cold when she saw the license plate.

No coincidence. It was her car.

She started towards the young man on the lawn, intent on finding out what was going on. Her own name, a gravelly prayer called out in the chaos, stopped her.

Joss stood on the other side of the driveway, eyes wide with an expression Nan couldn't quite decipher.

SHE WAS ALIVE. Whole and alive, and standing in his parents' driveway in rumpled hair and wrinkled clothes.

The first responders had dragged him inside to give a statement to the police officers who'd responded to the 911 call. The crew had still been extracting the passenger from the Volkswagen. No one had known yet exactly who was inside. Joss told them what little he'd seen, confirming that the car belonged to Nan, silently begging his phone to ring, for Nan's name to somehow miraculously turn up on his screen.

He'd come outside just as they extracted the woman in the passenger side. He selfishly prayed for it not to be the woman he loved behind the wheel. The sight of a disheveled young man, his head between his knees in the eerie glow of emergency lights, left him numb.

Looking up through the chaos to see her standing there, sleep-tousled and confused, shook him hard, replacing the numbness with a burst of fierce relief.

He jogged across the worn asphalt drive and swung her up, holding her tight against him. "I thought I'd lost you."

She leaned back as he lowered her to her feet. "You haven't lost anything."

"Nan?" Walt Fuller called out across the yard. "Is that you? Isn't that your car?"

Skirting the wreck, she and Joss joined Walt on the grass. She could see Molly through the window, on the phone.

Nan found herself in Walt's quick, warm, and unexpected embrace. "It is, Walt. I have no idea what's going on."

The young man under the emergency blanket tried to pick himself up from the grassy shoulder of the driveway, but he couldn't hold himself upright. One eye was badly bloodied.

Despite his injuries, the boy seemed somehow familiar. His voice was a barely audible croak. "Danny."

Nan left Joss and his father, and knelt next to the boy. He'd let the blanket slip from his thin shoulders, and his bare arms shivered in the cool air. His eyes were squeezed shut, presumably against the tears which leaked down his face regardless.

Nan tugged the blanket back into place and watched the crew peeling back the passenger side door of her car.

Danny? Not her Danny ... The boy's face sharpened in her memory. His arm slung possessively over Danny's softly rounded shoulders outside the high school. Nan fought down a wave of nausea. Her car was ruined, very likely stolen and crashed by Danny's boyfriend with Danny herself trapped and injured in the wreckage.

The EMTs returned and escorted the young man towards the back of one waiting ambulance, and Nan returned to Joss and Walt.

Molly joined them with a jacket for Nan, and the four of them huddled together while the firefighters extinguished the car and pulled Danny Beaudette from the passenger's seat.

"Excuse me, ma'am?" A young police officer approached the quartet, and directed his questions at Molly. "Mrs. Fuller, are you the one who called 911?"

"I am, Toby." When the young man flushed at the collar, Molly corrected herself. "Officer Tunney."

"Ma'am," Toby Tunney turned to Nan. "Is there anything you can add? Mrs. Fuller tells me this is your car?"

Nan lost hold of the panic held at bay by adrenaline. Through tears, she explained that it was her car, stolen from her driveway, but she'd slept through the whole thing. She started to explain her connection to Danny, but the officer's radio crackled and he excused himself to answer.

There was nothing to say as they watched the passenger's rescue from the smoking remains of Nan's Volkswagen. Nan caught the girl's profile in the flashing lights. No doubt now any longer that it was her Danny.

The young officer was speaking to her again. "Ms. Grady? Sergeant Lowry's on his way out. He says he'd like to talk to you. Can you stay?"

Joss took her hand when she nodded her assent.

Molly and Walt excused themselves and went inside. Lights blazed from the kitchen and mudroom.

Pete Lowry's first stop, after assessing the wreckage of Nan's car, was to speak privately with the young man now leaning against the rear fender of Officer Tunney's cruiser.

He approached Nan and the Fullers with a grim expression. "Excuse me, Ms. Grady." He rested his hands in his jacket pocket, but he jerked his chin in the direction of the teenage boy. "Mr. Kelley–Dylan–has a few things to say to you."

Nan peered around Pete Lowry. Dylan. She looked up at Joss. "Will you come with me?"

They approached the boy. Whatever she thought of him, in this moment he was a scared, hurt kid. One she was beginning to suspect had made a lot of bad choices.

From his tone, Sergeant Lowry seemed to feel similarly. "Dylan, say what you need to say to Ms. Grady, then I'm sending you to the ER. Your parents are going to meet us there."

Dylan Kelley flashed a stunned pair of brown eyes at the policeman before turning his reddening face to Nan. When he spoke his voice was a mutter. "Danny didn't do any of that stuff she says she did."

"A little louder, son," Sergeant Lowry prompted.

Something in the boy snapped. "It was me, alright? I broke your window and tagged your garage. I set the fire and shot out the window."

From somewhere within the bubble of shock that was rapidly sealing away Nan's emotions, she understood that Dylan was terrified he'd killed Danny.

A pair of fat tears rolled off Dylan's sooty lashes. He was coming undone.

"Danny was so pissed when the old lady left, and they had to move up to Kiln Hollow. We were up at Arcadia Falls and she was crying, screaming how it wasn't fair. How she couldn't live there, but strangers were going to be allowed all over the old lady's house, and she just wished it would burn down."

Dylan was gasping for air, sobbing with shock and grief. Nan squeezed Joss's hand while they waited out the boy's misery.

"I just thought I'd pull a few pranks, make the new lady sweat a little." He glanced up at Nan with ravaged eyes, and his voice dropped to a whisper. "I wanted to make Danny feel better."

Sergeant Lowry was gruff. "And you two decided to take Ms. Grady's car for a joyride tonight?"

Dylan sniffled. "Danny said she wanted to get out of town. She couldn't take it anymore up there at her uncle's place. I told her we should take her car." Here Dylan nodded at Nan. "We were going to leave it at the train station in Port Henry." He drew in a ragged breath. "We were just going to get the hell out of here, but Danny got cold feet. She tried to stop me. We were fighting over the wheel and I lost control of the car."

His eyes pled with all of them. "She isn't dead, is she?"

Nan stepped forward. "She's alive, just unconscious. We're going to deal with all of this after you get checked out."

Pete Lowry pulled aside the remaining EMT. Nan couldn't hear their brief conversation.

Joss touched her shoulder. "Why don't we go inside?"

She blinked at him. "What about Danny?"

Joss kept his voice low. "You're not going to be able to see her tonight, and I think you need to come inside."

Pete Lowry's agreement was swift and gruffly affectionate. It was easy to let Joss propel her through the Fullers' front door.

He sat her down at the kitchen table and put the kettle on for tea. Nan closed her eyes and listened to Joss move around his mother's kitchen. Surrounded by the warmth of Molly's space, the shock began to wear off. Questions surfaced, firing at the back of her eyelids from all angles. Nan voiced the most obvious one. "How did they get to the inn to take the car?"

Joss set a steaming mug in front of her. "Sugar? Honey?"

He was looking at her as if she might shatter, but this was an easy answer. "Honey."

He put a squat glass jar of honey down between them and sat, warming his hands around his mug. "I don't know. We'll get the answers starting tomorrow." He poured a dollop of honey into her tea.

Nan giggled. The laughter went sideways, bubbling up along with the sting of tears and a wave of weariness. "It is tomorrow."

Joss reached for her hand. "Can you hang on a couple minutes? I want to make sure Mom and Pop are okay, and then I'm taking you home."

She smiled for him. "I'll be fine here for a minute."

Joss took his mug and slipped out of the kitchen to find his parents. The sweet, citrusy tea called to her, but it was all she could do to keep her head up. Letting the exhaustion wash over her, she laid her head on her arms. Just a short rest, just until he came back for her.

WITH THE WORST of the emergency response chaos behind them, the valley was quiet again, but Joss imagined the inn's guests were still wondering what was going on. The idea of leaving his parents, of leaving Nan, was unthinkable, but he didn't want her business to suffer any more.

The answer came to him immediately. He pulled up Elisha's number and texted her, patting himself on the back for putting her number in his phone before her card had gone in the recycling. She wouldn't relish the late night intrusion, but she would know how to spin everything, at least until morning.

He found his mother tidying up his old bedroom. The rush of gratitude hit him hard and fast.

When Molly saw him, she threw her arms around him. "Where's Nan? Is she okay? And those poor children!"

Joss filled her in on as much as he knew, and let her know he'd texted Elisha to handle the inn's guests. "I'm going to take her home. I just wanted to make sure you two were all right before I left."

His mother didn't miss a beat, setting down the pillow she'd been fluffing. "You'll come by in the morning?"

"Of course." He pulled his mother into a hug and kissed her cheek. "Get some sleep, Mom. Tell Pop I'll come by early enough to help with the milking. I don't want him doing it all alone on no sleep."

"I will, hon."

Joss found Nan asleep at the kitchen table.

There were blue-gray smudges under her eyes, and her face was pale. She didn't stir when he nudged her, so he scooped her up and carried her upstairs to the room that had once been his, passing his misty-eyed mother in the hallway.

He laid her down on the double bed, slipping off her shoes and the fleece jacket his mother had given her. She shivered slightly and curled in on herself in her sleep.

With a fresh prayer of thanks for her presence there beside him, he pushed his hastily laced boots from his feet and crawled into the bed. He gathered her up against him and pulled a quilt over them, sparing his last waking thought to set an alarm.

The least he could do was remember to wake up and help his father with the morning milking.

CHAPTER 39

$\mathcal{N}$an awoke disoriented for the second time in twelve hours. Barefoot and still in the clothes she'd wore the day before, the clothes she'd been wearing when she ran next door. When her car crashed into her neighbor's tree.

She pushed a navy and yellow wedding ring quilt off her legs and sat up in the bed. The room was painted the color of sand with white trim. On the back of the door was a faded Thornton College banner. She could smell the lingering ghosts of tea and fresh bread.

Molly and Walt Fuller's house.

The room was dim because of the drawn curtains, but she could see daylight peeking through. She reached into her pocket for her phone to check the time, and found it empty. Doing her best to straighten her clothes and hair, she opened the door and went to look for her hosts.

The Fullers' second floor was as tidy and welcoming as the first, with three bedrooms and a bathroom. The doors were open to small but airy, light-soaked rooms. The floors and railings shone; Nan could almost feel the generations of hands that had worn down the finish. Downstairs, she found Joss at his father's desk, pencil in hand, at work on a drawing. She could see from the hunch of his shoulders that he was deep in thought.

"Good morning."

He rose and turned all in one motion, crossing the living room to kiss her. "Did you sleep well?"

Better than she had in weeks.

"I did." She looked at the grandmother clock on the wall with a sigh. "But I've left five guests without their breakfast, and god knows what they think."

Joss took her hands between his; he had the look of a cat in a creamery. "My mom met Kate over there earlier to put together breakfast for your guests, and I had Elisha do a little creative damage control last night." He looked over his shoulder to where the tree bore fresh scars from the crash.

A happy glow kindled in her chest. "I do love you."

Joss blinked at her. His lips curved slowly and he squeezed her hands. "You do?"

Realizing what she'd said, she blushed furiously. It had been quietly true for weeks. She'd only been wary of saying the words. "I do. I love you."

She wound her arms around his neck, stretching up on her toes to kiss him. He was still smiling when she teased his lips with hers. They kissed among the dust motes that floated in the mid-morning sun. Joss let his lips linger against hers when he pulled away to whisper, "Took you long enough."

"I owe you an apology, Joss."

"For making me wait for you?" He chuckled. "Hardly. I'm just glad you came around."

"For flying off the handle with you the other day." She laid her cheek against his chest; for the moment it was easier to apologize to the warm softness of his sweatshirt. "I was angry, and I lost my temper."

"I was being an ass." There was wry humor in his voice. "And if I have my way, it won't be the last time that happens."

She looked up at him, overwhelmed with the tenderness in his eyes.

"I'm not going anywhere unless you tell me to, and if we're going to be together, we're probably going to have an argument or two."

Nan blinked back tears. Her emotions were never far from the surface, and she still felt hollowed out from the events of the previous night. "I'm not going to tell you to go anywhere. I like you with me."

"Good." He kissed her forehead. "Now let's get you back where you belong. Kate was going to get Amanda to come in so you could go over to the hospital to see Danny, but I think she might want to see you before she goes back to Sweet Pease."

"Danny's okay?"

"She is. Pete Lowry called this morning to say that she's being held for observation for another couple of days, but she was awake and expected to be fine."

Nan let out a breath she hadn't been aware of holding. "I can't thank you enough for arranging everything."

It was Joss's turn to be serious. "I don't want you to thank me. I want you to know that I'm going to take care of you."

Nan inhaled and looked him in the eye. "I plan to let you, but," she said carefully, "you have to let me take care of you, too."

As PREDICTED, Kate had to hear everything they knew between the two of them before she left to get back to the bakery. At the end of the telling, she shook her head in disbelief. "Innkeeping isn't meant to be this dangerous a profession."

Nan sniffed. "Now you tell me."

Kate patted Joss's shoulder. "Thank god for your mom. Baked goods and flirting will only get you so far. Your mother knows how to charm."

Nan snuck a glance at Joss. "Baked goods and flirting is at least half the battle on a good day."

Joss caught her glance. "More than half from where I'm standing."

"Okay, you two. I'm still in the room." Kate snatched her purse from its spot by the door. "For about thirty more seconds." She smooched Joss's cheek and hugged Nan hard, giving her a pointed look. "We'll talk soon."

"Kate?" Joss called as the door was slamming behind her.

Kate popped her head back in.

"Where's my mom?"

Kate grinned. "Out back with the Mahers. The couple from Charleston. Talking flowers."

The door smacked the jamb, and Kate was gone.

Molly might have missed her calling. Nan and Joss found her giving the couple from Charleston a tour of the gardens in the back. The pair were each carrying a steaming mug and what looked like cider doughnuts.

Joss whimpered audibly. "Mom, please tell me there are more of those somewhere?"

Nan watched as Molly turned to Joss like a flower to the sun. Molly gave them both a warm look. "In the kitchen, under the pie dome." She excused herself from the guests from South Carolina and herded them into the house. Molly's focus switched quickly in her direction. "How are you, hon?"

"Shocked, still. But better rested than I've been in weeks." She smiled sheepishly. "Thank you."

"For not waking you after that awful thing?" Molly pulled the pie dome off a plate set on the island and doled out doughnuts to the two of them as if they were children coming home from school. "Katie Pease and I did okay over here, I think, and you got some much needed rest. We're neighbors. Friends. That's what we do."

Joss laughed. "It had nothing to do with wanting to get a peek at the third floor?"

Molly's cheeks pinked. "Maybe a little."

Nan left Joss to show his mother the Adirondack Suite and went exploring in her pantry.

Joss found her there a few minutes later, loading up a collapsible nylon picnic hamper.

"What are you up to?"

"A few treats for Danny."

"You shouldn't feel guilty."

"Joss," she said. "It's more than guilt. I let that poor girl shoulder the blame for things she didn't do, and she got hurt trying to stop her boyfriend from stealing my car."

Joss countered. "She got hurt because she got into the car with him to begin with. And she covered for him. Knowingly. You don't owe Danny anything."

Nan snapped the lid down. "I don't want it to be about debts. I want it to be about redemption and kindness and feeling like there's something I can do to help."

Joss's face softened and he reached for the handle of the basket. "Come on, we'll take my truck."

DANNY BLUSHED like fury when Joss and Nan arrived with the basket. She fidgeted nervously with her hospital-issue johnny, eyeing Joss like he was carrying explosives rather than flowers and baked goods. Sensing Danny's distress, Nan sent Joss to see if he could get any information on Dylan.

"How are you feeling?" Nan sat in the chair next to Danny's bed. Danny looked painfully young, stripped of her angry-teen uniform, stitched and bandaged and pale.

"Crappy." Danny sighed and tossed the TV remote on the tray table. She picked at a loose thread on her blanket. "Sorry about your car."

Nan got up and unwrapped the flowers Joss had carried in. She'd asked him to stop so she could run in for them, not knowing how they would be received. There were no vases, so she poured some water into an oversized plastic cup and arranged them as best she could. She looked out at the view of Thornton College's athletic fields, letting her question out into the empty space between them. "What happened, Danny?"

"Dylan was being an idiot."

Nan almost smiled. There was a ghost of adolescent exasperation in Danny's voice. She stayed at the window and let the girl talk.

"My mom's ... not around a lot. She has to drive pretty far for work, and my uncle doesn't take care of my grandpa real well. It's gross up there, and my uncle ... well, it's better when I stay out of the way."

Nan cringed, but stayed silent.

"Dylan likes me. He tries to be all tough, but he's not bad. He just does stupid stuff. He was trying to make me feel better after Ellie moved away and we had to leave the Swifts' house. Last night I had a huge fight with my uncle and took off on my bike to find Dylan. He told me he would run away with me, and I was stupid enough to say yes for five minutes."

Her breath hitched, and Nan turned. Danny's chin wobbled and tears welled up in her eyes. Nan went to the young woman and took her hand as the tears spilled over.

"I was so mad they left, the Swifts, and you had strangers all over the house, and you were living in my mom's room, and I missed the futon behind a screen that was my spot. Because we were okay there." Her words drowned in her sobbing.

Nan didn't know how to make her next words true, but she made a silent promise that they would be. "It's going to be okay." She stroked Danny's forehead, pushing the girl's lank hair from her damp skin. "Shh. I want to help you figure it out, but now you should be resting."

Danny calmed to a sniffle, turning her face away and closing her eyes. Nan stayed by the bed until Danny's fingers went slack in hers.

Joss found Nan dozing in the chair next to Danny Beaudette's hospital bed. He woke her gently. She leaned into him on the walk to his truck. In the midday sun, his mother's panicked phone call echoed in his memory.

... there's been an accident. A car clipped the oak tree ... we think it's Nan's car ...

He'd have said his heart stopped, but the truth of it was that his heart was already in the valley with Nan.

Next to him, she was drifting, eyes closed, but humming softly along with the radio. "Are you hungry? Do you want to stop at Kate's and grab something?"

She opened her eyes. "No. I just want to go home."

When they reached the intersection of County and Main, Joss turned the wheel west onto County Road.

His thoughts circled back to *home*.

Home, the farm, meant the lowing of the herd, the endless work, the weight of responsibility, the warmth of love and his mother's cooking. He'd tried–and failed–to make a home in shared spaces among concrete monoliths and industrial steel caverns. He fashioned a new one of his own in the cool of the forest, thin air, and first light.

And yet ...

Home was Nan Grady and her sun-drenched inn, surrounded by guests. Home was the sweet ache of wanting her beside him, the smell of her skin, the laughter in her whiskey eyes.

A tenth of a mile before the home where he'd begun, Joss pulled his truck into the home where he'd choose to spend the rest of his life.

If she'd have him.

CHAPTER 40

*J*oss nursed a beer on the back patio at Temple. The clear
evening sky revealed the first of the winter constellations. The last throes of Indian Summer were upon them,
but Thanksgiving was only a few days away.

Deirdre had opened a tab for him. All he needed was his friends.

Jack and Kate cruised in together, dazzling small town royalty.
Kate headed to the bar to give Deirdre their drink order. Jack sought
him out. Joss waved his friend over. He watched as Jack caught Kate's
attention, motioning to the table out back. Even their movements
were fluid, like choreography. It made him wonder if he'd have
enjoyed a brother or sister.

The Peases were a model of the nuclear family; he supposed not
everyone had it that good.

"Hey," Jack said, pulling out a chair. "What's with the emergency
summit? And where's Nan?"

Joss pulled a sip from his beer. "This isn't about the inn," he said,
"and I need you all here first."

"Who else is coming?"

With screenplay-worthy timing, Anneliese walked into the bar.
She intercepted Kate with the drinks. The two women spoke briefly

before Dee brought over a beer. Anneliese took it, and walked with Kate out to the patio.

"The gang's all here!" Kate said happily, plunking down next to Joss, leaving Anneliese in the seat closest to Jack. Anna scootched her chair a hair towards Kate.

"So, Joss," Kate continued, "what kind of surprise are we hatching for Nan?" She sipped at her drink, looking up at the group from under her lashes. "What?" she asked with a grin. "Isn't that why we've been called here tonight?"

Joss flushed. "She's right."

He dug into his jacket pocket, producing a ring box and a photograph. The two women gasped; Kate snatched the box and opened it. Jack grinned.

"Oh, Joss!" Anneliese spoke first; Kate only ran a reverent finger over the antique diamond.

"It came out great," Jack commented.

Kate snapped the box shut. "You knew?"

Jack smirked at his sister. "Man-code, Katie."

"Jack knew about the ring, but the next part is where I need everyone." Joss pushed the photo to the center of the table. "I'm planning to invite Nan up to the cabin tomorrow night. I'm going to ask her then." He looked at his cousin. "Anna, I need you to cover at the inn when she asks you."

Anna flipped the ring box open with a misty smile. "Done." She closed it gently. "I'm so happy for you guys."

Kate slid the ring box back to Joss and picked up the photograph. "So what's with the furniture catalog photo?"

"It's an engagement gift," Joss replied. "Provided she says yes."

"Which she will." Kate never missed a beat.

"You built it, didn't you?" Anneliese asked without looking away from the photograph.

"I did. I've been working on it on and off for a couple of weeks," Joss said. "I want to surprise her with it, and I'm going to need help." He looked at Jack. "You're going to help me disassemble it, move it, and reassemble it in Nan's apartment."

Jack took out his phone and went straight to swiping and tapping. "Count me in."

"Kate, you're in charge of distracting her."

"How long do you need?" Kate asked. "And how much notice do I have?"

"A couple of hours on Sunday afternoon should do it."

Anneliese spoke again, "I'll cover again at the inn. Kate can make it seem like her idea, so Nan won't feel bad about asking me twice in one weekend."

Kate flashed Anna an approving smile. "Okay, so Nan's going to come with me for celebratory mani/pedis in Burlington, where I will suddenly have a fiendish desire to see–" She whipped out her phone and tapped the screen. "A drippy romantic comedy. Because I am so depressingly unengaged." She looked back at Joss. "Of course, since Jack is in town, you two are off doing something manly, like golf –" She gave her brother a wink. "I will deliver the bride-to-be to Joss's parents' house," she continued, "where Molly will have whipped up a feast for her new daughter-in-law, and double back to the inn to relieve Anna so she can get home to her adorable little girl."

Joss, Jack, and Anneliese looked at her in wonder.

"At which point I will supervise bed linens before Jack drives me to our parents' house, where they will feed us." She set her phone down on the table and sipped her drink.

Joss put the ring box and the photo back into the bag. "And here I was, thinking this would be challenging."

"You forgot who you were asking for help. Now let me see that ring again," Kate said, holding out a palm.

Anneliese sipped her beer.

"Did you take him to that estate jeweler on Newbury Street that I love?" Kate asked Jack.

"I did." Jack did his best not to look too smug. "But he did the rest on his own."

Joss took back the ring. "I'm right here, you two."

"How are you going to ask her?" Kate teased. "All chivalry and bended knee, or wait for… later?"

"I'm sure she'll tell you all about it the next day," he said.

"You sneak!" Kate tossed a paper coaster at him.

Joss dodged the projectile with a laugh. "Well?"

"Of course she will, but that's not the point."

Anneliese finished her drink. "Guys? I'm going to head out. It's been a long day."

"See you, Anna. And thanks for coming by." Joss squeezed her hand.

Jack stood up as Anneliese did. "Anna."

Anna returned his gaze, but her eyes were guarded. "Jack." She excused herself and made her way through the crowd, leaving Jack standing.

"While you're up, you can walk me out." Kate checked the time. "I've got a couple of things I want to finish up in the kitchen before I go to bed." She left a ten on the table and flicked her wet straw at Jack. "Come along, brother of mine. And Joss?"

"Yeah?" Joss looked up at her.

"Well done."

NEIL DIAMOND AGAIN, Joss thought, climbing the stairs to the third floor. Nan was singing along with *Sweet Caroline* while she arranged flaming orange and red calla lilies on the dresser.

He slipped his arms around her waist, rocking her back against him to the rhythm of the music he couldn't hear.

She pulled her earbuds out and tipped her head back to kiss him. "Hi."

"Hi," he said. "You're really cute when you sing."

She turned, locking her arms around his neck. "You're just really cute."

He'd been thinking about kissing her the whole drive over, but it was Nan who stretched up to touch her lips to his. When he brushed his hand up her neck, the kiss blossomed. The citrus and spice of her skin, the feel of her under his hands. Her mouth tasted of raspberries and vanilla.

"Scones?" he said hopefully.

"Help yourself on your way out."

"You sending me home so soon?" he asked, pulling her flush up against him.

"Hey now," she scolded, "none of that. I have paying guests downstairs."

"We could give them their money's worth?"

"Joss!"

"I love when you're embarrassed," he teased, "your ears get pink."

She sighed and grinned, biting her lip.

"I love you," he said.

"I love you, too, but we still have work to do."

"Why work," he asked, "when I could be kissing a beautiful girl?" He leaned down, captured her bottom lip in his teeth; felt her shiver and relax against him.

"Joss?"

"Mmm?" his lips cruised her cheek, his fingers played at the small of her back.

"Go to work."

He pulled away. "You're so mean. And I was going to offer to make you dinner tonight."

"Ooh. Well maybe I'll reconsider my position." She snuggled in closer. "I love dinner I don't have to make."

"Can you get away to come up to the cabin?"

He watched her slip into her mental calendar and surface smiling. "If Anna or Amanda can cover, I can." She traced the waist of his jeans, leaving a hot trail of awareness in the wake of her fingertips. "But I can't stay."

The air was rapidly leaving his lungs. "I'll make sure you get home by dawn."

"Promises, promises." She kissed him, and shuffled him backwards towards to the door to the suite. "Take the scones," she offered. "And Joss?"

He turned at the landing.

"I do love you."

Joss headed out to his final meeting with Ellen Hill with an impossible buoyancy in his chest. It was going to be a very good day.

~

NAN WASN'T EXPECTING VISITORS, but Kate's contralto singing out from the foyer put a smile on her face nonetheless. She left the linens she was folding and jogged up the stairs from the basement laundry room, surprising Kate in the kitchen. "What brought you over?"

Kate blushed. "I was hungry."

"Liar," Nan stifled a laugh. "You own a bakery."

"Fine." Kate folded herself into a chair at the long farm table. "I just felt like a chat."

Nan opened the fridge and pulled out a pitcher of cold tea. "I always need a break from laundry." She poured glasses and sat down around the table's corner.

Kate sipped. Nan looked closely at Kate; there was something not exactly right about her.

"Is everything okay?"

Kate shook off the shadows in her eyes. "Yeah. Why?"

"You just seemed –" She was interrupted by Elisha bursting into the kitchen.

"I got it!"

Nan and Kate turned to her. Kate spoke first. "Got what?"

"The book deal! And the job here!" Elisha was crackling with pleasure. "I'm staying!"

"Here?" Nan was stunned. She'd never pegged Elisha for a small-town girl.

Elisha's laugh was somewhere between silver bells and a gong. "No, but in town. I'll have to rent a house! A little house or an apartment downtown…" She trailed off considering her options.

"Congratulations, Elisha," Nan said, getting up from her seat to hug her. "Tea? And cake! A new job and a book deal calls for cake."

Elisha floated into the seat next to Kate. "It's almost not even the most exciting news." She took the tea Nan offered. "The English department is bringing on a guest lecturer for the spring semester." The glass didn't even make it to her lips before the new professor's name blurted out. "Ewan Lovatt!"

Kate's face was blank, but Nan couldn't stop a smile. Ewan Lovatt was one of her favorite authors. "That's fantastic. He's amazing."

"I know." Elisha was gushing. "I've been to a couple of his readings. He's got this reticent charisma. Oh!" She took a plate of coffee cake from Nan. "I can't wait for the new faculty reception!"

Elisha waxed poetic about Ewan Lovatt over her cake and then vanished off to call her parents, who were on a Thai beach at the moment.

"I fail to see," Kate said, "why you two are so excited about a novelist."

Nan patted Kate's shoulder. "Do you remember when Henri Lesauvage did the master class in spun sugar sculpting? And you literally couldn't sleep beforehand?"

Kate rolled her eyes at the ceiling. "Fine. Yes. I get it. This Evan guy is a big deal." She glanced at Nan out of the corner of her eye. "If you're into those bookworm types."

JOSS WATCHED as Nan's VW pulled into his driveway. The sound of her tires on the damp, packed earth was improbably appealing. The ring box felt small, but very solid, in his hands. He set it on the window sill.

The pasta pot was nearly full, so Joss turned off the tap. He watched Nan close her car door and make her way to the front door as he set the pot on the stove.

He wasn't without skill in the kitchen; his mother had made sure of that, but the cabin on the Gap didn't have a whole lot of room for fancy preparation. What he excelled at was making the best of living in a creative, entrepreneurial community.

On his way up the mountain, after a long day finalizing the Hill

Barn project, he had stopped into the co-op. He'd picked up canned artichoke and walnut pesto, handmade pappardelle, and a jar of honey vinaigrette. He had a bag of his mother's greenhouse salad greens, and he'd dropped by Sweet Pease at lunch, leaving with a baguette for dinner.

When Nan had insisted on bringing something–*my gran raised me right*, she'd said–he'd put her in charge of the wine. He noted with pleasure the two slim bottlenecks protruding from her canvas market tote.

He opened the door to her hand, poised to knock.

He took her wrist, kissed her curled knuckles, and tugged her into a hug, deftly taking her tote bag at the same time.

"Hi," she said, laying her head on his chest and inhaling deeply. "You smell good. And you weren't lying. You are cooking."

Joss put the wine on the counter. She had brought a young Beaujolais and a California Zinfandel. He opted for the Beaujolais and, after setting her bag on the floor, rummaged around in a drawer for the corkscrew. "I'm not completely helpless," he replied, slicing the foil at the neck of the bottle with his utility knife.

He popped the cork, held it out for her.

"And you're the sommelier? I am impressed." She sniffed the cork with exaggerated delicacy.

He took the cork back, dropped it on the counter, and poured two glasses, setting them aside to breathe a little.

"I hope it's not an insult to your dinner plans," Nan said, amusement in her eyes, "but I was in the mood for brownies, and I stopped by Kate's on the way up here for a little dessert to go." She pulled a hot-pink pastry box, tied up with silver string, out of her bag. "Her toffee pudding brownies are a weakness of mine."

Joss's stomach growled, and he chuckled. "Kate's toffee pudding brownies are the perfect companion to any meal. I dare anyone to disagree." He pulled her close.

"I'm glad we agree on that."

"Would it have been a deal-breaker?"

"Possibly."

Her playful mood eased the lingering flutter of nerves in his gut. Joss touched his lips to hers. He'd only meant a brief, affectionate kiss, but she hummed appreciatively under her breath, wound her hands around his waist, stretched up on her toes, and dragged him under like a riptide.

He pulled her up, toes off the floor, pressing small kisses along her jaw, and carried her to the sofa. She kicked back her heels, kneeling on the cushions and drew him down with her. He was drowning, and it was bliss. The smell of her, the feel of her skin, her hair whispering against his face, her hasty indrawn breaths between kisses.

The hiss of the pasta pot intruded, and they pulled apart. Nan knelt against the sofa back, resting her cheek on her folded arms, watching him salt the water, toss in the pasta.

"You're a distraction, Beautiful." He set a timer.

"I like that," she replied.

He saw her there, perfectly at home on his couch while he made her dinner, and he saw his moment. She was glowing in the amber light, eyes sparkling, lips bruised pink from his kisses, and he loved her. Without reservation.

He plucked the ring box from the sill, pocketed it, and walked around to the couch.

Joss dropped onto his knees in front of her, took her hands. "I love you, Nan." The words he'd rehearsed all day flew out of his head, leaving him with the only two that mattered.

"Marry me?"

Her eyes widened, her smile beamed. "Yes," she whispered. "Yes."

He reached into his pocket for the ring box. Handing it to her, he was suddenly unsure.

She took the box, a slight tremor in her fingertips, and opened it. The light in her eyes dispelled his uncertainty.

"Joss," she breathed, taking in the ring.

Nestled in the dark velvet was an antique white gold filigree setting, with a princess cut diamond sparkling alluringly in its midst. The diamond had the buttery glow that so often defined old stones.

He'd known from the moment he saw the setting that it was right for her. Nan looked up at him with watery eyes.

"Do you like it?" he asked.

"It's perfect."

Joss pulled the ring from the box, took her hand. He slipped the ring onto her finger. Their eyes met over their hands for a heartbeat, before Nan threw her arms around his neck.

"We're getting married!" she cried, happy tears spilling over.

Joss held her there, reveling in the knowledge that she was going to be in his arms forever. The chirping beep of the timer from the kitchen counter reminded him of the pasta.

"After we eat." He was still grinning as he stood up.

Nan clung to him for a moment longer. One more kiss, and he took her hand. There was dinner to serve and the rest of their lives to start.

CHAPTER 41

For the first day or two, Nan woke up wondering if she'd dreamed the entire proposal. For nearly a week, she traveled at least two inches off the ground. For the first time since meeting Joss, she was genuinely pleased by the town's ability to disseminate news at speeds far faster than sound. It was easier to walk around the co-op with a space-cadet smile and little cartoon hearts spinning around her head, when everyone in town knew she and Joss were getting married.

She blamed the champagne bubbles that had replaced her regular thought process when she missed the setup for Joss's second surprise that week. Everyone's swift departure after her return from the movies was the first clue that something was up, and that her fiancé–*fiancé!*–had a hand in it.

She walked into the bedroom a step ahead of Joss, eyes closed. His hands rested on her waist, light and warm through her yoga pants, guiding her. She shivered as he grazed inquisitive fingers over the soft jut of her hip bone.

"Can I look now?"

He chuckled softly. "Nope. Not yet."

He held her fast as she started to take another step. Then, stepping forward himself, he wrapped his arms around her, molding their bodies together. She wasn't the only one anticipating.

She leaned into him, dropping her head back against his shoulder. He laid a trail of open mouthed kisses into the hollow beneath her jaw.

"Please?" Whether it was the kisses or the surprise she was begging for, she wasn't sure.

"Yes."

She opened her eyes to a bed. Not the bed that she'd bought at the flea market over the summer.

This one was a canopied fantasy of bent wood, twining branches with neither beginning nor end. The wood glowed in the moonlight. She longed to run a hand along the sinuous posts, to feel the satin hardness of the headboard under her fingers.

"Oh, it's beautiful." Her eyes stung with happy tears. "You made this." Not a question; a confirmation.

"For you."

~

SHE TURNED TO HIM, leaning back against a bedpost. With gentle fingers, he skimmed her forearms where her sweater sleeves were pushed back. Lips playful where her hair curled behind her ear, he let his hands wander to the buttons of her cardigan. He shivered when she reached for his t-shirt hem.

With infinite care, he kissed what skin he exposed, following an exquisite progress over her cotton camisole, from collarbone to belly. The rise and fall of her breath led the pace of his explorations.

He paused to slip the sweater from her arms, to help her out of the camisole. He moved his hands over her belly, upwards to stroke the soft underside of her breasts, slipping between lace and flesh to brush the peaks with his thumbs.

He drew down the slim lace straps and opened the catch, discarding the bra on the floor. She reached for him, winding her arms around his neck, eyes closed, lips parted, while he caressed, teased, soothed, and ignited again.

He nudged the pants off her hips; she shimmied them down, letting them pool into a shadow at her feet.

She became the explorer, tangling tongues, hands quick and sure as she tugged his shirt over his head. His heart turned over as she worked the buckle of his belt, unconsciously biting her lower lip in concentration.

She had him out of his clothes quickly, and his appreciation for her neat efficiency took on new meaning. In the luminous darkness of her bedroom, as she knelt to strip him of what clothing remained, a previously tethered part of his soul was cut loose.

She rose slowly, staying just arms' length away from him. She stood, naked save for one last swath of lace, and met his gaze. Slowly, her eyes never leaving his, she slipped off that last scrap of fabric.

And then she smiled. A secret smile full of power and pleasure. He reached for her and she went to him, pressing him back into the bedclothes.

Kneeling over him, she took his hands in hers and took him inside her, brought him home.

Time slipped away and moonlight gave way to darkness and stars through her bedroom window.

THEY BOTH WOKE in that same darkness, punctuated by different stars. Morning was creeping over the Green Mountains, pushing the starlight west.

"Do you know the history of the house?" His low voice promised a story as he linked his fingers with hers. "I've been meaning to ask you since we met, but I remembered it again working on this bed."

Nan snuggled into Joss's side. "I don't know the story. I know it was in Meg Swift's family before she married, but that's it."

"My grandfather's great-grandfather owned most of the valley when Faye Bartram got off the train in Port Henry and decided to stay. Her father owned the company that financed a railway expansion in Upstate New York just before the turn of the last century."

"Faye Bartram, railway heiress." Nan whispered. "I love her already."

"She was said to be an unconventional woman, loved to hunt and fish, dabbled in naturalism, and loved lavish excursions. She would organize hiking parties, mineral springs bathing, and extravagant country picnics away from her New York City social responsibilities."

"Ladies painting and sketching the mountains, wearing those wonderful wool bathing dresses to swim ... Joss, really? This was her house?"

"She never married, instead she put all her dowry money into the purchase of this land and the building of this house. She had a stable and a carriage house as well, but they were gone by the time I was around. It was her cabin, her personal retreat where she would host only those in her closest circles. Five bedrooms with bathrooms–the plumbing alone must have cost her an incredible amount, room for servants on the third floor. For a decade she summered here. She would come for months at a time, bringing her staff with her and never interacting with the town."

Nan could hear him leading her. "Until?"

"Until she met Oscar Pinckney. He was twenty years older than she was–and she was a dusty old maid of nearly forty–a wealthy, reclusive landowner from Boston who had a similar retreat on the shore of Lake Champlain. He rescued her when the wind died one afternoon while she and her friends were sailing on the lake. They conducted a shameless love affair that summer. He gave up his solitude and danced until dawn with her friends, they sailed and swam and fished together, but he never proposed."

Nan was breathless. "What happened?"

"Faye returned to New York for the winter, as she always did, and Oscar went back to Boston. Depending on who you ask, they carried on their affair between two cities, but I don't think so. He died the following spring, and Faye never returned to her cabin."

"She sold it?"

"No." Joss held her close. "She let the property fall into disrepair for ten long years, and then, one spring, she came back. Alone. She holed up in the moldy remains of the house. Folks said she was crazy, wandering the pastures at night calling for Oscar. There was a terrible fire a few weeks later. Her body was never recovered."

"My inn is haunted?" Nan was stunned.

"Not anymore."

"But it was?"

"Maybe? A young man came to town with his new bride over the winter. They bought the house, took a leased house in town, and left behind a team of carpenters and laborers to fix the property up. When they moved back in, there was a framed charcoal sketch on the table in their bedroom of an older man and a striking middle aged woman together in a sailboat, and a note asking them to love one another and to never waste a moment."

He paused and Nan shivered.

"It was signed, Faye Bartram."

Nan sighed, letting her imagination drift. "Do you believe the story?"

Joss stroked her hip under the blankets. "I don't disbelieve it. That couple's family owned the house until this year. They were Meg Swift's ancestors. And there was a lot of love in this house."

She rolled over and touched his cheek in the pale light. "There still is."

NAN WOKE to the chirping alarm on her phone. The day ahead promised to be a busy one, and she relished a few quiet moments. As her eyes adjusted to the fading dark, the bed transformed her bedroom into a fairy tale forest. She snuggled into the linens, redolent of lavender and the clean, toasty smell of sawdust and soap that was uniquely Joss.

He slept easily beside her.

She curled her fingers through the tips of his hair, the diamond on her left ring finger glinting in the first hint of morning light. Smoothing her hands over his shoulder, she shifted to press a kiss behind his ear.

He turned and met her mouth with his own. "Good morning," he whispered.

"Good morning." She wondered if he could hear the smile in her voice.

"I like waking up to you," he said easily, slipping his arm around her and rolling them together under the coverlet.

"Do I say I like waking you up?" She laughed. "Or is that the wrong answer?"

He pulled her tightly against him. She could feel him ready for her. "You'll always like waking me up," he said, kissing her. "Promise."

Reluctantly, she pushed herself away from him with mock severity. "You and I both have jobs to get to."

He touched a finger to the furrow between her brows. "I love when you're stern with me."

"I just love you," she countered.

Joss kissed her and swung out of the bed. He was gathering his clothes up as she was headed for the bathroom, and they danced around each other at the corner of the bed.

"You know, I hate to say it," he said, "but this bed is really too big for the space."

"Don't you dare try to take it away from me."

"I wouldn't entertain the thought," he said. "I value my life."

He stood a moment, contemplating the wall behind the headboard. "If you wanted, I could put in a covered porch off the kitchen, and expand this apartment out over it. That way, we could have a bigger master bedroom, and even a small second bedroom." He walked out into the living room, mentally assessing the structure and space. "Maybe even expand the bathroom."

Nan followed him out into the other room, realization dawning on her. "You said, 'We.'"

Her tone caught his attention. "I can live anywhere. You belong here, so here's where I'll be." He went to her and pulled her into a hug.

"I'll keep the cabin, but I sort of assumed we'd live here once we got married."

She laughed. She'd been so high on their engagement, so distracted by the miracle of loving him, that the practicalities hadn't yet occurred to her. She flushed. "Of course. Or maybe before?"

"Whenever you're ready for me, I'll be here."

Nan took his hands and looked up at him. "Consider yourself home."

TURN **the page for a sneak peak at Sweet Pease, book two in the Thornton Vermont Series...**

SWEET PEASE

CHAPTER ONE

CHAPTER 1

"I'm going to make one hell of a maid of honor."

Kate Pease laughed off the wobble in her voice and blinked back a threatening tear. She smoothed the fuchsia silk shantung over her hips and stomach, twisting to check out her own rear view in the three-way mirror.

Her best friend, Nan Grady, stood on a dressmaker's pedestal while an attendant laced up the wedding gown she was trying on. Nan was radiant; the creamy silk only accentuated her glow.

Kate blinked back tears. It wasn't every day your best friend found the dress she was going to get married in. "That's the one, you know."

Nan blushed happily. "I think so, too."

"There's no thinking about it. It's the one."

The two women regarded each other. Below the second story window, Boston's Newbury Street bustled despite the January cold. Nan's brilliant smile wavered; Kate rushed over and swiped gently at the yet-to-fall wetness in her friend's eyes.

"No crying. We are far too fabulous today for streaky mascara."

Lady Gaga suggested a bad romance from Kate's purse. When Nan snickered, Kate shot her friend a withering look.

She retrieved her phone from the bag and took the call with a grin. "Hello, brother dear."

"Did Nan pick a dress?"

"Yes, she found her dress." Kate winked at Nan, who was posing for the shop attendant's measuring tape.

"Did you leave anything for the other shoppers?"

Her brother Jack might taunt her about her shopping habit, but his own was just as bad… if not worse.

"You're mean."

"Can I make it up to you with an extravagant lunch?"

"You can."

"I have to go; client on the other line."

He gave her a restaurant name and a time, and Kate ended the call.

Nan looked over her shoulder while the attendant created a potential bustle in the skirt. "Lunch?"

"At that sushi place near Jack's office. And he's picking up the tab."

Kate watched as Nan took a moment to drink in her own reflection. The dress was a simple A-line; the corsetry emphasized Nan's lean waist and gentle curves. The skirt clung to her hips just a little before falling like water to her feet.

"Oh, Nan," Kate breathed, "you're gorgeous."

Thornton was in for the wedding of the decade. The Fullers, the Peases—who considered Nan one of their own already—and nearly half the county would gather to celebrate Nan and Joss Fuller's marriage at the Damselfly in June.

That they would all eat cake by Kate Pease, well that didn't hurt either. Especially given her business plans.

Placing the dress order was swift and expensive. Her thrifty friend was pale with sticker shock. Kate squeezed Nan's hand in solidarity.

Kate and Nan gathered coats and scarves and gloves, bundling up against the bluster of a Boston winter. Just as they struck out for the T station at Arlington Street, Nan's phone rang in her pocket.

"Hello, Anna?" Nan motioned for Kate to stop. "He just walked in? Well, we have room. Go ahead and check him in."

While Nan walked her friend and inn-sitter through the registration software, Kate's gaze lingered on a camel hair wool skirt in the window of a nearby boutique, and she slipped inside.

Kate picked up a few additional items on her way to the fitting room. Nan followed her inside. Her half of the conversation was clear across the tiny space.

"I'm as surprised as you are." Nan's smile was wide and gleeful. "I can't imagine why, though. The college must have offered him an apartment."

Kate waved to Nan, motioning at the fitting room door while Nan's eyes widened at whatever Anna was saying.

"He's what?" Nan laughed aloud. "I have to go. Kate and I are meeting Jack for lunch before we drive home. I'll be home in plenty of time for you to tuck Chloe in."

Nan waved to Kate from across the sales floor, pointed at her watchless wrist.

"Bye, Anna. Thanks for calling. Give Chloe a snuggle for me."

Kate whipped through her choices, but nothing was just right. She hung everything on the rack outside the fitting room and sought Nan out among the scarves near the register. She tucked her arm in Nan's and swept them out the door and down the street.

"What did Anna want?"

Nan squinted into the glittering winter sun. "I have a new guest. A surprise. Anna says he, and I quote, 'looks like Mr. Rochester.'"

"Oh, really?" Visions of Timothy Dalton's smoldering gaze danced in her head. She silently thanked her mother for making her watch old BBC dramas when she was home sick in high school. "I always did think Rochester was kind of dreamy."

Nan snorted. "Don't."

Kate grinned, wondering if the newcomer was her kind of dreamy. And if he was single.

~

Read Sweet Pease now!

ALSO BY CAMERON D. GARRIEPY

Children of the Parallels
Speculative Middle Grade Short Fiction

Parallel Jump

Parallel Hunt

ABOUT THE AUTHOR

Cameron D. Garriepy attended a small Vermont college in a town very like Thornton. She's missed it since the day she packed up her Subaru and drove off into the real world. Some might say she created the fictional village as wish fulfillment, and they would be correct.

She is the author of the Thornton Vermont series and the founder of Bannerwing Books, a co-op of independent authors. Prior to Bannerwing, Cameron was an editor at Write on Edge, where she edited three volumes of the online writing group's literary anthology, *Precipice*. Cameron appeared in the inaugural cast of *Listen to Your Mother - Boston*, and irregularly contributes flash fiction to the Word Count Podcast.

Since her time at Middlebury College, Cameron has worked as a nanny, a pastry cook, and an event ticket resale specialist. In her spare time, she cooks, gardens, knits, reads avidly, and researches hobby farming--chickens and goats are just waiting for her ship to come in. She writes from the greater Boston area, where she lives with her husband, son, and a geriatric pug.

Connect with Cameron online at www.camerondgarriepy.com
Hear first about sales and new releases via Cameron's newsletter—
subscribe at
www.bit.ly/cdgnewsletter
Join the conversation in Cameron's Facebook group at www.
bit.ly/thorntonfbgroup

ABOUT THE PUBLISHER

Bannerwing Books is a writers' co-op founded in 2012 by Cameron D. Garriepy, and completed by Angela Amman and Mandy Dawson. Currently residing on Slack, somewhere in the ether between Boston, Detroit, and Paso Robles, Bannerwing presents works by Stephanie Ayers, Ericka Clay, and Liz Zimmers, as well as collections featuring Andra Watkins, Kate Shrewsday, and Kameko Murakami.

www.bannerwingbooks.com

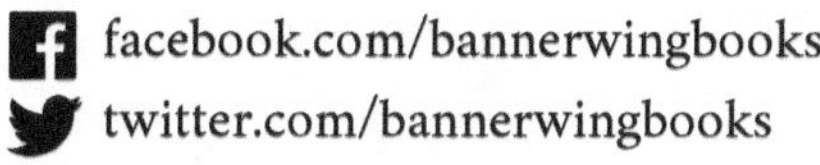

facebook.com/bannerwingbooks
twitter.com/bannerwingbooks